Phenomenal X

Hard Knocks, Book One

Michelle A. Valentine

PHENOMENAL X

Published By: Michelle A. Valentine Books, LLC

First Edition

Copyright © 2014 by Michelle A. Valentine Books, LLC

Cover Art: Romantic Book Affairs Designs

(stock photo purchased)

Edited by: Delphirose and Editing4Indies

For questions or comments about this book, please contact the author at michellevalentineauthor@gmail.com

Dedications

Valentine's Vixens: You ladies inspire me daily.
Thank you.

Other Books by
Michelle A. Valentine

Black Falcon Series Reading Order
Rock the Beginning (Black Falcon, #0.5)
Can be found in Stories for Amanda
or in the back of Rock the Beat
Rock the Heart (Black Falcon, #1)
Rock the Band (Black Falcon, #1.5)
Rock My Bed (Black Falcon, #2)
Rock My World (Black Falcon, #2.5)
Rock the Beat (Black Falcon, #3)

The Collectors Series
Demon at My Door

Coming 2014
Rock My Body (Black Falcon, #4)
Elite Invitation
Demon in My Bed

"Blessed are the meek, for they shall inherit the earth"—Matthew 5:5

Chapter
ONE

There's no better way to ruin a perfectly peaceful flight than sitting between two complete strangers. I always request an aisle or window seat if I can, but this flight was booked solid and the unhelpful lady at the check-in desk told me there was absolutely no wiggle room to change seats.

The older gentleman on my left keeps turning toward me and smiling, probably hoping I'll strike up polite conversation with him, but I'm just not in the mood to be nice. I'm leaving Portland, leaving behind the only life I've ever known, and the only thing I feel like doing is keeping quiet and praying that I'm making the right decision.

This morning my father went into one of his lecture-filled rages, telling me what a horrible person I was when I sprung it on him that I would be on the ten o' clock flight to Detroit to go live with Aunt Dee, his eccentric sister. My parents, especially my father, have always been great at controlling my life. Which is exactly why I'm leaving now.

I've followed his plan for the last twenty-one years, and it's brought nothing but heartache.

I'm ready to make my own decisions about what's best for me.

While the other passengers settle in around me, I quickly flick through my text messages. The anger in Father's messages is crystal clear. The same thing said a million different ways: for me to stop this nonsense of starting my own life, and come back home where I belong. Where I'm safe.

I shake my head and shut my phone off before slipping it into the seat-back pocket in front of me. "No can do, Father," I mumble to myself.

A mother and her twin sons fill the three empty seats in the row ahead of me. They are sitting in the first row, directly behind the wall that separates the first class patrons from the rest of us lowly coach passengers. If I had to guess, I'd say the twins are about twelve or so. Their brown hair pokes out from underneath the matching baseball caps they have firmly pulled onto their heads. The hats match their red shirts with some wrestling guy on it. I can tell it's wrestling from the logos. I remember sneaking around to watch the televised show with my younger brother when he went through a phase of loving that sort of thing.

Just then I notice an extremely tall, broad-shouldered man wearing jeans and a blue button-down shirt, with his sleeves rolled up to his elbows, board the plane. Even with his shirt on I can tell he's all muscle underneath it. The definition in his chest and arms is undeniable as the fabric strains against his pecs and biceps. Intricate tattoos cover every inch of exposed flesh on his arms, and I immediately know he's the kind of guy my mother always warned me about—which does nothing to decrease his appeal.

I bite my lip as my eyes scan further up and take in the dark hair on his head. It's got a little bit of length to it and is styled to messy perfection. His strong jawline has some light stubble, like he forgot to shave this morning, and the fact that his nose isn't perfectly straight—indicating it's been broken a time or two—only adds to his rugged good looks. The way he carries himself, chin up with a daring expression, exudes confidence. Everything about him says he doesn't take crap from anyone, which is a highly attractive feature in a man. And that body...*yowza*! It's absolutely delicious and belongs on the cover of a magazine. It's designed for masses of women to enjoy devouring with their eyes because in the flesh, that's exactly what I'm doing.

And I'm loving every minute of it.

My heart pauses for a beat the moment this man locks eyes with me. When I don't immediately turn away, a slight hint of a smile plays at the corner of his full lips. Briefly, I'm mesmerized, and then realize I'm still thinking about his body, and I'm biting my lip.

He winks at me like he knows exactly what's on my mind before he slides into an empty row of seats in first class. A short, thin man with a mullet and a beard takes the aisle seat next to him.

I lean my head back against the seat and sigh, feeling the heat in my cheeks. That man is dangerously sexy and way out of my league.

The two boys in front of me begin waving their arms above their head. "X! X! Back here! Can we get your autograph?"

The letter X is all I hear them chant over and over as the small man who boarded the plane last turns around and says, "Not now, boys. Phenomenal X is trying to rest." The hot guy beside him must be this "Phenomenal X" person because after the little man says that to the kids, he immediately leans over and says something to him. Mullet Man nods before turning back around to address the two boys. "Send something up, and X will sign one thing for each of you."

"All right!" exclaims one of the boys as they give each other a high-five.

The rest of the plane begins to buzz as the knowledge that a celebrity is on board the flight spreads. While I find the man extremely attractive, I have no clue who he is and I can't bring myself to get excited about it. I have too much on my plate to be interested in some guy who would never give someone like me the time of day.

Soon an assembly line forms as people begin to pass things up the aisle into first class. I almost feel sorry for him as it continues through taxiing, take-off, and while we are up in the air. The poor guy will probably develop writer's cramp before the flight is over.

After I turn down the stewardess' offer of an in-flight beverage, allowing her to assist the old man beside me who orders a tomato juice, I lean my head back and close my eyes. I try not to think about the one hundred texts Father is probably sending me right now, each repeating to me, over and over, that I'm running out on my problems back home. It isn't something I want to keep rehashing with him.

My eyes jerk open the moment something cold and wet covers my legs. My mouth drops open as I stare down at my tomato juice-covered lap.

This is *so* not happening to me.

The juice drips onto the floor, and I glance down at my shoes and the bag stuffed under the seat in front of me—everything is covered. I press the call light to request assistance from the flight attendant with cleaning up, taking care to hold my hands out away from my body.

The elderly man next to me frowns as he pushes up his glasses to survey the damage. "I'm sorry, young lady. These old eyes don't see like they used to. I didn't mean to knock that cup into your lap."

I can see the sincerity on his face and offer up a small smile because I don't want him to feel any worse. "Accidents happen. No worries."

The flight attendant approaches our row and leans over to turn the call light off before glancing down at me. "Oh, dear, looks like we've had a bit of a spill here."

I stare up at her and wonder how she can be so calm in this situation, but I can tell this is the type of woman who doesn't get worked up easily. There's not one strand of blond hair out of place in her updo, and her blue eyes sparkle with kindness.

I glance down at my soiled clothes. "Can I have a towel or something? I checked all my clothing, so I don't have anything extra to change into."

"Come on up front with me and we'll see if we can get you cleaned up," she replies.

I nod, grateful for her offer. "Thank you." Anything is better than smelling like rotten tomatoes for the remaining three hours of my flight. I glance over at the older man beside me. "Do you mind letting me out?"

He begins to move out of the way. "Of course not, young lady."

I follow the flight attendant through the first class section into the front galley of the plane. She reaches into a stash of canned club sodas and hands me one, along with a handful of plain white washcloths.

She frowns at me. "Sorry, it's not much, but try blotting it out the best you can. Taking out the smell will make your flight more comfortable. I would offer you a first class seat since I'm sure your seat is a mess, but unfortunately, it's all full."

"She can sit here," a deep, rumbling voice says.

When I look up, my gaze locks onto a pair of the lightest blue eyes I think I've ever seen. They're practically see-through. If I thought he was attractive from a distance that is nothing compared to the sight of him up close. The intensity causes my stomach to flip and my knees grow a little weak. I swallow hard. Considering every seat is filled, I find myself confused as to where exactly *here* is. As inviting as sitting on his lap for the next few hours may be, I don't want to open that naughty can of worms. He seems like way too much man for me. I don't think I can handle someone so...*intense.*

"You're willing to give up your seat for her, Mr. Cold?" the attendant asks.

He shakes his head. "No, but my manager will give her his seat."

Mullet Man's head jerks toward him. "I *will*?"

Mr. Cold rolls his neck and glares down at him with a stare so intense, it's almost frightening. "You have a problem with that?"

"N—no, of course not, X," he stutters, clearly intimidated by the beast of a man beside him. "She can totally have my seat."

Mr. Cold jerks his chin toward the back. "Then beat it."

Mullet Man quickly gathers his things and heads back to my tomato-stained seat in coach without another word. I glance over at the flight attendant but she simply shrugs and walks back down the aisle to continue passing out drinks.

I glance at the empty seat next to possibly the most attractive, yet scary, man I've ever come in contact with and my heart does a double thump. I can only imagine what sitting next to him for the next three hours is going to do to my cardiovascular system. My heart will never survive. It will explode from all the extra beats.

I pour the club soda onto the rag and begin blotting my jeans. I press and rub until practically every inch of my pants and shirt are soaked. Not exactly the greatest first impression to make on a celebrity, but this is the cleanest I'm going to get considering I'm thirty-five thousand feet in the air.

I sigh and then lay the now orange cloth on the drink cart in the galley and head toward Mr. Cold. I sit in the oversized gray leather seat, surprised at how much more room there is up here versus back in coach. I've always been curious as to what riding in first class would be like.

The weight of Mr. Cold's stare presses on me like a ton of bricks. I know I can't sit next to him for the next few hours and not say anything, so I might as well get it over with and thank him.

"Thank you for the seat. That was really kind of you."

His eyes drift down my body, and then back up to my face. "Don't mention it. You looked like you could use a little help, so I helped."

I roll my bottom lip between my teeth as he continues to gaze at me. His eyes are the kind people write songs and poems about. They're light blue and crystal clear. I've never seen someone with such intoxicating eyes. It nearly steals my breath every time I look into them.

Before either of us can say another word, someone passes a blank sheet of paper over my shoulder. "Give this to X. It's for a kid in the back."

I take the paper and slide it onto Mr. Cold's tray. "My, aren't you popular."

He nods and begins scratching his name across the sheet. "How about you?"

I furrow my brow. "How about me, what?"

He glances over at me and smirks. "Would you like me to sign something for you? A piece of clothing...bare skin, perhaps?"

I grimace because I don't exactly know what he's famous for. If I had to guess, factoring in the kids' reactions, I would say he's a pro athlete of some type. Still doesn't mean I need, or even *want*, his autograph—especially not on my bare skin.

"I'm good, but thank you."

He lifts his eyebrows in surprise. "That's a first."

Suddenly I feel bad for sort of insulting him. He was nice enough—if you call ordering a worker around nice—to give me a seat in first class. I should at least try and be gracious.

"I'm sorry, that was rude of me. If you would like to sign something for me...that would be great."

Mr. Cold chuckles as he hands me back the paper with his signature just in time for another autograph request to come from the back. "Don't ask out of obligation. I hate that shit. Do what you want, not what you think people want you to do."

His words hit me and remind me that's exactly what moving to Detroit is all about. Like a good little girl, I've always done what's expected of me. I went to a Christian college to please my father, and dated boys from our family's church so the guy would fit my family's ideal mold of what a good boyfriend should represent—all to please Father. None of it made *me* happy. Every time I wanted to explore the world, or taste some of the different fruits life had to offer, I was always reminded that some fruit is forbidden for a reason. Frankly, I was sick of always being told what to do and how to feel. I take a deep breath. It's time to start living my life on my own terms.

"You know what? You're right. I don't want your signature. I don't even know who you are."

His gaze snaps to me and my newfound toughness wavers a bit under the intensity of his stare. Panicking slightly, I feel the need to backpedal. "Don't get me wrong, I'm grateful for the seat, but I don't want an autograph."

He smiles and a tingle erupts in my belly before spreading through the rest of my body. He's got a great smile, and paired with those gorgeous eyes of his, it's a deadly combination of sexiness. I imagine many women have lost their ever-lovin' minds because of that smile.

"What's your name, beautiful?"

My heart does a double thud as I swallow hard and try to remember what my own name is. That smile is causing me to go a little batty myself. Not that anyone could blame me. After all, this stunning man just called *me* "beautiful."

"Anna Cortez."

His eyes dance with amusement.

"Cortez," he repeats.

The way my name rolls off his tongue sounds so sensual and naughty. It's almost as if he's trying to turn me on and make me squirm on purpose for turning down his stupid autograph. "Is that Spanish?"

"It is," I answer simply. "It means 'courteous.'"

"Ah, sassy and smart, I see," Mr. Cold teases. Or at least...I think he's joking. It doesn't seem like he's pissed or anything because he's still grinning. "It's nice to meet you, Anna Cortez."

"Likewise, Mr..."

Oh damn. Do I call him Mr. X? Or do I refer to him as Mr. Cold like the flight attendant did? I hate being stuck in these awkward social situations. I've never claimed to be a big people person.

Luckily for me, he fills in the gap. "You can call me Xavier."

Things begin to click for me. "Is that where the X comes from?"

"It is."

I lick my lips before I wonder out loud, "How about the 'Phenomenal' part?"

His eyes flick down to my lips and then back up again. "I could tell you, but I think it'd be a whole lot more fun if I showed you where that portion of my name comes from."

Why do I have the distinct feeling that this man has just propositioned me after sitting next to me for less than ten minutes? No one, other than me, gets into these jeans that fast. "I think I'm good without that too."

"You're a good girl, aren't you, Anna?" Xavier asks, trying to feel me out.

"I'd like to think so, but if you asked my father that question right now he might tell you I'm the spawn of Satan," I respond easily, and then immediately wish I could take the last part back. I tend to ramble when I get nervous, thus exposing all my secrets and this guy is the last person who needs to know my life history. Besides, it's not like he really cares anyhow. He's obviously one of *those kinds* of guys Father always warns me about. The kind who only wants one thing.

Xavier shakes his head. "I've met some actual demons from hell and trust me, beautiful, you're the furthest thing from evil I've been around in a long, long time. Your father needs a wakeup call. I could tell the second our eyes met that you were a sweet one."

"You...you noticed me...before?" I question, blown away that the little eye lock we shared when he got on the plane had made an impression on him too.

He goes back to signing his name and shrugs. "I always take in every inch of my surroundings, and any man would be a fucking fool if he didn't notice you."

I feel the blush creep into my cheeks from the full-on flattery. I've never had a man talk to me so...so...*bluntly* before. All the guys I've ever dated have been good guys. Polite, with proper manners. Xavier makes my toes curl with a simple look and a few dirty words.

Yep. I'm so out of my league.

It's difficult, but I jerk my attention away from this dangerous man next to me and study my nails, doing my best to keep my eyes from wandering back to my left. I can't help being intrigued by him. If I were the kind of girl who did naughty things with random hotties, I would be all over his offer to find out just how phenomenal he is—in a heartbeat. But as things stand, I'm still a good girl. I know I am, even if my father challenges that fact. All because I ran away from a man I'd promised to marry.

"You're quiet over there. Did I piss you off?" Xavier asks with what I assume is a tender tone but still has a touch of a natural growl to it.

I chew on the corner of my lip. "No. You didn't. I was just thinking."

"About..." he prods, and he glances down at my arm and zeroes on the spot where Father's too tight hold left some marks.

My hand instantly covers the small bruises, not wanting him to ask about them. Explaining how things got a little out of hand when I told my father I was leaving isn't exactly something I want to discuss with a man who I don't know.

I fold my arms over my chest, careful to keep the spot hidden, and stare down at my stained outfit, wishing I hadn't checked all my clothes. "Nothing you would want to hear about, I'm sure. No one likes to listen to a perfect stranger's drama. Besides, I'm positive my life is boring compared to yours—there's no autographs in my normalcy." I add a little teasing at the end to lighten the mood.

Xavier slides his index finger under my chin and then softly pinches it with his thumb, forcing me to look at him. "You're frowning. Why?"

His immediate concern for my happiness takes me aback, and I raise my eyebrows. I can't very well spill my entire tragic life story to this man, even though the sincerity of his intentions shine in his gaze. I didn't expect this type of reaction from him, so I'm thrown off balance for a moment, unsure of how to respond. "I, uh..."

His eyes never leave mine as he says, "A frown doesn't belong on a face like yours, beautiful. Ever. I'm just curious who put it there."

"No one put it there," I whisper, trying to block out that fact that this slight touch from him is sending my body into overdrive.

"Did your boyfriend upset you?"

I should say I don't have a boyfriend because I'm positive once Jorge discovers I left town with no intention of ever returning, he won't want to see me again anyway. Technically I'm single, and I have the feeling this is exactly what Xavier wants to hear from me. Spending the next few hours in such close proximity to him, I'll never be able to fend off his direct advances without eventually agreeing to have sex with him as soon as we land. If he knows I'm unattached, he's the type who'll never give up. No need to dangle a steak in front of a hungry lion.

"He isn't the problem. I'm fine, see." I give him a small smile, hoping he stops prying before I get caught up in my own lie about being taken.

"Not sure I'm buying that weak-ass smile."

His lips pull into a tight line, and I fully expect him to release me, but he doesn't. Xavier's fingers stay in place, burning into my skin. "It's fine if you don't want to say what's on your mind. I get that. But no more frowning for the rest of this trip, or I might be forced to find other ways to make you smile just to piss your boyfriend the fuck off."

His finger traces down my neck and across my collarbone, leaving a trail of fire in its wake.

My mouth drops open and I can't stop myself from asking, "What kind of ways?"

Damn my stupid curious brain. That just set him up for all kinds of dirty talk.

He tries to fight back a smile, but it doesn't work. It comes at me in full, glorious force. "More ways than that sweet brain of yours could ever imagine."

He leans into me, and I can't do anything more than tense because his hand slides up the side of my neck in a very intimate gesture. He's close enough that, if I pushed forward a couple of inches, our lips would meet in what I imagine would be an earth-altering kiss.

"I could do things to your body that most women only dream about while reading their dirty romance novels, and I promise you'd fucking enjoy it."

I stare up at him speechless. Wow.

Just...*wow*.

I can't believe he just said that to me.

Xavier licks his plump lips. "No strings attached, and your boyfriend would never have to know." He leans in and whispers in my ear, "I just want a little taste."

My breath hitches and I close my eyes. The thought of allowing this man to have his way with me is very tempting. So tempting in fact that, for a moment, I seriously consider agreeing. The opportunity to possibly have the best sex of your entire life doesn't come along every day, and I can tell just by looking at Xavier Cold that his skill in the bedroom likely knows no bounds.

He would be the perfect act of rebellion. Going against everything my life currently represents—a representation I'm desperate to break away from.

I want to say yes to him, I really do, but no matter how hard I fight to break away from the good girl persona, I know random sex with a stranger will never be my kind of thing.

I open my eyes and they instantly lock on his cool blue ones. I take a deep breath and whisper, "No."

His brows shoot up, like he can't believe he's just been turned down.

"*No?*"

My chest begins to heave. For some strange reason, turning him down is hard. It's like my body is defying my brain and becoming aroused, even though my head is screaming for me to run as far away as I can.

Xavier sucks in his bottom lip and slowly pulls it between his teeth. "You don't seem so sure about that *no*, beautiful. You want to change your answer? I'll be gentle with you, I swear. You don't have to be afraid of me."

"I, uh..."

I, uh...what? There's nothing to even consider here. I don't know why I'm having such a hard time giving him a firm no—one that sounds like I mean business. Even *I* realize I'm throwing him mixed signals by allowing him to touch me and whisper dirty promises in my ear.

Desperate to get myself out of the intense mess I've allowed to go on too long, I push him back a bit and turn to the middle-aged, brunette lady sitting across the aisle from me. "Do you have any blank paper, please?"

She nods and reaches under the seat in front of her to retrieve a bag. After digging around for a moment, she finds a small notebook and rips out a page. "This is all I have."

I return her smile with one of my own. "Thank you. It's perfect."

I turn and redirect my attention to Xavier, who watches me with a mixture of amusement and curiosity. "The only thing I would like from you is your autograph. *Nothing* more."

I lay the paper on his tray, but he doesn't take his eyes off me. "That's all, huh?"

"That's all," I confirm.

He adjusts the paper on his tray and then glances back up at me. "We'll see."

This little game with him is exhausting. If we keep this up, by the end of the flight I'll either want to kill him or screw his brains out, and neither of those things are on my scheduled to-do list on the path to starting my new life.

I lean my head back and shut my eyes, and pray I can sleep my way through the rest of the flight. Ignoring the dangerously sexy man sitting only inches away from me is the only way I'll stop my body from taking him up on his offer.

Chapter
TWO

Anna

A gentle nudge on my forearm startles me, and I'm quickly jerked back to reality. I've just fallen asleep while sitting next to a ridiculously delicious man. Quickly running my fingers around the corners of my mouth, I make sure I haven't drooled all over my face.

God, this is so embarrassing. I just pray I wasn't snoring. I got very little sleep last night while I lay awake in my bed, dreading the thought of facing my father. The possible scenarios of what he would say when I told him I was leaving Portland to move across the country had played on a continuous loop through my mind, all of them ending with my father not supporting my choice and trying to stop me—which is exactly what happened. I'm just glad I knew enough ahead of time to make arrangements for my neighbor, Kayla, to wait outside my house with the motor running so I could make a quick getaway. Father had no intentions of allowing me to follow through with my plans, which is exactly why he left me no choice but to sneak out of my house and into Kayla's car the moment he turned his back.

Leaving home was the hardest thing I've ever done, but I had to go. I couldn't take being smothered any more.

"The pilot just announced that we'll be landing in approximately thirty minutes, so I thought you would like to know," Xavier says. "You fell asleep so quickly I figured you were exhausted, so I didn't bother you. I have to say, you're different from most women I've met, Anna."

Curiosity gnaws at me as to what exactly he means by that, and I can't help asking, "Different how? Because I refuse to sleep with random men who proposition me?"

He shrugs. "No, not that. I just don't recall that I've ever bored a woman to sleep before. You didn't even seem the slightest bit fazed with me sitting next to you when you zonked-out. Matter of fact, you seem indifferent toward me, which is refreshing...in an odd way."

I laugh. "You *prefer* when people deny your requests?"

The corner of his mouth turns up, revealing what I'm sure is his best panty-soaking smile. "No, but I admire how you stick to your principles and don't back down. Most women aren't like that."

I smile. "I do believe that's a compliment, Xavier."

His grin gets even bigger. He's clearly pleased with himself. I bet in that sex-crazed brain of his, he thinks he's getting somewhere with me.

"So, what's in Detroit?"

My mind stumbles, not ready for such a simple question. I was fully prepared for more sexy banter.

"A fresh start."

His expression turns quizzical, so I explain. "I need to start over, I have family there. My cousin Quinn and Aunt Dee have offered to help me out."

Xavier glances back to coach, where his manager occupies my old seat. "I know the old man you were next to isn't your boyfriend, and the woman on the other side of your assigned seat isn't your girlfriend, so I'm thinking your boyfriend isn't on this flight with you. He's not apart of this fresh start?"

I take a deep breath. Since we're off this plane in a few minutes, and I'll never see this man again, I may as well come clean. A little truth can't hurt.

"No, he's not. No one I know from Portland is."

He raises his eyebrows. "The boyfriend isn't going to come after you?"

I shake my head. "I sort of ended things with him."

"Is that why you're running away from Portland? Can't face breaking some poor schmuck's heart?" he asks with a playful tone.

I fold my arms across my chest. "I assure you that I didn't break Jorge's heart."

He smirks. "You don't honestly believe that, do you?"

"Why wouldn't I? Jorge and I were never really in love. Our families are close, and us being together was expected." If arranged marriages were still legal, that's exactly what would've happened with Jorge and me. We were more like siblings than anything else. I loved him, but not in the way that made me know deep down he was "*The One.*"

Recognition flashes across Xavier's face. "So you're escaping an overbearing family that tries to control your life. Aren't you afraid that your aunt will try to push more things on you that you don't want?"

He's good. He's practically figured out my entire life story with just that little bit of information. I should shut my big mouth right now and not indulge him further, but it's actually nice to talk to someone about this—especially since it seems like he understands how my family tries to push their beliefs on me. It's like he can connect with me on some level.

"Aunt Dee isn't like that. She's really cool. The exact the opposite of my father."

He nods. "I grew up like that myself—in an overly religious household. It's rough living with people who are passionate over certain...beliefs."

Xavier pauses for a beat before he asks, "So how pissed is your dad that you took off without his consent?"

My mouth drops open a little. "How did you know that?"

He shrugs. "You're a good girl who has a controlling father, it's not hard to figure out. You want freedom. I can sense it on you from a mile away. I understand why you're leaving."

"You do?" Surprise rings in my voice. No one other than Quinn and Aunt Dee have empathized with me before. Most people from back home will freak out and call me a fool once they figure out I left. People don't understand that sometimes ideas of perfection in a family get carried a little too far. It's nice that he seems to get it.

"I do. Being trapped in a life that you didn't choose is no fucking picnic, no matter how good it may appear to people outside of the situation. I've been there myself. So, yeah, I get it, and I don't blame you. No one should be forced to live their life in any way other than how they choose."

I stare at him, amazed he knew exactly what I was thinking. He's been where I'm at, and he doesn't look down on me for running away from my life. For a moment it's easy to forget he's a sexy celebrity and not just a regular man—one I would like to get to know better.

"It's nice to hear someone agree with me for a change. I don't like defying my father but I felt like if I didn't get away, I was going to drown in a world full of ideas and beliefs that I don't necessarily agree with."

"When you say beliefs, I'm going to assume you mean religion."

I sigh. "Yes. Not that I'm a non-believer, I just don't like having it shoved down my throat all the time."

His blue eyes search my face. "You really are a sweet girl." Before I can reply to that statement he continues. "I'm glad that you refused me. I'm no good for you."

With our gazes locked, I suddenly forget why I was so put off by his advances in the first place. Maybe my assumptions about him were wrong. He would make an excellent friend—if I weren't so insanely attracted to him.

"You don't seem so bad to me. You're easy to talk to."

He swallows hard. "That's because you don't know me. Believe me, beautiful, I'm bad fucking news. A nice girl like you should run away from me as quick as you can."

My chest heaves while the intensity radiates off him and wraps itself around me. Something about him pulls me in, and I can't explain why I suddenly feel like we are kindred spirits, both running from something. I know he's not good for me—he even said so himself—but I can't stop my stupid body from being attracted to him.

My eyes drift down to his lips, and the thought of what they would feel like on mine washes over me. I imagine they're demanding yet gentle, all at the same time. Thinking like this is dangerous and will lead me down a road I'm not sure I'm ready for, but I can't help doing it.

"You can't keep looking at me like that. I want you. If you give in to me, there's no going back, and you're not ready for someone like me. I don't have the best self-control, and I'm a very selfish man." His voice is tight, like he's struggling between what he *should* do and what he *wants* to do.

Just like I am.

He leans in closer and runs his nose down the length of my jaw, pausing for a brief second to kiss the soft skin beneath my ear. My breath catches and I clench my thighs together to calm the ache he's just created between my legs. It gives me some relief, but my damn naïve curiosity won't let his last words go.

"How am I looking at you?" I whisper.

He tugs my earlobe lightly with his teeth. "Like you're begging for my touch." He inhales deeply through his nose and then growls, "I haven't even kissed you yet, and I'm already fucking hard. Spend the night with me. Let me show you just how good I can make you feel."

I close my eyes. Even though his dark promises of passion are tempting, I can't give in to him. I don't willingly give my body over to complete strangers.

"No," I say again, so faintly that I barely hear it myself.

His tongue teases the bare flesh on my neck. "I don't typically beg, beautiful, but if begging gets me access between those creamy thighs, I will. Just give in to your desires."

He's right.

And, damn it, I hate that he's right. I do want him, more than anything I've ever wanted in my entire life. He pulls back and stares into my eyes, searching my face for permission to pleasure me.

Electricity zings between us, and every nerve ending in my body comes alive. My willpower falters a bit. How many times can I turn down something I really want? If I'm being honest, right now, my body craves nothing more than to experience sex with this powerful man, even though my logical mind knows it's wrong, and I've always been more of a "follow your head, not your heart" kind of girl. I stare into his eyes, willing the word "no" to tumble from my lips again, but no sound comes out.

The landing gear unlocking from the underside of the plane causes my pulse to race under my skin. I need to make a decision because I know the moment I step off this plane I'll never see Xavier again.

The plane jolts, and the tires screech against the runway, but Xavier's eyes never stray from mine as he awaits my answer. While we wait to exit the plane our eyes remain locked, and a thousand scenarios run through my head. I don't even realize that we haven't said a word to one another for several moments. No words are needed to know what we are both thinking. It's impossible for me not to sit here and stare at him, and not imagine his mouth on mine.

The flight crew opens the door, and all the passengers around us stand and begin exiting the aircraft. I swallow hard as his eyes drop down to my lips and then back up to my eyes.

"What'll it be, Anna Cortez? Are you in, or are you out?"

My heart bangs in my chest, but as much as I would like to experience what he's offering, I have to stick to my guns.

"I'm out."

I stand and turn to exit, but freeze when Xavier grabs my wrist, my skin igniting from his mere touch. My eyes snap down to my hand as he stuffs a paper into it. I flick my gaze back up to his and a grin plays along his lips. "Let me know when you change your mind."

He releases me and immediately my skin craves his warmth again. I consider tossing his autograph back down at him, but for some reason a part of me wants to keep it so I can be sure this time spent with him wasn't just a dream. It'll be a nice memory to hang on to. That Phenomenal X is real and, at one time, was very attracted to me. I tighten my fingers around the paper and take a deep breath.

"Goodbye, Xavier."

Before he has an opportunity to make any more sexy promises, I turn and flee the plane, stuffing the paper into my back pocket. My heart still beats a million miles a minute. I need to find a place I can calm down and regain my composure.

Once I'm safely in the terminal, I dash into the first ladies' room I find. The urge to splash cold water on my face surges through me. I definitely need to cool off, but I don't want to totally ruin my makeup, so I resist. I pull my long brown hair back and then pull it to one side as I rest my hands against the counter and stare at myself in the mirror.

I'm searching hard to find what someone like Xavier would find so appealing about me. My button nose and dark hair don't exactly stand out against my tan skin. My green eyes are only thing I've always been complimented on. The light color against everything else dark really seems to *pop*.

I sigh and reach into my back pocket for my phone. I need to call Aunt Dee, and I need to get out of this place and as far away from Xavier as possible. A growl escapes my lips as I frantically begin patting the empty pockets of my jeans. "Shit," I mutter to myself.

The last time I had my phone was on the plane when I shut it off after checking my father's messages. I didn't bother grabbing it from the seat-back pocket when I moved. My shoulders sag when I realize I didn't grab my bag from under the seat either. I'm going to have to go back and hope I can sneak on the plane and get it.

I make my way down through the terminal back to the gate I just came from. It's completely empty and I'm afraid to try and get back on the plane. The last thing I need is TSA all over me. I lay my head on the gate counter, trying to not lose my mind, but my stomach clenches and I'm about two seconds from having a nervous breakdown.

It's gone. My phone is gone.

Deflated, I flop down on the nearest seat. Great. Just great. I move out to a new city and before I even set foot onto its soil, I lose my belongings. Numbers for everyone back home are programmed into that phone.

I shake my head in disgust. I'll never hear the end of it when Father finds out about this. I rub my forehead and fight back the building tears.

"Excuse me, miss? Can I be of some assistance?" a somewhat familiar voice questions. I glance up as the same flight attendant who helped me when I had tomato juice incident approach me from the gate. She offers up the same sweet smile she gave me when she spoke with me before. "Are you all right?"

I sniff, fighting back the tears. "I'm missing my phone and my bag. The last place I had them was on the plane—before I changed seats."

She nods in agreement. "Mr. Cold asked me to let you know that he has your belongings."

My eyes widen. "He does?"

Relief washes through me, only to be flushed away when I realize I have no way of getting in touch with him again. "I have no way of reaching him."

She tilts her head and I hear the questioning tone in her voice when she says, "He said you have his number?"

I knit my eyebrows in confusion. *I have his number?* What's he talking about? The only thing he gave me was...

Wait a minute.

I reach in my back pocket and pull out the paper containing his autograph, or at least I thought it was his autograph. I unfold it slowly and take in the thick, manly scroll.

Anna Cortez,

Call me when you change that no. I'll be waiting.

Xavier

I swallow hard as I stare at the number listed below his signature. Even in a simple note, his commanding tone makes my insides jitter.

A war rages within me. The exhilarated half of me is excited that I'll likely see Xavier again, but the rational half knows that means I'm in for trouble. Trouble I'm not sure that I can resist.

However, one thing *is* clear, if I want my phone and other personal belongings back, I have no choice but to call him.

Heaven help where it may lead.

Chapter
THREE

I head out into the warm Detroit summer and spot my family the moment I'm outside. Aunt Dee and my cousin Quinn wait in the loading zone for me as I wheel two large suitcases packed with all my clothes and shoes. I kept my eyes peeled at baggage claim, hoping to see Xavier and reclaim my items so I could be done with him for good, but there was no sign of him anywhere. The fact that I'm going to have to call that sexy beast of a man looms over me.

Aunt Dee greets me with a warm smile as I approach. "Anna, sweetheart, how are you? You look beautiful, darling, absolutely stunning, except for that hideous stain all over you. Looks like someone doused you with their drink."

"It's great to see you, Aunt Dee."

I giggle at her words, laced with a thick Spanish accent, as I take in the multicolored bandana tied around her head in a chic, yet fashionable way that blends into her hairstyle. Like I said, Aunt Dee is a little eccentric. She's an artist—a painter and a sculptor—and her creativity typically carries over into her wardrobe. Much like the tie-dyed maxi-dress she has on. "I hope this stain comes out. I didn't bring a lot of clothes."

"I know just the trick to get it out once we get home." She pulls back and inspects me from head to toe. "You look so much like your mother. Doesn't she, Quinn?"

I glance over at my cousin who is wearing a pair of cut-off shorts and a black tank top. Quinn has always been whom I would consider the most beautiful person in our family. We're exactly the same age, but it's hard to compete with her gorgeous brown hair and legs that go on for days. She's drop-dead gorgeous, and every man around always notices her. She's not stuck on herself though, which makes me love her even more. She's about the most down-to-earth person I know.

Quinn smiles at me before wrapping me up in a hug. "I'm so glad you're here, Anna. We are going to have so much fun this summer."

"Aye, girls...but not too much fun," Aunt Dee warns. "Your father would have my head on a stick. He is the last person on earth I want on my back."

Quinn pulls back. "How did this morning go?"

Allowing my eyes to flit back and forth between my aunt and cousin, I frown. They know how bad it was for me back home. We talk all the time, and Quinn is like a sister to me. If it weren't for their support, I wouldn't have had the guts to walk away like I did. "It was bad. I'm sure he's still blowing up my phone telling me that I'm making a huge mistake."

Aunt Dee shakes her head. "That's where your father and I differ in opinion, Anna.

Marrying a man you don't love to please your family is a much larger mistake. He should want happiness for you, not sorrow."

I nod. "I can never thank you enough for giving me a place to escape to."

She cups my face. "It's no problem, sweet girl. I wouldn't want my Quinn to be forced into something like that and, someday, I hope your father will change his mind and see that what he was trying to do was wrong."

Emotions build inside my chest, making me nearly burst as I fight against them. I don't want to have a breakdown right here on the curb at the airport. I swallow hard.

"Me too," is all I can whisper.

My aunt's face twists with pity. "Awww, come on. Let's get you home, yeah?"

A single tear slips from my eye. It's not until this very moment that I realize how serious all this is. For the first time in my life the unknown is staring me in the face and I'm scared shitless, yet exhilarated at the same time. I've never felt this free—this alive.

Quinn takes one of my suitcases and loads it into the trunk of her mom's Prius. "I can't believe you fit all your stuff in two bags. It would've taken at least ten for my shoes alone."

I shake my head and smile. "You and your shoes. I've never known anyone more obsessed with them."

She grins, and it lights up her gorgeous features. "I'd like to think only Imelda Marcos could rival me. I would love to peek in that lady's closet."

I roll my eyes as we shut the trunk. "I could think of so many better things to do with my time than explore an eighty-year-old woman's shoe collection."

Quinn's eyes widen like I've just cursed her out. "Are you *kidding* me? The woman is famous for having over three thousand pairs of shoes. Aren't you the least bit curious to see that?"

I laugh as I get in the backseat and Quinn slides in up front next to her mother. "Honestly, I find it a little disgusting and wasteful to have so much excess."

She shakes her head as she fastens her seatbelt. "Always the realist, aren't you, Anna? One of these days something is going to break you out of that conservative shell of yours."

"You know I've been this way since birth, Quinn. It'd take a real miracle to change my views after twenty-one years," I answer, a hint of amusement in my voice.

"No. Not a miracle, Anna—a man," she teases. "We're going out tonight to find you a hot piece of male ass to loosen you up."

My mouth drops open, completely mortified that Quinn is talking to me like that with her mother around. It would be one thing for her to say that to me when we were alone, but it's absolutely mortifying in front of an audience. My father would've given me a stern lecture and forbidden me to ever see Quinn again, even if she was flesh and blood. He wouldn't care. Someone like Quinn doesn't fit his mold.

When I don't reply, Quinn glances back over her shoulder, gauging my reaction. "Come on, Anna. Mom is completely cool. She's a single woman too. She gets it. Don't ya, Ma?" Quinn nudges Aunt Dee's elbow with her own.

Aunt Dee nods. "I do, but dear, you have to remember how Anna was raised. She isn't used to people being so open and free."

Quinn sighs. "Uncle Simon is too hardcore. I can't even imagine living with him. It must've been torture."

I adjust in the seat. It's hard to hear someone else confirm that your life has been a living hell. I mean, I've known for a while now that I haven't grown up like most people, but it's been the only life I've ever known. Even though Aunt Dee and Quinn promised to help get me on my feet, it still wasn't easy leaving.

There are so many things that are uncertain now, but I'm ready to face whatever comes at me, head on.

"Oh, and I talked to my boss about you yesterday. Andy says he can use another waitress since the one he just hired quit, so the jobs yours if you want it. All you have to do is fill out an application and you can start right away," Quinn informs me.

I smile and place my hand on her shoulder. "I'll never be able to thank you enough. I'm truly grateful"—I put my other hand on Aunt Dee's shoulder—"to both of you."

Aunt Dee pats my hand. "You're more than welcome, dear."

I lean back in my seat. No matter how many times I thank them, it's never going to be enough. It's like they have given me a chance to live life my way for once. I'll always be grateful.

"Anna, I know you probably don't want to think about this right now, but I think you need to give your father a call and let him know you're safe. My big brother will worry himself to death if he doesn't at least know you're with me. He's probably worn a path in the marble floor and driven your poor mother crazy by now," Aunt Dee says as she merges onto the freeway.

I sigh. "I can't. I lost my phone on the plane."

"Oh, shit," Quinn says. "Do you have the insurance plan so you can get a new one?"

I shrug. "No idea. Father pays the bill. But it should be okay because I know who has it and I have his number, so I can get it back. All I have to do is call him and make arrangements to get it...and my purse."

Quinn jerks around in her seat, concern written all over her face. "Anna, I know this being on your own thing is new to you, but you cannot make friends on airplanes. You never know what kind of whack-job you're sitting next to. How did a stranger end up with your things anyhow?"

I glance down at my soiled clothing and replay the moment I met Xavier in my head while I explain what happened on the flight.

Quinn furrows her brow. "So some rich guy has your stuff and wants you to call him."

"I guess, if you want to look at it that way."

"Looks like he took a special interest in making sure he'd get to see you again." She smiles. "Girl, sounds like you've got more game than I gave you credit for. That must've been some conversation on that flight because he could've easily turned it into the flight crew."

I roll my eyes and feel my face heat up, revealing a blush. There's no way I want to repeat the things Xavier said to me. I shouldn't have allowed him to speak that way to me. I should've stopped him, but I'd be lying if I said I hadn't liked it. "You're ridiculous."

Quinn gasps, making a big show of being shocked before nudging Aunt Dee's arm again. "He's hot, isn't he? I know that look."

I raise my eyebrows. "What *look*?"

She smirks. "The one that says I-just-met-a-really-hot-rich-man-that-totally-wants-to-jump-my-bones-and-I-just-might-let-him. Trust me, Anna, I've had that look a few times myself." She laughs. "So tell me all about him."

"Quinn, I don't really know him," I say.

"You spent four hours next to the man chatting. That's longer than most first dates, so spill, sister."

I laugh at her forwardness. "I hate to disappoint you, but I slept most of the way."

She twists her lips. "You must be one hell of a sleeper to get a man that sprung without much conversation. Come on, Anna. At least tell me his name."

I lick my lips as his face pops into my mind. "Xavier."

"Oh, *rawr*. That's a definite hot guy name. Tell me more. What's he look like? Details, girl. De-tails."

I chew on my bottom lip. "He's really tall, has really broad shoulders, tattoos and he's sort of..."

"Oh my God, what? The suspense is killing me," Quinn whines.

"He's famous," I blurt out.

Quinn's eyes widen. "Who is he? If you say Xavier is Ryan Reynolds' real name I will wrestle you for his phone number."

I chuckle. "No, it's not Ryan Reynolds. I would've probably freaked if I sat by a celebrity I actually recognized."

She frowns. "So he's not super famous, just a little famous?"

I shake my head. "Oh no, he's popular. I'm just not sure what for. He signed autographs the entire flight."

She tilts her head to the side and her eyes drift up toward the ceiling. "Hmm. I don't know anyone famous by the name Xavier and I study the tabloids proficiently, so he must be known by something else."

"Does Phenomenal X ring a bell?"

"Ring it? It fucking smashes it! I can't believe you didn't know who he was! He's only *the* hottest man in wrestling, and the newest playboy to grace the cover of all the magazines." She tsks. "You really are the most sheltered human on the planet. This needs to be rectified immediately."

"And how do you plan on making me worldlier?" I tease.

"Easy." She grins and the wicked twinkle in her eye scares me a bit. "You're going to start by sleeping with a known bad-boy."

I shake my head. "Oh, no. No way, Quinn. I don't do things like that."

"Maybe old Anna didn't, but new Anna will. You came out here to live a little and be free. What better way to experience true rebellion than messing around with a guy who's the exact opposite of everything you're used to. Plus, as a bonus, Uncle Simon will hate it. It's a total win-win for you." The confidence in her tone tells me she believes what she's saying down to her soul.

"I don't know, Quinn. That's a huge step for me. I'm not sure I can sleep with some guy I barely know. That's crazy." I glance over at Aunt Dee who is shaking her head at Quinn's evil-genius plan.

I sigh. "How about we compromise? I'll call Xavier and ask him to meet us somewhere so I can get my stuff back. I'm not promising to sleep with him though."

"As long as we can meet him in a bar or something, it's a deal. I'll need some liquid courage to speak to that beast of a man." She claps her hands together and then digs through her Coach bag to find her phone. "Get his number out. We're setting this up before you have a chance to talk yourself out of it."

If I didn't desperately need my phone back, I'd never call Xavier. Just the memory of the way he made me feel without really touching me on that plane is enough to make me nearly combust. I'm in way over my head here, but Quinn's right. I need to do the exact opposite of what I would normally do. I hope I know enough to keep me afloat once Quinn shoves me into the shark tank.

The folded paper is still in my back pocket, so I lean forward and retrieve it. "Can I borrow your phone?"

She hands me her phone wrapped in its sparkly diamond case. "Be assertive. Tell him to meet you at Gibby's Bar on Third tonight at nine o'clock. Don't give him a chance to gain the upper hand. With a man like Phenomenal X, you have to take control and show him you aren't the kind of girl who will take his shit. You call the shots and he'll be eating out of the palm of your hand in no time."

A lump builds in my throat as I dial his number. After three rings a distinctly male voice answers the phone. "Speak."

The cold way he answers the phone throws me off guard. I open my mouth to speak, but no words will fall from my lips. All of the witty things I wanted to say to him fly completely out the window.

Quinn nudges my leg, pushing me to say something so I just blurt out the first thing that comes to mind. "I want my phone back."

Xavier chuckles into the phone. "Is that any way to say thank you after I rescued your belongings? Ask me a little nicer and I might just give you what want you want."

"I, um..."

God, what is wrong with me? He has me stuttering like an idiot. This man is infuriating. I wish I wasn't at his mercy, but until I get my things back it looks like I have to play nice with him. "Is there any way you can,"—Quinn nudges me again and again mouths to have him meet us tonight—"meet me at Gibby's on Third tonight and bring my things?"

"That's a really public place, beautiful. I was hoping the next time I saw you, we'd be somewhere a little more secluded, if you know what I mean," he says, amusement lacing his voice.

"No way," I fire back.

"What's wrong, Anna, don't trust yourself to be alone with me? Would it really be so bad if I found my way into those panties of yours?" he teases and the tingle that rippled through me on the plane comes back with full force.

"Please," I say with a chuckle, attempting to make a show that he's not getting to me. "I don't know where you get off believing for one second that you'd be able to get inside my underwear. It's not happening, X."

Quinn's mouth drops open and her eyes widen as she gets the gist of the conversation I'm having with this absurdly sexy man.

"So it's 'X' now, is it? I thought I told you to call me Xavier. X is reserved for people who don't know me." All traces of the playful tone have been erased from his voice.

"I *don't* know you," I answer without any hesitation, because other than the fact he makes my body crazy, I know absolutely nothing about him.

"Not yet." His reply is simple, but confident. "But you will. I'll see you tonight, beautiful."

Before I have a chance to say anything else, the line goes dead. I pull the cell away from my ear and stare down at it.

Shit.

Why do I get the feeling that I'm in for it? I run my hands through my hair as I hand the phone to Quinn. The knowing grin on her face only adds to the gnawing feeling in the pit of my stomach that Xavier Cold is about to be the tornado that flips my world upside down.

Chapter
FOUR

Up or down? That's the classic debate most women face when trying to get ready for a night out. I thread my fingers through my brown hair and pull it up off my neck as I stare at myself in the mirror. I twist my head from side to side. Of course I want to look sexy, but I don't want to give Xavier the impression that I'm easy. I'm far from that.

"Oh, my God, Anna. I can't believe you were sitting next to professional wrestling's resident badass. Not to mention one of world's sexiest men alive—according to the last magazine I read. You got to sit next to this tasty treat of a man for nearly four hours...how did you keep from spontaneously combusting right there on the plane?" Quinn wonders out loud as she lies on her belly, scouring the Internet for information on Phenomenal X. "I don't think the guy takes a bad picture, ever. He does the whole 'fuck me' vibe without even trying. Since you're so adamant you aren't into him, you might have to stop *me* from jumping his bones in public."

I allow my hair to fall loosely around my shoulders. Down it is. "Why would someone like him be into someone like me?"

Quinn's eyes snap up in my direction as I spin away from her dresser mirror to face her. "Puh-*leese*, Anna. Please tell me you're not one of those self-loathing chicks who can't see her own beauty. I know you're smarter than that."

I shake my head. "It's not like I just said I was ugly, Quinn. I just meant that he's a celebrity and I'm...well...boring and plain."

She shoves herself up from the bed. "Boring, yeah...I might have to agree with you on that one because if a guy like Phenomenal X showed the slightest bit of interest in me on a plane, we'd be joining the mile high club in a snap—even *if* I had to turn myself into a human pretzel to make it work in that tight as hell bathroom."

She laughs at herself as she makes her way over to me, and spins me back around to face the mirror. "But, Anna, *plain* you most certainly are not. We are Cortez women. We are naturally beautiful. No man can resist our charms when we use them. It's a gift from the deities, designed to help us maneuver this crazy manmade world."

I stare at Quinn through the mirror. "Easy for you to say. You're beautiful."

Her hands slide up on my shoulders. "Not as beautiful as you. I've always been insanely jealous of your nose and green eyes."

My eyes widen at the thought that my drop-dead gorgeous cousin thinks I'm prettier than her. "Really? I can't believe I'm going to admit this out loud, but I would kill for your legs."

She chuckles. "Lots of working out, babe, but don't discount that rockin' bod you've got going on. I'm sure if you allowed yourself to see it, you'd notice that men flock to your beauty." She sighs. "So you see, you have all the tools to be confident—you just need a little experience in how to use them. And you're in luck because I just happen to be an excellent flirting instructor. You can practice tonight on Mr. Sexy."

I frown. "I doubt all the training in the world can help me gain enough courage to flirt with him."

All the overtly sexual comments he made, and the way my body instantly reacted to him, flood my brain. A man like Xavier, who has already shown that he is well versed in how to arouse the opposite sex, is not the ideal candidate to be honing ones flirting skills on. He's the kind of guy a girl like Quinn can handle. But me? I've only had one serious boyfriend my entire life, and as much as I would like to say I attracted Jorge on my own, I can't even take credit for landing him. If it weren't for my father, that relationship wouldn't have happened either.

"Hey." Quinn taps the top of my head. "Whatever's rolling around in there just forget it. Whatever you're thinking about right now, think the opposite. Today is the first day of your new life—out with the old, shy Anna, in with the spunky new one. It's time the rest of the world got to experience some of the fire that I know is hiding inside there. I've seen spunky Anna before and I like her. It's time to explore the world."

That's the second time today someone has encouraged me to be the me who's deep inside—to do what I feel, instead of what I think I should do.

I nod and smile at Quinn. "You're right. That's what coming here was supposed to be about. I need to learn to loosen up and live a little, and a sure thing like Phenomenal X feels like a good place to begin. I'm so tired of being the good girl, Quinn. The Goody-Two-shoes nobody ever wanted to be real friends with. Did you know I didn't get invited to one single party in high school because kids were afraid I would narc them out?"

Quinn frowns and strokes the back of my head. "Oh, Anna, girl, that's terrible, but I'm sure college was much better, right?"

I shake my head and fight back the tears that threaten to expose the years of sadness that plague me to this day. "Not really. By that time Father had set me up with Jorge who went to another Christian college across the state, and I never accepted any invites to any parties because I was afraid of upsetting Jorge or Father. Even though we're not together a lot, I still feel like you're my closet friend. You're the only person who's ever been really there for me." I wipe a lone tear from my eye and sniff. "Ugh. Admitting that makes it all sound even lamer."

She wraps her thin arms around my shoulders and pulls me in for a tight hug. "Screw all the assholes who can't see how awesome you are. I'll gladly accept the title of your best friend."

I laugh softly and hug her back. "Thank you, Quinn. I feel like you and Aunt Dee rescued me."

She pulls back and smiles. "What are best friends for?"

A couple hours after our heart-to-heart we're seated at a corner booth at Gibby's. Quinn is doing her best to attempt to get me drunk for the first time, and so far it's working.

The fruity drinks she's been supplying me with are delicious, and I can't really taste the alcohol.

I throw back the rest of my drink and Quinn smiles. "Atta girl! Liquid courage, baby. You're gonna need it the moment sexy X gets here."

The moment he walks in the room, it's like the air in the room becomes charged, and I feel a pull toward him. Even in the crowded room, my gaze instantly finds Xavier. My eyes stalk him as he walks across the room to the bar, most of the heads in the place turning as he passes by them.

His presence in a room is one that's hard to miss.

Xavier leans against the bar casually, an elbow resting on the hardwood behind him as he chats with a blond woman and the short, mullet-man I recognize from the plane. Xavier's broad shoulders fill out the black dress shirt he's wearing and like before, he has the sleeves rolled up to his elbows. His gaze drifts away from the company standing before him as he scans the faces in the busy bar.

The instant our eyes lock, all the air whooshes from my lungs. Everything in me screams to look away—that this guy is trouble with a capital T. I should be scared out of my mind that he's staring right at me with those piercing blue eyes—but no matter how much I know I need to fight it, the intense need to find out what his skin feels like sliding against mine pushes me to allow this to happen. I have never lusted after a man like this before and as I realize that I'm undressing him with my eyes, my face flushes and I break our stare.

"Oh, good Lord," Quinn murmurs next to me as she snuggles closer to my side in the booth. "The pictures do not do that man justice. He's sexy as hell, and staring at you like he's ready to eat you alive."

"He's not looking at me like that."

Heat creeps up my neck again, surely deepening my blush. I risk another glance in his direction, and he licks his plump lips before pushing away from the bar, grabbing something off the counter in the process. Quinn's right. He *is* staring at me like I'm the tastiest thing on earth as he slowly approaches me, much like a tiger stalking its prey.

I swallow hard as my heart thunders in my chest. My eyes grow wide as I stare at Quinn.

"What do I do? I'm not ready for this. I can't do this."

Nervous energy spreads through my body and I'm not quite sure how to handle myself. I've never felt this anxious before. The only thing I can think to do is flee from this dangerous man because I already know what's on his mind. The urge to run right out of this bar before a full-on panic attack hits me is at the forefront of my mind as I rapidly become overwhelmed by his presence.

She places her hand on my bouncing thigh and holds it steady. "Calm down, Anna. I know this feels like I'm throwing you to the wolves, but you can do this. Think about what we talked about on the ride over here. You have the tools, remember? Don't let him gain the upper hand at any point. You call the shots. You lead the conversation. Don't let him sweet talk you into anything you aren't ready for, and above all remember that I'm here for you. Just say the word and we'll split."

Her words of comfort help a lot, but they don't change the fact that I'm in a completely new environment. Not only is this my first time at a bar, and the first time I've ever had alcohol, but it's also the first time I've ever allowed myself to think about giving my body over to a man to do as he pleases, just because I want him so much.

Xavier's heady stare bores into me as he approaches our table with a wicked grin. "Anna Cortez." He holds my purse out in front of him with one thick finger. "If I didn't know any better I would say you left this behind on purpose, just to see me again."

I roll my eyes at his cocky tone. "You wish."

His grin widens even more at my snarky comment as I stand and reach for my bag. He quickly wraps his fingers around it and jerks it just out of my grasp, teasing me like one would do to a puppy with a toy. This is pure entertainment for him. I grit my teeth as he holds it out again, only to repeat his silly little game of "keep away." The taunting causes a low growl to escape from between my teeth.

I throw my hands on my hips. "Give me back my stuff, you...you...big *jerk*."

He throws his head back and laughs heartily which only pisses me off more. I'm not trying to be funny. Can't he see I'm being serious?

Those mesmerizing blue eyes twinkle with amusement. "Oh, a temper. I like that. Careful, good girl, you're going to lose that title soon if you get me all riled up with your feisty little attitude. If

I get too turned on, I'll have no choice but to take you right here in this bar."

I curl my lip in a mock show of disgust, pretending like I wouldn't love to know just how worked up I'm getting him. I walk around the table to face him, determined to get my things back. "Like I said, *X*, you wish."

The easygoing vibe and boyish charm he exuded only seconds ago disappears as he allows me to wrap my fingers around the strap of my purse that still dangles from his finger. The moment I have a firm grip on it, Xavier grabs me by the waist and pulls me tight against his body—the purse wedged between us is the only thing keeping our chests from colliding. I stare up at his face, fully aware of every point where our bodies touch.

Hands.

Hips.

Knees.

His hand pressing tightly against the small of my back.

The crazy idea of pushing forward a few inches and finding out what those sexy lips of his taste like zings through me, and I bite my lip, causing his crystal-clear blue eyes to drift down to my mouth before slowly moving back up to meet mine. "You're right, beautiful. *I do* wish."

My mouth gapes open. Normally I would have responded with some sort of witty comment telling him he didn't have a chance with me, but I can't deny the way I crave him.

I'm not sure how long we stay there like that, gazing into one another's eyes, waiting for the other to make the next move, or at least say something, but before I'm ready Quinn's voice drags me back to reality. "Anna, do you want to finish your drink? The ice is melting."

Her subtle way of giving me an out if I need one isn't missed by Xavier as we remain locked together. "I should get back to that drink. I can't let it go to waste," I murmur.

Xavier nods, like he understands things are moving a little too quickly for me. "Drinks, like most things, are always the best before time melts away the taste, leaving things bland and watered down. Everything is better when it's fresh which is why I never miss an opportunity when I see something I like. I'm a firm believer in jumping on things right away."

He stays tangled up with me, gauging my reaction to his words—words I don't believe have anything to do with a drink. It's more like the idea of this crazy connection we seem to feel toward each other is just a passing phase, but one we should act on right away.

The waft of cold air hits me hard as he pushes away from me, and I instantly crave the warmth of his body back. I fold my arms around my purse and hug it tight against my chest to keep my fingers from reaching for him. I feel like this is my moment to tell him that I want him—to make some sort of move on him to let him know I'm interested in him. But it's just not me. I'm not that forward.

So instead of telling him that I want him to take me somewhere and prove to me how he got the name "Phenomenal," I stand there like a scared deer caught in the headlights of an oncoming car. I swallow hard and search for anything to say to kill the awkward vibe that's growing between us.

"Thank you for returning my things."

A corner of his mouth lifts up, revealing a tiny smile.

"It was no trouble." His eyes flit between me and Quinn, who is no doubt watching us like a hawk. "I'll let you get back to that drink."

Before I have a chance to say anything else, Xavier turns on his heel and heads back to the people he left at the bar.

My shoulders relax now that I'm no longer pinned under the intensity of his stare. I don't know what it is about him but he makes me feel crazy, which is so not like me.

Quinn grabs my arm and then drags me back down in the booth next to her. "Holy shit that was intense. That guy is so hot for you. Whatever spell you've put him under, you must teach me. I didn't know you had that in you."

"I didn't do anything, Quinn," I answer.

"Exactly!" she exclaims. "A guy like him isn't used to a women not responding to the smallest bone he tosses their way. You've done exactly what I told you to do on the way over here. You've maintained the upper hand."

I really hadn't set out to play some kind of angsty sex game with Xavier, but it seems to be exactly what we're doing. Problem is, I'm not so sure what my next move is supposed to be here.

"Just look at him." Quinn nudges my arm. "He can't keep his eyes off you."

I glance up and find his gaze firmly fixed on me. The blonde who entered the bar with him and Mullet Man affixes herself to him, running her finger slowly up and down his forearm. A twinge of jealously rolls through me, even though I know

I don't have any right to be envious. It's not like we're dating or anything.

Xavier glances down at the woman and shakes his head before pushing her fingers off his arm. Her face twists as she crosses her arms over her chest and then plops down next to him like a sulking child who's just been told no.

"Looks like Blondie doesn't handle rejection well," Quinn snickers and I smile.

"I would never go after a guy like that," I reply.

She grabs her drink off the table and tips it at me. "And that, my friend, is exactly why you have his attention."

I risk another glance in his direction, but he's not looking at me this time. His attention is tuned to Mullet Man who appears to be telling him a story while wildly gesticulating with his hands. There are, however, a new pair of eyes pointed my direction. The beautiful blonde beside Xavier shoots daggers at me with her stare from across the room and if looks could kill, I'd already be in a body bag.

Not wanting any trouble, I quickly look away and do my best to immerse myself in conversation with my cousin. Before I know it we are laughing and making plans for how much fun we are going to have this summer. Quinn goes on and on about how great her job at the bar is and how she promises I'm going to love it—especially the tips.

"Your boss does know I don't have a drop of experience as a server?" I ask as I start on my third drink of the night.

Quinn waves me off. "Hotness outweighs what a résumé says any day, Anna. Trust me on that."

"I'm just really nervous. It's my first job. Father is going to kill me when he finds out I'm choosing to serve drinks in a bar rather than using the degree he shelled out so much money for."

"We all have to start somewhere. Plus, it's not like there's hospitality management positions just lying around for recent college grads. Besides, most of us have to start from the ground up," she assures me.

"What are we talking about ladies?" My attention snaps to a tall, dark-haired man standing in front of our table with a couple of drinks. "I'm Brad, and this is my friend, Jared. Mind if we join you?"

My eyes flit to blond guy, Jared. He's wearing a hopeful smile that makes his brown eyes twinkle. Both guys are pretty cute. Nowhere near as attractive as Xavier, but cute nonetheless.

I glance over at Quinn, and she shrugs, pulls out a flirty grin, and turns her attention back to the two guys in front of me. "I'm Quinn, and this is my cousin, Anna."

Brad takes that as an invitation and takes a seat next to Quinn, sliding one of the beers he brought with him in her direction. "What brings you girls out tonight?"

Quinn explains we're just out having a drink to unwind, and I take a second to glance over in Xavier's direction as Jared slides a chair from the table beside us directly in front of me. Despite the obstacle I can still clearly see Xavier glaring at Jared's back, watching every move he makes.

"I'm Jared." I smile at him politely as he extends a hand toward me.

"Nice to meet you," I say after shaking his hand.

I know getting to know new people is high on Quinn's list of fun activities for us this summer, but I still can't help feeling awkward. My flirting skills need some work.

"So, umm, are you from around here?"

I can't tell if Jared's actually interested in me, or if he's just taking one for the team so his buddy can talk to Quinn. I shake my head and finish off my drink, feeling my toes start to tingle. I giggle as I wonder if this is what it feels like to have a buzz. "Nope. I'm actually from Portland."

"Wow. Are you just visiting or what?"

"I'm a transplant—moved here today, actually. Quinn is my new roomie."

I flick my tongue around in my mouth, amazed by how foreign it feels in my mouth as I speak, and giggle again. I lift the glass to my lips, but grow disappointed when I remember that it's empty.

"I really like these things. They taste so fruity. You can't even taste the alcohol."

Jared grins and taps my empty glass. "Let me get you another drink."

I rest my chin in my hand and smile, thinking of how nice Jared seems. "That would be great."

When he gets up, I glance around, noticing there are a lot more people in here than an hour or so ago when we first arrived. Just then a voice pipes up over the low music that was playing, and a DJ announces that he's taking over before an up-tempo song blasts through the speakers.

"Oh!" Quinn squeals in my ear. "I love this song! Let's dance, Anna."

She nudges me out of the booth before turning around and shouting at Brad to watch our seats. Typically I'm not a "dance in public" kind of girl, but with the way the liquor has me loosened up, and the heavy thump of bass pounding through me, all I feel like doing is letting go.

She stops at the edge of the floor. "Let's give them a little show, cuz."

I laugh as she grabs my hands and starts rocking her hips to the music, forcing me to follow her lead. "Where'd you learn to dance like this?"

"I should ask you the same question, girl. You've got some moves."

I grin. "My undergrad degree is in dance. I've always been fascinated. There was a girl in one of my classes who taught me a few freestyle moves and introduced me to the beauty of top forty pop."

"Oh, if Uncle Simon ever found out, you would've been toast." She laughs and tosses her dark hair around. "Whip your hair around. It drives guys crazy!"

I mimic her actions just as I feel a hand slip up on my hip and see Brad push up behind Quinn.

"You look great out here. Very sexy!" Jared says in my ear as he hands me a drink.

"Thanks!" I shout so he can hear me over the music as I lift the drink to my lips.

My arm stops in mid-air, and I stare down at the fingers wrapped around my wrist. My vision follows the thick fingers, to the wrist, up the tattooed arm, broad chest, finally resting on a light-blue pooled iris. Xavier's jaw flexes as he stares over my head at Jared, who has completely stilled behind me. "Don't *ever* take a drink from a random guy. That's lesson one in this cruel reality, beautiful. Not all guys are nice."

He grabs the drink from my hand and slams the plastic cup down on the floor, splattering its pink liquid all over a group of guys standing a little too close watching the action unfold. With a sharp tug he pulls me behind him, effectively putting a wall of muscle between Jared and me.

Xavier stares down at Jared, his fingers flexing into fists at his sides. It's like he's ready to rip into my would-be dance partner. "You think I didn't see what you put in her drink back there, motherfucker? There's no way in hell I'm going to allow a little pecker-stain like you to attempt to drug this girl and get away with it."

All the blood drains from Jared's face, leaving his skin pale, and his mouth hanging open in shock. But more frighteningly, he doesn't deny the accusations. Xavier shakes his head in disgust. "You just gave me the green light to end your fucking world."

Jared raises his hands in surrender and takes a step back. "Hey, man. I don't know what you think you saw, but I don't want any trouble."

Xavier rolls his shoulders. "You should've thought about that a few minutes ago because trouble is my middle name, and my foot has been twitching all night to kick your fucking ass."

"I'm sorry, okay." Jared's voice shakes as his eyes flit to Brad, who seems content on staying the hell away. "We'll just go."

Some friend you've got there, Jared, leaving you to hang out to dry.

Xavier shakes his head and laughs darkly. "Go? You think I'll let you just leave after that shit? You must be out of your fucking mind."

Jared turns to leave but Xavier grabs him by the bicep, turning him back around before drawing back his fist to crush every bone in Jared's skull. The instant I realize what's going on I gasp.

I can't let this happen. He can't get into trouble over me.

I wrap both of my hands around his elbow, clinging on for dear life as I scream, "No!"

Xavier jerks his gaze to me, his thick eyebrows knitted in confusion. "You don't want me to pound this punk?"

I shake my head vigorously. "I don't want you to get into any trouble. He's not worth it."

"He's not, but *you are*."

The intense connection that always pulls me to him assaults me full force and I can tell he feels it too.

I stare into his eyes as I cling to him, my fingers woven together so tightly that they're numb, while he waits for me to give the word to destroy Jared. I have to remain calm and try to defuse the situation before things get ugly, and Xavier gets arrested for murdering a man while defending me.

"Let him go and we'll leave."

His hard eyes soften a bit. "Together?"

I nod. "Anywhere you want to go."

A wicked smile cracks his face, and a weird tingle erupts in my belly. Maybe I shouldn't have promised that—who knows what's on that naughty mind of his. But if that means walking out of here without Xavier in handcuffs, I'm game.

Xavier directs his attention back to Jared. "Looks like it's your lucky day, fucker. You should kiss the ground this angel walks on because she just saved your fucking life."

He releases Jared's arm. "Don't let me catch you in here again. Beat it, you fucking pussy."

Jared and Brad push past Quinn, wasting no time getting as far away from us as possible. For a second I feel a little guilty for ruining my cousin's fun—Brad seemed nice enough—but the old saying that goes "a man is known for the company he keeps" rolls through my brain, so Brad's probably a date rapist too. In a way I guess I kind of saved her, well, Xavier saved her—us.

Quinn smirks as her eyes drift down to where I'm still tightly clutching my sexy savior and I quickly detach myself from him, only to be instantly reconnected with him when he grabs my hand and tugs me toward the exit. I turn and wave at my cousin as I'm pulled away.

He stops at the bar, where the blonde and Mullet Man sit chatting, a couple of empty beer glasses in front of them. The blonde's nostrils flare as she rakes her eyes over me from head to toe. Clearly she's not one bit impressed by me or my clothing. Her eyes zero in on my hand, held tightly inside Xavier's thick fingers, while he gives Mullet Man some instructions. "Make sure Anna's cousin gets home safe, Jimmy."

"No problem, boss."

Xavier takes a step but doesn't make it far because Blondie hops into his path. "You're not leaving with her." She glares at him with icy blue eyes.

He scoffs at her order. "Watch me, Deena."

Mid-pivot, Deena grabs his arm, but he jerks away like he's been stung by a bee. "I told you to never touch me again."

She narrows her eyes. "If you walk out that door with her, I'll quit—right here, right now."

"Promise?" he asks with a sarcastic tone to his voice as he pushes past her and tugs me along behind him, not giving her a second glance.

I, however, can't fight my stupid curiosity and turn around to catch her reaction. The look on Deena's face makes me believe she's growling and given the chance, she would pound me into oblivion.

I don't know who she is, or what kind of relationship she and Xavier have, but one thing is perfectly clear—Deena is pissed and believes I'm messing with something of hers. Alarm bells ring immediately as I return my gaze to take in the beautiful, strong profile of the man leading me out of the bar. He warned me that he wasn't a good guy, and by the looks of things, he leads a complicated life—stardom and women—that I'm sure I don't want to get mixed up in.

But for the life of me I can't fight the crazy attraction I feel toward this man. And after the way he just came to my rescue back there, I'm not sure I want to anymore.

Chapter
FIVE

Xavier pulls me around the side of the building and then we cross the street, hand in hand, heading toward the parking lot. I open my mouth to start asking questions, but quickly close it because a lot of the things I want to ask—like who in the hell is that Deena woman—aren't any of my business. After all, he doesn't owe me an explanation, we're still practically strangers, but I would like to hear how he knew what Jared did.

"How did you know Jared put something in my drink?" I ask as we weave through the tightly parked cars in the downtown lot. At first he doesn't answer, he just keeps walking straight ahead, pulling me along, so I decide to try again. "Were you watching me in there?"

Xavier licks his plump lips, and my mind instantly goes back to the thought I had on the plane about those lips, and what they'd be like to kiss. "I was standing right beside him when he ordered, and I saw him slip something in it."

My heart sinks a little. He wasn't watching me all night like I secretly hoped. "I've read all about guys drugging women in bars just to have their way with them, so thank you for saving me from that experience."

"With or without the drink shit, I wouldn't have allowed you to leave with him," he growls. "Whether you realized it or not, you were leaving that bar with *me* tonight."

I know him saying that may be considered barbaric, and crazy, but my stomach still does a flip. The thought of him being jealous and possessive over me turns me on so much I can barely see straight. But I don't want him to know that.

"Pretty sure of yourself, aren't you?"

We finally reach a matte black motorcycle wedged into a small corner space and he turns to face me. That magnetic stare of his, leveled on me, nearly steals my breath. Fire shoots through me from where our hands remain connected and suddenly I crave more of his skin on mine.

"You're a good girl, Anna. I'm not going to allow some undeserving asshole to come in and take you away to hurt you. Not going to happen. Not on my watch."

I bite my tongue, wanting to say a million things but only allowing myself to ask a simple question. "And are *you* deserving?"

His lips tighten into a line and he shakes his head. "I'm the most undeserving motherfucker in the world...which is why I'm best suited to protect you from pricks like me."

I furrow my brow. He may come on a little strong at times, but from the few interactions I've had with him, I can tell he's got a good heart. Today alone he's helped me out three times.

"I think you're wrong about yourself, X— Xavier."

I stumble over his name, remembering the command he gave me earlier to call him by his full name. "You're a good man."

"You say that now because you don't know me, but *I* know me, and I'm speaking from experience."

I take a deep breath and shrug. "Guess you'll have to prove me wrong then. I'm an excellent judge of character. I know a good person when I see one."

He chuckles. "Are you always so positive?"

"Are you always so negative?" I fire back automatically.

"You know what they say about a positive and a negative together, don't you?" Xavier teases as he grabs the handlebars of the bike and throws his muscular leg over the seat. Immediately my eyes are drawn to the way his jeans hug his legs, distracting me from the question he just asked. All I can think about is how powerful and strong he must be.

Before I know it I begin undressing him with my eyes, wondering if sex with a man like him would be as great as I've read about in books and seen in the movies I've snuck around to watch.

He smirks and hands me a helmet. "Looks like science is correct. They do attract."

Blood rushes to my face as I realize he's caught me staring at his crotch and I'm not sure how to respond. It's not like I can deny it or anything.

I want to die.

I take the helmet from his outstretched arm and plop it on my head. "Where are we going?"

Xavier reaches over and buckles the strap under my chin, his fingers feathering across my skin. "I would say back to your place, but I doubt you'd let that fly, and quite frankly, I'm not up for being turned down again today." I raise an eyebrow, and his lips pull into a lopsided grin. "That's what I thought. Hop on, beautiful, and I'll take you somewhere special." He holds out his hand. "Trust me?"

"Yes."

The answer slips out in a low whisper. I know I shouldn't, but I can't help this overwhelming feeling of safety I have when I'm with him. Like he can save me from anything. After all, he's already proven that he can.

I slip my hand into his. "I trust you."

That cocky grin of his turns into a full-on, heart-stopping smile. "Good."

He gives no further explanation of where he plans on taking us, just grips my hand tight as I swing my leg over the bike and squish my body against his. My thighs wrap around his hips, and he positions my hands so I'm practically bear-hugging him. My fingers trace the hard muscle beneath his t-shirt and my entire body tingles.

I've never in my life been this turned on by a man. There's something about him that makes me crave to be wild and out of control. He's like freedom, wrapped up in one sexy package. A package that has me thinking about doing things that I shouldn't.

My breasts press firmly against his back, and my nipples pucker beneath my blouse as they rub against the thin pieces of material that separates our skin. I close my eyes and snuggle into him tighter.

"Hang on tight, babe." Xavier fires up the engine and the bike roars to life as he pulls out of the lot.

The entire machine vibrates beneath us as we zip through the streets of Detroit and adrenaline flows through my veins as I press tightly against Xavier. This is the first time I've ever been on a bike, and the ride is exhilarating and sensual all at the same time. I've never been offered such a dangerous ride before, not that I would've been brave enough to ever go, but I didn't hesitate for a second before hopping on this bike with Xavier. He seems like he knows what he's doing, so I trust him.

I've never felt this wild and free—like I could do anything and everything. My first day out on my own, and I'm already breaking every one of Father's rules. I've never felt so alive.

When we stop at a red light, Xavier drops his feet off the pegs and onto the ground, balancing our weight with ease. He takes the opportunity to rest his hand on top of mine as they cling to his chest, and his thumb rubs over my fingers, causing butterflies to go crazy in my stomach. The small movement feels affectionate, like he's reassuring me that I'm safe with him. It's almost enough to make me not care that I still don't have a clue where he's taking me.

Almost.

I should have demanded to know where we were going instead of being a lustfully blinded twit, willing to go anywhere with a sexy stranger.

The light switches to green, and he puts his hand back on the handlebars, sending us forward in a blur once again. I'm not sure how long we ride, but it's long enough for me to relax and feel somewhat comfortable on the bike, comforted by the continuous purr of the motor. I lay my head on his shoulder and snuggle closer to him, inhaling the spicy scent of his cologne mixed with some sort of soap and something distinctly male. As if it's even possible, smelling him turns me on even more.

Before I know it we are just outside the city and pulling into one of those all night diners. Xavier backs the bike into an empty space and cuts the engine. I slowly peel myself off of him, and he twists, extending his hand to help me off the bike.

He reaches for the strap under my chin. "First ride?"

I reluctantly nod, unable to lie because I'm terrible at it. "Yes. How could you tell?"

He lifts the helmet off my head and chuckles. "I think the claw marks etched into my ribs are a telltale sign."

I cover my mouth with my hand as a gasp escapes from me. I knew I was hanging on for dear life at some point, but he didn't let on that I was hurting him. "I'm so sorry. Did I hurt you bad?"

Xavier shakes his head and a strand of dark hair falls across his forehead as he lifts his shirt to assess the damage. My eyes zero in on the washboard abs on full display in front of me, each muscle clearly defined and very...lickable.

Oh, Lord. Did I just think *lickable*? *Who am I?* I've never in my life referred to a man as lickable before. But in all fairness, I've never had a man like Xavier flash me his unbelievably ripped body before either, so I'm going to chalk it up to unexplored hormones.

The urge to run my fingers along his skin pushes me forward a step. I bite my bottom lip as I trace the angry red marks just above his stomach. I swallow hard. His skin is even softer than I imagined.

"We'll have to work on relaxing your grip a little, but it'll get easier every time we do it," Xavier says, breaking me out of my lustful daydream.

I jerk my hard away from him and he pulls his shirt back down before shoving himself off the bike. "You think we'll be doing this again?"

He smiles as he straps the helmet to the handlebars. "I think we will. You and I are going to be great friends. I already know it. And friends hang out with each other all the time."

"Friends?" I question, trying not to sound let down by the idea of only being Xavier's friend. "What makes you think we are *just* friends?"

He raises a thick eyebrow and smirks. "Come on, Anna. You've made it perfectly clear that I'm not your type, and that you're never going to sleep with me, so I've come to accept that. I'm happy to play the friend and protector role while you find your footing here. Detroit's a tough city. It'll eat a girl like you alive if you don't have someone watching out for you."

"And why would you be willing to do that for me?"

"I guess it's because I haven't met someone as sweet as you in a long time, and I would like to see you stay that way. You need a guy like me around to keep all the assholes away," he replies matter-of-factly.

I fold my arms over my chest. In just the short time we've known each other he believes he can read me just like that? Maybe he needs a curveball thrown his way. "Maybe that's why I came out here—to get mixed up with the wrong kind of man and make a few mistakes."

He smiles and takes my hand. "You shouldn't say things like that to a man who's a walking mistake, and one who would like nothing better than to take you home with him."

There he goes again with that suave dirty talk that makes me want to jump his bones.

He doesn't give me a chance to reply, just tugs me toward the door of the diner. The place isn't packed, but isn't entirely empty either. The white tile floor is worn but clean, and the booths look like they've seen better days. The open kitchen in the middle of the restaurant allows all the patrons to watch exactly what's going on with their food as it's prepared.

The counter is packed with mostly gray-haired old men making small talk with each other, and the waitress, wearing a blue uniform, who is refilling their coffee. None of them seem to notice that we've come in until the woman glances up and spots us.

A huge grin spreads across her face, making her round face appear even more like a perfect circle. Her dark hair has a lot of gray streaks through it—very noticeable because of the way she has her braids pulled up—and she seems more like a grandmother rather than a rabid wrestling fan.

"Xavier Cold!" she exclaims as she sets the pot down and scoots around the counter. "Boy, you better get over here and give me a hug!"

The moment she embraces him, Xavier wraps his huge arms around her petite frame. "It's so good to see you, Nettie."

She pulls back and then abruptly smacks him on the arm. "Boy, what's the meaning of staying gone for over two years without a goodbye?"

He closes his eyes and sighs. "Come on, Nettie. You know I hate writing."

She shoves her hands onto her tiny waist. "Would it have killed you to call us more often than twice a year?"

He nods. "You're right. I'll try harder, I promise."

She narrows her eyes at him. "You'd better. Just remember you aren't too big for old Nettie here to whoop your butt if you don't act right." Nettie's eyes flick to me. "Speaking of acting right, who do we have here?"

"Nettie, this is Anna, my...*friend*."

Being introduced as just his friend hurts a little. I know we've just had this talk, and this is exactly the kind of relationship I *should* have with Xavier, but it doesn't stop me from wanting him. The fact that he's given up his pursuit so quickly stings.

I extend my hand and Nettie's smooth, brown skin makes contact with mine. "It's very nice to meet you, Nettie."

"Mmmm hmm, you too." She lets go of my hand and her gaze returns to Xavier. "I can tell she ain't from around here. Way too sweet. Don't you be taking this pretty little girl down to the Block, Xavier, you hear me? A girl like her doesn't belong down there. Hell, a girl like her doesn't belong in a dump like this either."

"I heard that!" the cook yells from across the counter.

She waves her hand dismissively. "Oh, hush, Carl. Ain't nobody talking to you. Go 'head, Xavier, sit wherever you want, honey. I'll bring you out some water."

"Hey, Carl," Xavier tosses over his shoulder as he pulls me toward a corner booth.

"What up, X! Good to see you, brother," Carl answers as he pulls the white cook's cap off his head, wipes his brow with a dish towel, and goes right back to cooking without washing his hands, grossing me out a bit. But I refuse to be rude.

Xavier sits across from me. "Don't mind Carl. That skinny little fucker is harmless."

"I heard that too! Don't forget who taught you all those wrestling moves before you went and got a real trainer. I can still take you," Carl taunts Xavier.

Nettie smacks Carl on the butt with a dishtowel. "Hush, you old fool. Everybody here knows you didn't teach our boy a damn thing. So quit flapping your gums and get back to what you're actually good at—"

Carl waggles his bushy, white eyebrows at Nettie. "You know what I'm good at."

Nettie twists her lips. "Yeah, cooking, fool. Now get back to it. I've got a hungry bunch here tonight."

Carl shakes his head and laughs as Nettie brings us out two waters and places them on the table. "You want the usual, honey?"

Xavier shakes his head. "Not today. I'm on a new protein diet to help build muscle. I'm trying to bulk up."

"Lord, sugar. Your arms are already big as tanks. What'cha want to get any bigger fo'?"

That's a very good question, Nettie.

He shrugs. "I've been thrown a bone to go after the championship belt and I have to be in top shape. I want the higher-ups in the biz to know how much I want it. How seriously I take my job."

"If you take your job any more seriously, honey, you'll put one of them boys in the hospital...for real."

"You know all that's fake, Nettie. We're professional. Everything we do is choreographed and thought out ahead of time."

"Mistakes happen, child. You should know that better than anyone else." She gives him a pointed look, but he doesn't say a word. It's like he doesn't have to. These two have such a history they can communicate a thousand meanings in just one look—a look that passes me by because I'm clueless as to what in the world she could be talking about.

"So that's meat and egg whites for my boy. What about you, Anna, what'll it be?" She turns her attention back to me.

I glance around and notice most of the other patrons are having breakfast, so I figure that's a safe bet. "Um, I'll take the pancakes and sausage."

"Oh, I like this one—she's got a healthy appetite." Nettie nudges Xavier's arm with her hip as she writes down our order on the notepad. "You can bring her around any time."

Xavier rolls his eyes while Nettie cackles before turning to head toward Carl. "Sorry about that."

I smile, liking the idea that Nettie is teasing him to lighten him up. "Not a big deal. I think it's funny that she treats all the girls you bring in here like that."

He rubs his scruffy chin with his fingers. "I've actually never brought a girl in here before."

I raise my eyebrows. "Really? I find that hard to believe. You're trying to tell me that this isn't where you bring all the girls who turn you down for sex? Hoping that by bringing them here it will impress them and get them to change their minds?"

He bites his bottom lip. "Does this make you change *your* mind?"

The way he rakes his teeth slowly over his bottom lip draws my attention to that stupid, sexy mouth of his. I force back a sigh as I once again find myself thinking about kissing him. If he weren't so attractive, continuing to pretend that I'm not interested would be a hell of a lot easier.

Finally, after focusing on his last question, I shake my head.

"While I find it ridiculously charming that this place humanizes you, it doesn't change my answer. I still won't sleep with you."

His lips stay together, but one corner turns up into what appears to be a knowing grin. "That's what I thought. So maybe we need to establish some friendship boundaries, so there's no confusion about our relationship."

I take a sip of water to quench my suddenly dry throat. "What kind of boundaries?"

"You know, some basic rules so we don't give each other any mixed signals about moving past the 'friend zone.' I'm a big fan of specifying exactly where one stands."

I rest my chin in the palm of my hand. "I suppose you already have some of these rules in mind?"

Xavier smirks and holds up a finger. "Rule number one: no getting naked in my bed."

I laugh. The thought that I'd ever be brave enough to strip down and hop into his bed on my own is comical. There's no way I'll ever muster up the courage to do that. "I don't think you'll have to worry about that one."

I hold up two fingers, ready to add some boundaries of my own. "Rule number two: no kissing."

He shakes his head. "That rule sucks. Friends kiss. That's not one I'll abide by."

"Not open-mouthed they don't," I argue.

He sighs and holds up two fingers. "Amended rule number two: no open-mouthed kissing."

The thought of his lips on me in any form gets my blood pumping, but as long as I know there will be no tongue involved, I think I'll be able to control myself. "I can live with that."

"Third and last rule," he says while holding up three fingers. "If either one of us starts developing feelings for the other person, we have to tell them. We don't want any pent-up sexual frustration building between us."

I lick my lips and bat away the idea that the ship containing all of my lust for him has already sailed, but he doesn't need to know that. It's not like I'll ever act on them. "They sound like three solid rules to me."

"Agreed," he replies as Nettie returns with our meals.

"What are we agreeing to over here?" Nettie asks.

Xavier pulls his fork out of his rolled up napkin. "We were just establishing the rules of our friendship, Nettie."

"Friends, huh? Okay, if you say so." The doubt in her voice is clear. "I've never known you to have a girl as a *friend*, Xavier Cold."

He shrugs as he cuts into his eggs. "What can I say? Beautiful here, is different."

Nettie smiles at me and winks. "Different is good, honey."

She doesn't give me a chance to reply, or ask what she meant by that exactly, before she walks away and tends to the other people in the restaurant.

Chapter
SIX

Anna

Xavier clears his plate and orders seconds before I even make it through a quarter of my food. When I give him a quizzical expression, he simply shrugs and informs me that muscle burns a lot of energy and constantly needs to be refueled.

I take a sip of my water as I eye his broad shoulders and wonder how much time he spends perfecting his body. "So is that all you do?"

He leans back and stretches his arm along the back of the booth, making himself comfortable. "Eat?"

"That, and work out? Do you ever have time for much else?"

He shakes his head. "Typically, no, but right now I'm on vacation."

I twist my lips. "You vacation in Detroit? Shouldn't a vacation be somewhere tropical or something?"

He lifts an eyebrow. "What's wrong with Detroit? I was born and raised here."

I quickly try to backpedal, not meaning to offend him. "Nothing. I like it here so far."

A smile pulls across his plump lips. "I'd like to think that's your way of saying you like me, considering you just got here today."

I fight back a smile. He's right. Xavier has made the first day of my new life more exciting and invigorating than any other day I can remember. "I do like you."

He leans into me, licking his lips. "Still not enough to change your 'friends only' rule though, right?"

"Right," I quickly agree. "But it is nice to have someone to talk to."

He nods. "I know exactly what you mean."

Xavier's next round of food comes to the table, and Nettie smiles at me. "So, Miss Anna, are you a wrestling fan?"

I shake my head. "No, not really."

"You've never seen my boy here perform? He's really somethin'." She pats his shoulder.

"To be honest, Nettie, I didn't even know who he was until my cousin told me today. Then she pulled videos and photos up of him on the internet."

Xavier chuckles, drawing my attention to him. "You really had no clue who I was, did you?"

I shrug. "Hate to disappoint you, but not everyone's a wrestling fan."

"Maybe you'd like it if you gave it a chance." Xavier glances up at Nettie after checking his watch. "*Tension* will be on in a few minutes. Let's turn it on and make my girl a fan."

"You got it, sugar." Nettie makes her way over to the counter and grabs the remote for the television hanging on the wall, changing it to a different channel.

After the commercial break, a hard rock intro blares through the speakers as the words *Tuesday Tension* flash across the screen, followed by clips of wrestlers beating the crap out of each other. When Xavier's face appears in the montage, I'm mesmerized by the cocky grin on his face before he tackles another man down onto the blue mat, using enough force to make me flinch at the thought of physical pain.

"That was one of my favorite matches."

Xavier's words draw my attention back to him.

"Do you ever get hurt?" I quiz, wondering how someone can subject their body to so much and be able to walk away without a scratch.

The corner of his mouth lifts up into the same cocky grin I saw moments before on the screen. "You worried about me?"

"More like curious...and worried too, I guess," I admit. "I don't like to see people in physical pain."

He shrugs. "I can't say that I've never been hurt, but I'm damn good at my job—as are most of the guys on the show. We wouldn't be there if we didn't know what we're doing. The goal is to never really hurt one another, but to put on a good show. Give people their money's worth."

"So none of it is real?" I ask as the show plays on in the background.

"The show has writers. Every storyline is well thought out. Sometimes they get inspiration from things actually happening in our lives, but the pain—when we do actually get hit—hurts like a motherfucker. The guys who make it in the business know it's mind over matter. The key is to turn off the part of your brain that experiences pain—to shut everything out. Being able to do that is going to make me the champ one day. My body can take punishment," he explains.

"Is that a goal of yours? To be the champion?" I ask, trying to figure out what makes him tick.

He nods toward the television. "That's the goal of every man on the show. It's the ultimate prize, and people will do whatever it takes to get it."

I wrinkle my nose. "That sounds pretty cutthroat."

"Believe me, beautiful, my job isn't all rainbows and fucking sunshine. I've got to watch my back constantly. A lot of the guys are pissed I've climbed to the top so fast. They don't think I've earned a shot yet, even though our boss believes I have."

I stare into his eyes. "*Have* you earned it?"

His gaze drops down to the table as he says, "I've been through some shit in my life. Nothing I've ever achieved has come easy. I've fought for everything I've ever gotten, including working my way to the top of *Tension*. There's no one more dedicated to the job than me. So, yeah, I've earned it."

I open my mouth to dig a little deeper because I'm so curious about him, but quickly shut it. So many questions race through my mind—like what kind of shit has he been through?—but I've only known the man a few hours, and I don't want to come off sounding like a nosy pest. But the curiosity burns through me like a pesky itch begging to be scratched.

Before I go against my better judgment and pry anyway, a voice on the television calls out Xavier's wrestling name loud enough to jerk my attention back to the show. The man with broad shoulders and rippled muscles shoves his dark hair back off his face and points his black eyes directly into the camera.

"Phenomenal X, how convenient you choose now to take a personal vacation. What a load of crap. Such lies you tell all these fans who support you!"

The crowd boos the man, but it doesn't stop him. "Why don't you tell them all the truth, X? Tell them all that you're too afraid to face me again after you cheated your way to a win last Tuesday. We both know who the better man is. Why don't you tell them all how much pain I caused you? No, you're too ashamed to let the world see how jacked-up your face is thanks to me. I want a rematch!"

I glance over at Xavier, who is focused intently on the screen. His hands ball into fists as they rest on the table in front of him. Whoever this man is, he certainly seems to be getting to him. If all this was so fake and scripted, why is he getting so angry?

The man on the show leans his elbows on the red ropes casually, like he's completely comfortable being a jerk on national television, and holds the microphone up to his lips. "Whatever your reason for running, X, know that I'll be right here when you get back—ready to kick your ass all over the place."

Music blasts again as the man drops the mic into the ring and smirks as the camera zooms in on his face.

That guy gives me the creeps. "Who is that?"

Xavier's nostrils flare a bit, like the mere thought of this man disgusts him somehow. "That's Rex 'The Assassin' Risen. He's the other guy the boss is looking at as a contender for the belt."

"As in the championship?" I clarify.

"Yeah," is all he says.

I tilt my head. "I take it you don't like him very much?"

He shakes his head. "Fighting outside the ring is strictly prohibited, and we all sign a contract that states that we won't do it. We fight— we get booted, without hesitation. There are too many guys chomping at the bit to take our spots for the company to worry about loose cannons. Assassin has begged for an ass beatin' for a while, but the fucker knows I won't touch him. He gets under my skin, and he loves to push my buttons."

"So what did he do to antagonize you? Was it over a woman?"

His brow furrows. "What makes you assume that?"

I shrug. "Seems like that's one thing you're willing to fight over—contract or not. You were ready to pound Jared over me back at the club earlier, so I just assumed."

"You assumed wrong. I don't fight over women."

"So then why did you protect me? You didn't hesitate for even one second to call out Jared." I try to point out how he's just contradicted himself.

His blue eyes search my face, like he's looking for answers to that very question for himself. "I don't know how to explain it, and I'm sure I'll fuck this up when I try to because it sounds crazy even to me."

I reach over and touch his hand, wanting to hear his reasons so badly I can taste it. "Try."

His tongue darts out and licks his lips. "Have you ever felt a connection with someone without even knowing them? When I look at you, I see goodness. I've not had a lot of good shit happen to me in my life, so when I see something pure, I'm drawn to it."

I trace my fingers over his hand. "What do you mean? You have an awesome career, you're famous...how is that not good?"

"That stuff isn't real. It can all go away in a heartbeat." He pulls away and rubs his face. "I told you I'd fuck this up. I guess what I'm trying to get at is that I'm alone. Other than Nettie and Carl, I have no family—no one. I've been on my own a long time, not living the way I should, and at one point I dug myself into a hole so deep, I wasn't sure I'd make it out alive. It's not a life many people want to get mixed up in. Working here saved me. Detroit is a rough place, so when I see a nice girl like you coming into a city filled with pricks like me, I worry. I don't want you to become jaded down the road when the world's cruel realities set in. You have too much light to be clouded by the dark."

I smile. It's crazy to think he's so compassionate about me after only a few hours and while his intensity is unfathomable, I'm completely flattered. "So you're saying you want to become my personal bodyguard and protect me from the big bad city?" I tease.

He reaches back for my hand and laces his fingers through mine. "There are lots of things I would like to do to your body, but yeah, if you want to look at it like that, guarding it from other guys is definitely a top priority."

I giggle as heat rushes to my face. Oh, how I would like to tell him to do with me as he pleases, but I know I'll hate myself if I allow some man I barely know use me like that. I may not have much experience with men, but I've seen enough in movies and read enough books to know that a lot of men toss women aside after they get what they want from them. Even if that man causes tingles to explode throughout every inch of me with one simple touch. I don't think I could do that if he didn't love me.

Gah! I have to stop thinking about him that way. Every time I think about him, my stupid brain thinks of sex—more specifically, what sex would be like with him. How it would feel. How he would taste.

I need a subject change. Fast. "So how long are you on vacation?"

"A little over a week. You going to miss me when I head back out on the road?" He smiles, fishing for information.

I shrug, trying not to take the bait, but eventually give in and smile. "I might. You are my friend, and official bodyguard in Detroit, after all."

He rubs his thumb over the side of my hand. "What about you? What are your plans now that you're all settled in and have started making friends with the locals?"

"A job, I guess. Quinn got me a job at Larry's Bar and Grill with her. I start tomorrow."

The idea of having my first real job scares the crap out of me. It's not like I'm doing this for pocket change—this job will be the only means I have of supporting myself. I have zero job experience, and even less of an idea of how to be a good waitress. If I fail at this, I don't know what I'm going to do.

"What's that look for?" Xavier asks, pulling me out of my thoughts of impending failure. "No frowning, remember?"

"Sorry, I'm nervous about tomorrow. I should probably be getting back to Quinn's so I can rest up for my first day of work."

"I'm sure you'll do great." He glances down at his watch. "You're right, it's getting late." He leans over to the side, fishes his wallet from his back pocket, and lays several one hundred dollar bills on the table before setting his plate on top of it.

My eyes widen. Holy crap! He's rich—like can-buy-anything-he-wants-rich—and yet he's generous. All the wealthy people I know are tightwads. They would never leave a tip like that, family or not.

"You are so nice."

"It's the least I can do. They did a lot for me when I had nothing," he answers simply.

The sweet gesture of leaving that money for Nettie tells me so much about his character, and only reinforces the first thought I had about him being a good guy—whether he wants to believe it or not.

Xavier stands and extends his hand down to me. "Ready, beautiful? Let's get you home before you turn into a pumpkin."

I take his hand and laugh. "Did you just reference a princess story? Macho guys like you aren't supposed to do that."

He pulls me up against his side and wraps his arm around my shoulders. "We do if we're hoping to be a woman's Prince Charming someday."

The idea that this sexy, beast of a man is trying to impress me causes my stomach to flip. If he keeps this up, those damn friendship boundaries we established will go right out the window because I won't be able to stop myself from jumping his bones.

Being on the back of Xavier's bike is more comfortable the second time around. I press my chest against his back so tightly I swear we share the same skin. It's crazy how seeing him around his...family, I guess is what he calls them, and getting into his head a little bit changes my perception of him somewhat. While he's still a very intimidating human being, I know under all that toughness is a man with a good heart. Everything he says to try and push me away, like telling me he's not a good guy, only makes me like him more. It's like he'd protect me from anything that would hurt me—including himself—which is a very endearing trait in a man. If he wasn't leaving soon and wasn't a known womanizer, I could see myself falling for Xavier Cold.

But he definitely isn't the relationship type. He's the let's-have-some-fun-and-forget-each-other type, and that is a type that I most certainly do not partake in.

The moment Xavier pulls up in front of Aunt Dee's place, the thought occurs to me that I never even gave him directions. The moment he kills the motor, I hop off the bike and yank the helmet off my head, unable to stop myself from asking the question flashing in my brain.

"How did you know where I lived?"

He grins mischievously. "Your cousin Quinn isn't the only one who knows how to track down someone's information."

My teeth glide over my bottom lip, curious as to why he would go to all that trouble, and wondering what else this man knows about me. "I'm not certain that stalking me on the Internet would be that interesting. I'm boring."

His eyes twinkle. "Boring is relative, Anna. Someone who graduated with a degree in hospitality—with honors—and a minor in dance, doesn't seem that boring to me."

I shake my head. "You found all that out on the *Internet*?"

"I didn't, Deena did."

Deena? The blonde from the club? She hates my guts and probably loathed that task. I'm surprised she didn't fill his head with a bunch of lies about me while she was at it. "She work for you or something?"

He nods, and shoves his dark hair back off his face. "Yeah, or at least she did until she threatened me a little while ago. I don't do well with threats. Giving me an ultimatum of any kind doesn't work. She knows that. I do what I want, when I want. It's a shame because she was a decent PA."

I scrunch my brow. "What's a PA?"

"A personal assistant," he clarifies. "Jimmy is going to hate doing all my personal and managerial shit until he finds a new one."

Xavier sounds like he might be a handful. "So you have two people that basically follow you around everywhere?

"More or less. I didn't ask Deena to come out here with me though. She showed up on her own." The moment he says that everything falls into place. No wonder that woman hates me.

Even though it's none of my business, I ask, "Do you sleep with all your assistants?"

He smirks. "Is it that obvious?"

I laugh. "No woman would follow her boss unless she had to. And the look she gave me back at the bar—"

"She's threatened by you," he interjects.

"Why? Has she not seen herself?" I can't imagine anyone who looks like Deena feeling threatened by the likes of me.

Xavier taps my nose. "You obviously haven't seen yourself, Anna. Every man in that bar was watching you tonight, wishing they were the lucky bastard who got to take you home."

"That's why you said I was leaving with you whether I knew it or not, wasn't it? You were protecting me from all the pricks in Detroit again, weren't you?" I tease him, throwing his definition of every other man in the city back at him.

He winks. "What are friends for?" Xavier cranks the bike alive, and over the rumble he says, "See you around, beautiful."

He doesn't give me a chance to ask him when that will be before he speeds off into the darkness. A thousand questions dance through my mind as it replays the day I've just spent with this intoxicating man. I know never seeing him again would be the best thing for me, but I can't stop the longing for him aching inside me. Xavier Cold is one bad man I pray I get the chance to know better.

Chapter
SEVEN

The brush runs through my hair, and I stare absently into the mirror while my thoughts drift to Xavier. Ever since he dropped me off last night, I've had him on the brain. I know we're just friends, but I have this unyielding desire to be more than that. The problem is, I know what he wants from me, but I'm afraid to go there because I don't think I can give myself over to him just one time and be okay with him walking away. I know I'll want more, and he's not the relationship type.

I'm afraid of getting my heart broken.

"Come on, Anna, we're going to be late. If there's one thing Andy hates, it's tardiness, so hurry your cute ass up. You want to make a good impression on your first day," Quinn calls from her bedroom—*our* bedroom now.

I finish pulling my hair up into a high ponytail and rush out of the bathroom. "I'm ready."

She appraises my outfit—black shorts that read "Staff" across the butt and a bright green shirt with "Property of Larry" across my chest. "You look great!"

I tug at the shorts, wishing they were a little longer. "I'm not so sure about this outfit, Quinn. It's not very *me*."

She grabs her keys off the dresser. "Isn't that the point? I thought you wanted to do the opposite of what you'd normally do."

I frown. "It is, but it's all a little much to get used to at one time."

She wraps her slender arm around my shoulders as we walk toward the front door. "I promise it won't be so bad. All the girls dress like this. Trust me. You'll be thanking me when you're counting your tips."

Quinn drives us to work in her Honda, and fills me in about the job and what I can expect. I nod in all the correct places, trying to pretend I'm not a complete mess inside. My nerves are in overdrive. Who knew starting a job would make me feel like a crazy person?

We pull into the parking lot of Larry's, and I stare at the brick building, anxious to get inside while simultaneously wishing I could run away.

Quinn must sense my unease, because she pats my arm. "Don't worry. You're going to do great."

I give her a small smile. "Thanks. I'll try not to let you down."

The moment we walk in through the back door, clearly marked "Employees Only" my nose is assaulted with the smell of fried, greasy food. Bodies flit around the tight kitchen so quickly I'm not sure where to point my gaze first. Two guys, wearing green t-shirts with the same slogan as mine, wave to Quinn from behind the grill. I fully expect my cousin to be polite and greet our coworkers, but instead she raises her left hand as we pass and flips them the middle finger.

"Quinn, baby, don't be like that," the taller of the two guys whines.

She doesn't even glance in his direction, and the cook frowns. I'm not sure who he is, but he's cute with floppy brown hair and boyish good looks.

It appears Quinn hasn't told me everything about this place.

The blond cook beside the one who just spoke to Quinn allows his eyes to roam over my body, spending a noticeable amount of time on my chest.

"Did you bring us fresh meat, Quinnie?"

"Fuck off, Tyler. Don't even think about it. Anna is off-limits." She stops dead in her tracks and directs an evil stare at the brown-haired cook. "That means you too, Brock. You come near her or me, I'll shank you where you stand."

Tyler holds up his hands in surrender. "Damn, Quinnie, who pissed in your Wheaties?"

She narrows her eyes at the two men. "Ask your butt-buddy."

Tyler immediately whips his head in Brock's direction and gives his arm a small shove. "Did you two break up? A fucking warning would've been nice, dude."

Brock shrugs, like he can't come up with a better explanation than that.

My eyes widen. She never even mentioned a boyfriend to me before, and by the sounds of things, the breakup was pretty recent. Even Tyler, who seems to know them both appears stunned, like the news is shocking.

"Unbelievable!" Quinn mutters before tearing through the kitchen.

"Quinn, wait!" Brock calls after as he chases her through the door, leaving me alone in the kitchen with Tyler.

He flips the meat sizzling on the grill and shakes his head, a strand of his shaggy blond hair falling in his eyes. "Those two are nuts. I can't keep up."

Curious, I ask, "Have they been together long?"

Tyler lifts one shoulder in a noncommittal answer. "On and off for the past couple of months, I guess." He looks up at me, a flick of recognition flaring in his brown eyes. "You're her cousin, right? The one from Seattle or something?"

"Portland," I correct him. "I'm Anna."

He laughs. "The name I got—right around when Quinnie was warning me to stay away from you."

I laugh too, feeling strangely at ease with the guy. He seems harmless, and he must be pretty close to my own age. I can see Tyler and me being friends. Working here might actually be fun, and not the terrifying place I expected it to be.

Feeling the need to fill the dead air lingering between us, I attempt to make small talk. "Have you been here long?"

"Close to a year. Quinnie and Brock have been here longer. Brock's my cousin," he adds.

"Glad to hear I'm not the only one who had a little inside help getting a job," I tease.

Tyler rakes his eyes over me again and then shakes his head, an amused smile on his face. "I don't think you would've had a problem without your cousin's help."

From out of nowhere a short, balding man smacks Tyler on the back of the head. "No hitting on our new employees."

"Ouch! Jesus, Andy, I was only being friendly," Tyler wails.

"Flirt on your own time. You." Andy turns his attention to me and I hold my breath ready for a word of warning as well. "You're Quinn's sister, Annie, right?"

"It's Anna, and I'm her cousin," I correct him.

"Whatever." He points to himself. "I'm Andy, welcome aboard. We're short-staffed today, so I'm afraid there won't be much time for training. I'm going to give you some tables."

He stalks toward the door to the left and when I don't immediately follow behind him, he raises his eyebrows at me. "Well, come on." He waves at me to follow him. "We don't have all day. Dinner rush is in two hours, and you have a lot to learn before I toss you out there."

I follow Andy into what appears to be his office, although I swear it feels more like a storage closet with all the supplies stacked around his tiny, metal desk.

He opens the desk drawer to the right and pulls out a couple of papers. He slaps them down on the desk, along with a pen, and then pours four antacid tablets into his hand, and popping them in his mouth. "This is an official application and a W2 form. Fill them both out, make sure you mark your tax-withholding information down correctly, and lastly, sign our accountability form."

All of that sounds pretty standard except for the last one. "What's the accountability form for?"

"It's our theft policy here at Larry's. We're a small, family-owned business, and my father, Larry, came up with it to help protect us if we suspect an employee of stealing from us. It basically says if we suspect an employee is stealing in any manner, they will be terminated with no questions asked."

"Sounds fair enough."

"Good. Glad you're on the same page. Leave the papers on the desk once you complete them, and then go find Quinn. Tell her to start you on dinner prep."

And just as quickly as he appeared, Andy's gone again, leaving me no time to ask any questions at all.

I sit down at the desk and make quick work of the paperwork. Seeing as I'm only twenty-one years old, with absolutely zero work history, there's really not much for me to write down. The tax form trips me up a bit, but after reading it carefully, I figure it out.

I stack the papers neatly on Andy's desk and head back out into the kitchen. Brock is back at the grill next to Tyler, but Quinn is nowhere to be seen.

Tyler glances up at me and smiles. I'm sure he notices the clueless expression on my face. "Hey, Anna. You lost?"

I nod. "Can you tell me where I can find Quinn? Andy told me to find her when I was through with the paperwork he gave me."

Brock jerks his head toward the dining area. "She's on the floor."

"Thanks." I turn to head that way when Brock's voice stops me.

"Tell her I'm sorry, would you? And that I admit I'm a complete idiot and that she was right. She won't listen to me." His brown eyes appear pained, and he seems sincere.

"Sure thing."

Whatever's going on between them feels very intense, and that's a mystery I need to get to the bottom of. I push through the swinging kitchen door, wondering why Quinn didn't tell me about Brock before, and find myself in a dimly lit pub. Dark-green berber carpet stretches from wall to wall, while tables and booths fill the rest of the space. Behind the expansive wooden bar is a hardwood floor and a window that opens to the kitchen. A couple of plates of prepared burgers and fries sit under a heat lamp, waiting to be served.

A tall redhead with slender arms and legs stands behind the bar, drying beer mugs before stacking them underneath the bar. She's beautiful in that non-traditional sort of way, and I immediately consider how great her tips must be with boobs as big as hers.

When she catches me openly watching her, she rolls her eyes. "You the new girl?"

I nod and walk over to introduce myself, wanting to make a better impression with her than I had with the two cooks and my boss. "Hi. I'm Anna."

Her green eyes flick down to my extended hand, but she makes no attempt to reciprocate the greeting. "Look, I don't train newbies, I don't give pointers, I don't share my tables, and the bar seating is mine. Above all, stay the hell away from my regulars. If you're looking for a friend, don't come sniffing in my direction. If you want to keep your job here, just learn to stay out of my way because Andy listens to everything I say. Got it?"

I swallow hard, not missing her blatant disdain, or the fact that she seems to run this place. It doesn't take a lot to realize that she's one woman I don't want to piss off.

"Got it."

She raises an eyebrow. "Good."

Just then Quinn approaches the bar and her brown eyes flit from me to the redhead and then back again. Her pretty pink lips twist before her gaze snaps toward the unfriendly bartender. "Alice, don't be a fucking bitch. Anna's cool, so lighten up."

Alice folds her thin arms across her chest. "Don't expect me to cut her any slack just because she's related to you, Quinn."

"I'm not asking for any favors. I just want you to act like a human being instead of a demon bitch from hell. Try and pretend you have a heart for a change, would you? It's her first day. Soon enough she'll learn to stay away from your evil ass."

I'm quietly impressed by the way Quinn goes right back at her, not allowing her to push her around in the slightest.

Alice rolls her eyes and returns to drying the mugs. "Whatever, Quinn. Just makes sure she knows the rules."

Quinn waves her off dismissively. "Yeah, yeah. You're the queen bee, and the rest of us are lowly peons. I think she can handle it." She moves behind the bar and picks up the waiting burgers, placing them on her tray before turning toward me. "Come on, Anna, let's get you trained up."

"Thanks for that," I tell her the moment we walk away.

"No problem. Alice is all bark. Don't let her get to you."

I smile. "I'll try my best." I snap my fingers, suddenly remembering Brock's message. "Oh, Brock wanted me to tell you that he's a complete idiot, and he's sorry."

Her lips twist. "He did, did he? Well, he's got the idiot part right. Not sure what I ever saw in that clown."

"How come you didn't tell me about him?" I question.

She shrugs. "I don't know. Mom doesn't even know about him. It's like what we shared, I wasn't ready to share with the rest of the world or something. I felt like people would judge me for wanting to date a fry cook."

I touch her arm. "Who cares what people think? If you're into him, and he treats you well, that's all that matters, right?"

She sighs. "I know, you're right."

For the next hour I follow my cousin around, attempting to learn everything I can. As we work, I relentlessly try to extract more information about her and Brock, but she's tight-lipped about the situation, still not ready to share more with me yet, so I respect her boundaries. Quinn's great at her job, and she's a thorough teacher, but all the information she's throwing at me is enough to make my head spin. Who knew there was so much more to this job than just memorizing menus and bringing customers their correct food orders?

"Dinner rush will start soon. Andy wants you to take a few tables tonight since we had a waitress quit," Quinn says as she wipes down a table. "Any guesses why she quit?"

I snicker after I glance over at the bar. "Enough said." Alice is busy flirting with a couple customers sitting at the bar and doesn't notice my stare. "Is she always so mean?"

Quinn laughs. "It's okay to call her a bitch, Anna. Uncle Simon isn't here to bust your chops."

"You're right." I nod and laugh with her. "She's a major bitch."

She gives my arm a nudge. "Atta girl. The sooner you learn not to take her shit, the better off you'll be. Andy doesn't listen to her half as much as she thinks. He only puts up with her because he fucks her from time to time when he and his wife go through a dry spell."

"Eww."

The image of my new boss and Alice getting it on turns my stomach a bit. Andy isn't exactly hideous, but not the type I would figure Alice to go for. "Why does she do that?"

Quinn shrugs. "Alice is a slut. She sleeps with anyone she thinks has a little bit of money."

I grimace. "How can she allow them to use her like that?"

She gives me a pointed look. "She's using them just as much as they're using her. Have you seen what she drives? No one can afford a brand-spanking new Mustang on our salary. Those things are like thirty grand."

I raise my eyebrows. "Some guy gave her *that* just for sleeping with him?"

Quinn laughs. "Sex done right can make a man do just about anything. Your vagina is your strongest weapon—always remember that. It can make any man putty in your hands." She grins when something catches her eye. "Speaking of man-putty, I see a delectable piece of man-meat now. I think it's time to give you your very first customer."

I scrunch my brow as I try, unsuccessfully, to read her face. Quinn nods toward the bar and I point my gaze in that direction just in time to see Xavier take a seat. Alice immediately dashes over to him, leaning across the bar so he can get a direct shot of her cleavage down her v-neck t-shirt.

"You better go save him before Alice tries to stake her claim," Quinn says.

"I can't go over there. She'll kill me," I complain. "Besides, he might not even be here to see me."

She rolls her eyes. "Get real, Anna. Of course he's here for you. Now, go get your man."

I clutch the pad tightly in my hand as I walk over to where Alice is attempting to engage Xavier in some flirty conversation. Her gaze immediately cuts toward me, and I swear a chill runs down my spine as I take in her fiery stare. I swallow hard, silently praying I'm not making a total fool of myself and that he actually might want to talk to me again. After the way he rode off last night, I wasn't sure I'd ever see him again.

The moment his blue eyes meet mine, my breath catches. It's almost enough to stop me dead in my tracks. I can't read whether or not he's glad to see me, but I take another couple of steps forward to reach the end of the bar.

"You need something, newbie?" Alice says with ice in her voice. "You know this is my section, right. I'm sure Quinn explained the boundaries to you."

I nod, biting my lip at the same time. Going up against Alice for Xavier's attention wasn't exactly the plan, but I can't back away without letting her know that he's not hers for the taking. Which makes no sense because he's not exactly mine either.

I shift my nervous gaze to Xavier, and I notice he's no longer looking at me, but glaring at Alice, who is oblivious as she stares at me through narrowed eyes. He hadn't missed the snide tone in her voice either.

Xavier pushes back from the bar, and Alice flicks her gaze in his direction. "Looks like I sat in the wrong section then."

Xavier takes my hand off the bar and pulls me behind him, leaving Alice to stand there with her mouth agape as we head toward Quinn's section. I risk a glance back, and she's glaring at me.

Uh-oh. I think I've just made an enemy.

Quinn's mouth twists as she tries to hide her smile as we approach. "Funny seeing you here, X."

He gives her a slow nod like they've spoken before. "Quinn."

Xavier stops at the corner booth. "Is this your section?"

"Yes. It's one of the only four tables Andy gave me to start with today," I answer, and he slides into the seat. He raises his eyebrows and gestures toward the seat across from him. I shake my head. "I can't. We just came off a break."

He grabs the menu from the end of the table. "So, what's good here?"

I pull my pad and pen from my back pocket. "Burgers seem to be really popular today."

Xavier folds the menu and says, "I'll take three of them and a water."

I lift my brow as I write that down and repeat the same question I've heard Quinn repeat all day. "Okay, do you want some pink or no pink in your hamburgers?"

"Some pink, but I don't need anything on them, including the buns."

I laugh as I think about what he ordered last night when he took me to the diner. "All part of your bulking diet?"

He smiles, and I swear my knees grow a little weak. "You're a quick learner. You don't need a job, do you?"

I tear a sheet off the notepad and stuff it back into my pocket. "And work for you? No way. Besides, I think I'm going to like it here."

His large hand drapes over his heart. "That stings, beautiful. I thought we were becoming such good friends."

"We are friends and I want it to stay that way, which is why I could never work for you. I have a feeling you're a diva, and I'd be suppressing murderous tendencies before the week was over," I tease.

He smirks. "I'm far from a diva."

"You say that now, but I think having two people constantly working for you makes you seem a little needy. So, like I said, DEE-VAH."

"If you worked for me, I promise you'd like it, and it'd be a whole lot more fun and lucrative than the little service gig you've landed yourself here."

I think about the fifteen dollars in tips Quinn has shared with me sitting in my pocket, and the minimum wage that's wracking up on the clock, and I can't help but be curious. "How much more?"

"The PA position pays fifty grand a year," he says matter-of-factly. "And if you want the job, it's yours."

Oh, that's tempting. Working with Xavier every day, getting to stare at him as much as I want while I get paid well for it—that's a single girl's dream job. It sounds perfect, but I'm sure that's what Deena thought when he offered her the same position...right before she slept with him. And look where that got her. I can't allow that to be me.

I *won't* allow that to be me.

I slide the slip of paper between my fingers to distract myself from staring into those baby-blue eyes of his. "Thanks for the offer, but I don't think I can."

He drums his fingers on the table in front of him, and it's almost as if he read my mind because he asks, "Is it because of Deena?"

My gaze jerks up to meet his. "No."

The corner of his mouth pulls down into a one-sided frown. "It wouldn't be like that between us, you know."

I twist my lips. "Is that what you told her when she started too?"

For some strange reason the thought of him with another woman causes a painful burn in the pit of my stomach, and I can't stand looking at him a second longer.

I turn to walk away, but his hand darts out and grabs my wrist, holding me in place. "I would never treat you like that. Deena knew what she was getting into. She knew there would never be anything real between us, and she chose to give it up to me anyway. Our agreement with one another was crystal clear."

I flinch. "So that makes it okay?"

"She consented, Anna. I never promised her a wedding ring." I can hear the defensiveness in his voice.

"But you'll promise me one?" The question leaves my mouth so quickly, it even surprises me.

He lets go of my hand. "A ring is something I'd never promise anyone. I'm not the marrying type."

I know it's stupid, but the small hope that had built inside of me that something between Xavier and me would eventually happen—no matter how much I fought it—just got crushed to smithereens. I know he's a player, and even Quinn says the tabloids link him to dating several women at the same time, but I can't snuff out this stupid connection I feel with him. But if it's never going to be serious between us, I wish he'd just leave me alone and quit tormenting me with the idea that he might actually see me as more than just an easy lay.

I swallow hard, attempting to steady my voice. "I'll have your food out to you as soon as it's ready."

"Anna..."

I don't turn around because I know if I look at him, I'll crack. Knowing you'll never have something you really want is a terrible feeling, and something I wouldn't wish on my own worst enemy.

Chapter
EIGHT

After working eight hours, and standing up pretty much the entire time, my feet are on fire, I'm exhausted, and I lay my head back against the headrest as Quinn drives us home.

"It'll get easier, you know—the more you do it. Your body will adjust after a week or so," she tells me.

I sigh as I finish counting the tip money that's in my lap. "I hope so. It seems like so much work for fifty dollars in tips."

"I told you that I'd share the money X left. I still can't believe he left a *five hundred* dollar tip. That guy has it bad for you." She waggles her eyebrows. "What happened between the two of you, anyhow? I thought you two were getting along after hanging out last night?"

I shove the loose strand of hair that has fallen fom my ponytail behind my ear. "I don't know. We're friends, I guess, but—"

"You're so horny for him it clouds your judgment?"

"No!"

Quinn rolls her eyes as she turns onto the next street. "Oh, come on, Anna. This is me you're talking to. It's okay that a man—a mighty sexy one, I might add—turns you on. I don't see how you've gone this long without allowing him to ravage you. He obviously wants to."

I pinch my bottom lip between my teeth. While I don't want to admit exactly how much I think of him doing that very thing to me, she's right. Even after he's made it perfectly clear that there would be no long-term future for us, I still can't believe I'm entertaining the idea of giving into Xavier. I just don't want to get hurt.

"I see that look," Quinn says, snapping me out of my thoughts.

I grimace and shake my head. "I don't have a look."

She raises her eyebrows. "Yes, you do. And I'm telling you right now, Anna, you've got to learn to let go of all of those preconceived notions that sex is bad. The entire world is not going to judge you for wanting X. Hell, half of the world wants a piece of him for themselves! Be young. Have a fling. He's sex on a stick!"

"Quinn!" I scold her.

"No, Anna, fuck that. I want you to admit to not only me, but *yourself*, out loud that it's okay to want to have crazy, premarital sex with a bad-boy."

"*What*?" I ask, completely flabbergasted. "Who tells someone to say that kind of stuff?"

She grins as she pulls up to the curb in front of her house. "A best friend, that's who. Now say it."

"Quinn—"

"Anna, so help me, if you don't grow a pair of lady nuggets right now and admit out loud how you really feel, I will ship you back to Uncle Simon tonight."

"This is so ridiculous," I huff.

She folds her tan arms across her chest. "Do it, or we are not getting out of this car."

"You're relentless." I pinch the bridge of my nose as I sigh. Might as well just give in. "Fine. I want to have..."

She gestures for me to continue. "Crazy..."

"*Crazy*, premarital sex with a bad-boy. There, I said it. Happy?"

She shakes her head. "Say it one more time with *feeling*, and admit that you want that bad-boy to be wrestling's sex god, X."

I rub my face. This is freaking painful, but I know she won't give in until she wins. That's the thing about Quinn—she never gives up if she believes she's right.

I take a deep breath and close my eyes. "I want to have sex with Xavier." The moment those words leave my lips, the mad rush of shame that I know I should feel for thinking such things isn't there. It's really quite the opposite. It feels good to finally get that off my chest because for the past couple of days, that's all that's been on my mind.

Quinn claps her hands and squeals. "Don't you feel better?"

I smile. "Yeah, I actually do. I think you need to go back to school and get a psychology degree. How did you know that would help me?"

"I'm a student of human nature. I knew you wanted to let that man into your pants the moment I saw you wrestle to get your purse back from him."

"Ugh. That! He can be so frustrating. He's gotten under my skin so quick."

She laughs as she opens her door. "And that, Anna, is how I know you like him. There's a fine line between love and hate. They both cause your body to react in a similar fashion. Each of those emotions creates such intense feelings that one can easily be mistaken for the other."

"I never said I hated him. He just...I don't know." I sigh as I get out, and we head into the house together.

"A guy like X is new territory for you. While I highly advise a fun fling with a bad-boy, I don't recommend catching any feelings for him whatsoever. Look at the mess between Brock and me."

My pesky curiosity is back in full force. "What did he do to upset you, anyhow?"

She shakes her head as she slides her key into the door. "Let's not talk about him. Brock and I are history. No need to hash out boring details about something that's over."

"Okay," I agree, allowing her completely off the hook. I should press her like she just pressed me about Xavier, but I have the feeling she isn't ready to talk about whatever is going on between them yet. So, for now, she gets a pass, but if tension keeps up between them at work then she's going to have to fill me in. If Brock has done something horrible to her, I want to hate him right alongside her, not keep on delivering messages from him.

The moment we step inside, I hear Aunt Dee call us from the kitchen, "Hey, girls! How was work?"

I toss my purse on the counter as I walk into the kitchen. "It was great. Everyone was really nice."

Aunt Dee glances up from the pudding she's making on the stove. "Even Alice?"

"Well..." I grimace. "Everyone but her."

"Aye, when will that chica ever learn to lighten up? Even evil needs a holiday."

I laugh. "You sound like Quinn."

"Ah, correction. You mean *Quinn* sounds like *me*."

Quinn struts into the kitchen in her pajamas, raking her fingers through her long, dark locks. "I sound just like what?"

"Me," my aunt clarifies.

Quinn pulls some grapes from the fridge and pops one into her mouth. "Definitely not. You won't catch me making pudding at nearly midnight. You're a weirdo."

Aunt Dee chuckles as she pours the pudding into a glass bowl. "A creative mind is always a strange one, honey."

Quinn pulls herself up on the counter and dangles her long legs as she eats her grapes. "Ma, guess what? I already got Anna to admit she wants to shag Mr. Sexy."

My mouth instantly drops open, and Quinn winks at me before she pops another grape into her mouth. I'm never going to get used to how open she is with Aunt Dee.

"Oh, good choice Anna. I peeked outside when he dropped you off last night. He's a handsome one, that one is." Aunt Dee licks the spoon before tossing it into the sink. "When are you seeing him again?"

My shoulders sag. "I don't know. He came into Larry's today, but things didn't go so well."

She tilts her head and pokes out her bottom lip. "I'm sorry, baby. Maybe it'll all work out. If he's smart, he'll see what a catch you are and come to his senses."

"That's the thing. I'm pretty sure that's all he wants—to *catch* me."

Aunt Dee walks across the kitchen and stops in front of me. Her dainty hand pats my cheek. "I wouldn't be so sure. A man like him doesn't have to work hard for women. He sees something special in you, or else he wouldn't have put in this much effort."

I give her a sad smile. "He told me he doesn't get serious with women."

"Maybe he's not ready to allow himself to have feelings for you, but if he gets to know you, he'll feel different. You're impossible not to love." She kisses my cheek, and for the first time in a long time, I feel unconditionally loved. There's no judgment from her when I tell her about my issue with Xavier. Instead, she encourages me to hold on to hope. "Anna, please at least think about calling your father. He misses you."

I nod even though I have no intentions of speaking to him yet. "Okay."

She pats my cheek. "Goodnight, girls."

The moment my aunt locks herself in her room, the unmistakable sound of a motorcycle rumbles to a stop outside.

Quinn grins. "One guess who that is?"

I suck in my bottom lip, trying to hide my grin as I dash to the front door and pull it open just as Xavier steps onto the concrete stoop. "Hi."

His blue eyes flash in surprise. I'm sure the way we left things earlier has him wondering why I'm suddenly so happy to see him. It's amazing what a little soul searching and a shove from your family can accomplish.

"Hey, Anna. I...um...shit."

Xavier rubs the back of his neck and looks away as if he needs a moment to regain his composure before his eyes are able to meet mine again. "I had fifty different speeches prepared for you. I practiced on the way over, but none of them sounded like good enough apologies. Nothing I can say will make what I said any less shitty, but *I am* sorry. I just thought you should know."

For some reason I'm getting the impression that this is a huge step for Xavier. It's good to know he's at least recognized that there's enough of a connection between us for it to matter that he's hurt my feelings. I'm sure the word "sorry" isn't one that he says a lot.

The sudden need to comfort him overwhelms me and I reach out and touch the warm skin on his bulging forearm. "I'm sorry too. I shouldn't have pushed you."

His lips pull into a tight line. "Don't do that."

"What?" I ask, completely surprised and immediately jerk my hand away. This isn't exactly the reaction I imagined when I apologized in return.

Xavier's eyes soften. "You were right to say what you said. I know I use women, and I'm sure that's probably what you think I want to do with you, so don't apologize for standing up for yourself. Never allow yourself to be used, or be forced into something you don't really want. Don't apologize for asking for respect. You deserve it."

I stand a little taller. "Okay. I'll remember that for next time."

His mouth pulls into a one-sided sexy grin. "Next time? Are you saying we're still friends?"

I laugh and roll my eyes. "Yes, as long as our friendship rules still apply."

"Good." He grabs my hand without warning or apology, and pulls me toward his bike. "Then we're going for a ride."

I pull the door closed behind me and follow him down the path.

This is crazy.

I've never known anyone to have a friendship like this. I shouldn't let this go on, because I know he's going to end up breaking my heart. If he keeps being so sweet to me, I will fall for him. No question. I know myself well enough to know that if this continues it *will* end badly for me, but I don't have the willpower to turn him away. I want to be near him, even if it'll never mean as much to him as it does to me.

Xavier hops on the bike and stands it up between his powerful thighs, stretching his hand out to me with a huge grin on his face. "Hop on, beautiful."

And just like that, I'm a goner.

I'm in so much trouble.

Lots and lots of trouble.

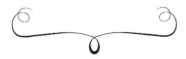

Riding through the streets on the back of Xavier's bike is unbelievably freeing. The wind rushes across my skin, and I close my eyes, resting my cheek against his back. The muscles in his back work under his shirt with every turn of his wrist, and the smell of his spicy cologne mixed with soap lingers on his skin. When I'm close to him like this, it makes me forget every reason why I should stop this thing between us before it gets too complicated. Distance gives me clarity—the ability to see that I should stay away. There's just one problem.

I don't want to.

I could stay like this forever, which is bad, but I don't care.

Xavier turns into the parking lot of the same diner he took me to last night. The streetlights illuminate the area, and the neon in the restaurant's window gleams "Open 24/7," inviting hungry people in at all times of the day.

Xavier flicks the kickstand down with his boot and then slides his sunglasses onto the top of his head. "I hope you're hungry."

I take his hand and swing my leg off the bike, the muscles in my thighs still tingling from having such a powerful machine vibrating between them. "Starving, actually. My nerves were too on edge to eat at Larry's during my lunch. Besides, I didn't have any money."

He furrows his brow. "You moved to a new city with no money?"

"I have money...just not a lot of it. I knew I could wait until I got to Aunt Dee's to eat, so it really wasn't a big deal," I say, trying to make light of the situation.

"No, Anna. Not eating is a very big deal. You're a tiny thing. If you don't eat, you could faint and hurt yourself. From now on, you eat." The authoritative tone in his voice is impossible to miss. "And if you don't have money, you call me. Understood?"

My lips twist as I try to figure out why this is such an issue for him. So I skipped a meal—no big deal. "You're being a touch ridiculous, don't you think? I don't understand why you're turning this into a 'thing.'"

Xavier shoves himself off the bike, and I can't help but notice how delicious he looks in the blue jeans he's wearing. "Let's just say I know what it's like to be hungry and do whatever you have to in order to eat. Someone like you should never have to experience that. Rough living can make you a hard person."

My eyes roam over his sculpted shoulders and travel down the length of his torso. It's hard to imagine this well-fed man ever being hungry, but the words from his lips indicate that he's had to struggle.

"That must've been tough. Did your family—"

I cut myself off before my curious mind steps in and asks for answers that are none of my business. Heat rises up my neck and into my cheeks, surely creating a blush at the thought of my own brazen attitude. "Sorry. It's none of my business."

When I attempt to look away, Xavier slides his index finger under my chin. "You can ask me anything, beautiful. I can't promise I'll always answer, but you can ask all you want. I like knowing that you're curious about me. Your questions allow me inside that mind of yours. But you should know up front that I don't talk about my family."

I open my mouth to ask him why, but think better of it. It's probably smarter to honor his wishes because I, of all people, know that sometimes families suck. Maybe he's trying to forget his past just like I am?

"I understand."

He gives me a sad smile and takes my hand, pulling me toward the entrance of the restaurant. "Hope it's okay that we came here again. It's the one place I can relax when I'm in town. It's like—"

"Home," I say, filling in the answer for him after remembering how at ease he was there last night.

After a moment of contemplation, he nods. "Yeah...something like that."

The moment we step inside I notice the place is empty. Nettie glances up from the broom she's using to sweep the floor and a huge smile warms her face. "Boy, two days in a row! How did I get so lucky?" She leans the broom against the counter before she makes her way over to us. After a quick embrace with Xavier, Nettie turns her attention back to me. "I think this is a record. Carl, you seein' this?"

Carl turns around from the grill that he's scrubbing. "I see it, woman. I ain't blind."

Nettie tsks at Carl. "No one asked for your lip. Go back to cleaning."

I chuckle at the banter between them. "Are you two an item?"

Nettie raises her eyebrows and slides her eyes toward Xavier and then back to me. "Who? Me and Carl? That old fool wishes!"

Xavier shakes his head. "Come on, Nettie, I know when this place is dead you two have a little alone time back in the storage closet."

Nettie throws her hands on her hips. "Xavier Cold, I have the mind to take you out back and tan your hide for talking to me like that."

He tips his head back and a deep laugh rumbles out of him. "It's not as big of a secret as you think, Nettie. Everyone knows you and Carl are a thing."

She folds her smooth brown arms over her chest. "I have no idea what you're talking about."

"Sure you don't."

I don't miss the wink Xavier throws her way before pulling me toward the same corner booth as last night. I slide into the seat across from him. "Why do they hide being together?"

Xavier shrugs. "Who knows. They're both crazy as hell, but together they work. I don't know why they hide it. I've known for years."

I rest my head in my hand as I lean in. "How exactly do you know them?"

"I used to work here."

I glance around at the ripped booth seats and worn checkered floor and try to imagine Xavier working here. I can't imagine him as anything other than a powerful wrestling icon, so it's hard to picture him scrubbing floors and serving meals. "How long ago was that?"

"When I was seventeen, Nettie and Carl offered me a job," he answers right before Nettie sets two glasses of water down.

"You two want the same thing as last night?" she asks.

"Yeah, I do. Beautiful?" Xavier asks and I nod. "Same as last night, Nettie."

"Will do, but this time don't be leaving no heap of money. We don't want you wasting your money on us." She swats his shoulder.

"Speak for yourself!" Carl calls from the stove. "He can leave me all the cheddar he wants."

Nettie whips her head in his direction. "You're going to get it if you don't stop!"

Carl swirls a white towel around. "Hot damn! Just what I like to hear."

Nettie rolls her eyes and Xavier laughs. "You two kill me."

"I'll bring your food out as soon as it's done," she says shaking her head and marching toward Carl, who she promptly smacks in the back of the head.

"They're great," I say.

Xavier's eyes turn almost nostalgic. "They really are. I'm lucky to have them."

While I find it endearing that he loves his old co-workers so much, it also breaks my heart. How evil must his own family be for him to be closer to strangers?

"So you've known them for eleven years?" I ask, still curious about his relationship with them.

He lifts his right eyebrow. "And how would you know that?"

Heat floods my cheeks. Busted. "It's simple mathematics. You said you worked here when you were seventeen, and I know you're twenty-eight...so I figured it out."

"I suspect you learned my age from the Internet stalking you and Quinn did." His lips twist.

I roll my eyes and fire back, "Just like you learned where I was staying when you dropped me off last night. I didn't give you the address."

He shrugs. "I always look into things I'm interested in."

I take a sip of water to quench my suddenly dry throat. "Are you saying that you're interested in me?"

He stares directly into my eyes. "You know I am. But I can never be involved with you, so for that reason, we're friends. And that's all we'll ever be."

I can't help asking, "Why is that?"

He licks his lips before he grazes his top teeth over his bottom one. "I know that the kind of relationship I like to have with women will never fly with you. I can't just use you, Anna. I respect you too much for that."

My heart races in my chest as I think about the desire building inside me. Desire for Xavier. I know I haven't known him long, but I feel like we've spent a lot of time together already. The thought of never getting to find out what a night with him would be like scares me, almost to the point where I'm willing to bend my own morals just to find out.

"What if I wanted to have a relationship like that with you?"

Xavier shakes his head. "You say that now, but I know you'd regret it later. Girls like you—you're the long-term commitment type. That's something I can't promise."

"You keep saying that, but I don't understand why you think so? How do you know that you're not my type? You've done nothing but keep me safe and watch out for me in this new city. You're a great guy. I really like you."

He furrows his brow and pulls his lips into a tight line. "You shouldn't."

The intensity in his stare causes me to swallow hard. "W—why?"

"There's more to me than just the persona that the public sees. There's darkness inside me that no one should have to experience, and that's what I'm trying to protect you from. No one should have to live with my demons but me."

The harsh reality hits me. There's a lot about Xavier Cold that I don't know. Some obvious issues he's dealing with. He refuses to talk about his family, and he believes that he's *evil* somehow. With all that being said, I still know there's a lot of good in him—whether he sees it or not. I'm a perfect stranger, and he's been there for me since the plane ride from Portland. He just needs to see that he's a nice guy and that he's not completely bad like he believes—that he deserves happiness too. Everyone does.

I reach over and touch his hand. There's a slight flinch, and his harsh expression remains, but I don't pull back. I want him to know we all have secrets we'd like to hide from the world.

"We all have things that haunt us—things we'd like to forget. The key is to not allow them to get in the way of our happiness."

Xavier runs his hand along his scruffy jawline. "Not everyone's meant to have happiness, Anna. Some of us are meant for the dark."

"I don't believe that."

He levels his eyes on me. "That's because you've got a good heart and like to believe that everyone is a good person underneath. I knew that from the moment you refused me on that plane. A girl like you...you aren't meant for a guy like me."

His tone is meant to scare me off, I can tell, but it's doing the exact opposite. It's pulling me toward him. Telling me to make him see that he's wrong.

Nettie sets our food down on the table in front of us, redirecting my attention from Xavier and his self-loathing for the moment. As soon as the sweet smell of pancakes wafts around me, my mouth waters. Xavier wastes no time digging into his steaming food while I take my time applying butter to my pancakes.

"How long you got with us, Xavier?" Nettie asks as she leans her hip against the booth.

"The rest of the week, and then I have to fly to Atlanta for *Tuesday Tension*. If all goes well, I'll be heading into a title match soon."

"You sure are moving up. Did you hear that, Carl? Our boy is gon' be champion." she calls over her shoulder.

"I never had a doubt he would be. Not after the way he pummeled half the neighborhood around here." Carl chuckles as he leans against the counter and stares up at the ceiling with a nostalgic twinkle in his eye. "Did you tell your little girlfriend here about the first time you met us?"

Xavier swallows his food. "We're just friends. And no, I haven't told her. She doesn't need to know about that."

"Ah, come on, X. It's funny now. You're not the same punk kid that came in here the first time. Go on. Tell her. She'll get a kick out of it," Carl says, antagonizing him.

That pesky curiosity of mine rears its beast of a head again, and I join in with Carl's teasing, desperate for any glimpse of this man's past. Desperate to know him better. "Please?"

He shakes his head. "I was stupid. It's not worth repeating."

"Not worth repeating? Man—"

Nettie cuts him off. "Hush, Carl. If Xavier doesn't want to tell this girl about his past, let it go. I'm sure he's got his reasons. Even though he should be proud of everything he's overcome."

"Well if he wants to keep who he is a secret from her, he shouldn't have brought her 'round here. The girl is bound to find out sooner or later."

Xavier scrubs his hand over his face. "All right. Fine." He turns his gaze back to me. "When I was seventeen, I robbed this place. I was hungry, needed money and it seemed like a good target since it was open late. I just didn't anticipate the old man over there getting the best of me. Once Carl had a hold of me, it was over. No running away."

I flinch. That's not exactly a great story. That's sad and tragic—not to mention mind-boggling—since I know he used to work here. Looking at him now and trying to picture the young man who must have been at the very edges of hunger to resort to such a violent act makes my heart ache. Even though I haven't known him long, I sense that he's not one for pity, so I do my best to keep my face straight as I ask, "I thought you said you used to work here?"

"I did."

My eyes flit to Nettie and then back to Xavier. "You robbed your own employers?"

"Sugar, he didn't work here when he did that. That's what landed him the job," Nettie says as she pats Xavier's shoulder.

The skin on my forehead creases as I furrow my brow. "I guess I'm confused. Why would you give him a job if he tried to steal from you?"

Nettie waves me off. "The boy was hungry. We all do crazy things when we don't have any other choice. We figured the law wouldn't do a thang for 'dis boy but corrupt him more by throwing him in jail. So instead of calling the cops, we offered him a job."

My eyes drift over to Xavier, and he frowns as he gauges my reaction. That explains his rough edge. He was a street kid. He had to grow up tough. I'm not sure what he experienced with his family, but whatever it was, it was bad enough that he still doesn't want to discuss them now. It's obvious they mistreated him, but I wonder to what extent.

I straighten my shoulders and give Xavier a small smile, attempting to reassure him this doesn't sway my opinion of his character. "Looks like you're right, Nettie. He appears to have turned out just fine."

A flicker of relief washes over his stoic expression as Nettie says, "I agree. He's made such a turn around. The hardest part was—"

Xavier cuts her off. "It's getting late, and we should really get going. How much do I owe you?"

"It's on the house," she replies as she gathers up his empty plate. Xavier rolls his eyes and fishes out his wallet, placing a few hundreds on the table again. "Boy, if you don't put that money away—"

Xavier pushes himself out of the booth and wraps an arm around Nettie's shoulders. "Don't be a pain in my ass. Take the damn money."

She sags against him. "You know you don't have to do this every time you come in here. We'd love you if you were still broke."

He kisses the top of her head. "I know." He releases Nettie and extends his hand to me. "Ready, beautiful?"

Other than the roaring engine of the bike, the ride back to Aunt Dee's is quiet. It's taking every inch of my self-control to bottle up all my questions about his past. I want to know about him so badly it physically hurts.

Xavier parks his bike next to the curb and kills the engine. After I remove my arms from around his waist, I hop off and hand him his helmet.

He swings his leg over the bike, and I raise my eyebrows. The expression on my face must give away my surprise because he chuckles as he says, "Relax, I'm just walking you to the door. Lots of creeps around at this time of night."

"Bodyguard mode?"

Another chuckle has his eyes crinkling at the corners as he shrugs. "Can you blame me for wanting to protect that smokin' little body of yours?"

His words make me blush and run my fingers through my hair, desperate to draw attention away from my reddening cheeks. It's crazy how simple flirty phrases from him can cause my heart to flutter.

He takes my hand and pulls me toward the front door. "What time is your shift tomorrow?"

"Not until four."

He chews on his bottom lip as we step onto the landing. "Do you have any plans afterward?"

The smart thing for me to do is cut this off now. We both know that this can never be a long-term relationship since he's leaving soon, but I can't keep myself away from the torture that I know lies ahead. "I'd like that."

Xavier's smile widens. "Great. I'll come to Larry's and pick you up. When is your shift over?"

"Eleven." This feels like a date, and I know I shouldn't get my hopes up, but I can't help the pure elation that engulfs me at the thought of spending more time with him.

"I'll pick you up then." His eyes drift down to my lips.

"Okay." My mouth betrays me and, completely ignoring one of our friendship rules, drifts open.

My heart thunders in my chest. Oh my God. This is it.

I'm finally going to feel his lips on mine.

I close my eyes. The heat from his skin radiates around me, and my chest heaves. I want this more than I can even express, and I can't wait to finally move to the next level with him.

The moment his lips press against my forehead, my brow furrows and my shoulders sag as my hopes are instantly crushed.

Xavier chuckles, knowing he's teasing me as he pulls away. "I believe no open-mouthed kissing was your rule, not mine."

I twist my lips and fight the sudden urge to kick myself. My stupid good-girl rules are coming back to bite me in the ass.

"Right." I sigh.

"I'll see you tomorrow," he says as he presses his lips to my forehead again. "Goodnight."

He pulls away without another word, and my entire body sags.

As he turns and heads toward his bike, my eyes instantly focus on his backside. There's no denying the man has a great ass. I don't think any woman in the world would disagree with me on that. But just like most dangerous things, it's forbidden for a reason, and I can't allow myself to get swept up in what feels like the beginning of an epic romance. His words of warning should be enough to scare me away, but they don't. There's no fighting this pull I feel toward him, no matter how foolish I know I'm being.

The last few days have been a blur. My life has consisted of working and Xavier, and it's been perfect.

I finish applying my lip-gloss just as Quinn walks into our room. "Is Mr. Sexy coming to pick you up again tonight?"

A heated blush creeps into my cheeks. "Yes."

"Damn. That man has it bad for you." She slides in next to me and checks her hair. "That's what—the fifth night in a row?"

"Sixth." I giggle. "But who's counting?"

She bumps her hip into mine. "You, obviously. Are you sure you aren't having sex with him yet? It's pretty hard to believe that one of the sexiest men on the planet picks you up from work everyday, just to take you to some crappy diner, without even getting desert, if you know what I mean."

I shrug. "We're friends. There's nothing sexual going on between us."

Quinn tilts her head. "It's only a matter of time before that happens, Anna. X isn't stupid. He knows a girl like you can't be rushed. How many days until he's off vacation?"

"Two." My shoulders sag.

I haven't dwelled on the idea of what it will be like around here once Xavier leaves. Since I arrived, we've been practically connected at the hip. My new life consists of working at Larry's and spending my nights at the diner with Xavier. I'm not ready for him to go yet.

"Aww." Quinn wraps her arm around my shoulder. "Don't look so sad, Anna-Banana. When he leaves, I'll take you out and we'll go hottie hunting to take your mind off him."

I frown. "What about Brock? Aren't you two working things out?"

She rolls her eyes. "We are, but he's an ass most of the time. I don't know why I even bother with him. If his ass didn't look so great in a pair of jeans, I'd be a lot less forgiving every time he pisses me off."

I laugh. "I don't know if I'll ever understand your relationship with him. You guys fight way more than you are nice to one another. If I didn't know you two had something going on, I would swear you were mortal enemies."

Quinn snorts. "There's a thin line between love and hate, Anna. Remember that."

A few hours later I find myself immersed in loud chatter of the restaurant patrons, trying to keep up with the orders. The crowd at Larry's tonight is insane. It's Bike Nite, and who knew there were so many riders in Detroit? Andy says tonight's revenue helps sustain the business throughout the month when it's not as busy. There's not even a spare moment to chat with Quinn or the guys back in the kitchen.

As I punch in my next order I glance down at the clock on the computer, calling to Quinn, "We close in two hours. Does this slow down soon?"

She props her tray on her hip. "Yeah, this should be the last of it. Once we get these customers served, things should begin to die down." I slide over and allow her to punch her order in. "Speaking of dying, did you see how pissed Alice got when X came in and avoided the bar area, heading straight for your section? I thought her head was going to explode. Her face was as red as her hair. You would think after all the times he's been in here and passed by her section, she would accept he's not interested."

I laugh. "She hates me."

"Fuck her," Quinn barks. "There's a word for girls like her that starts with a 'c'. That bitch is mean, and I think it's funny X doesn't give her the chance to shove her fake boobies in his face."

I shake my head. "You're too much."

"Believe me, she deserves a little torture. Alice has had things go her way around here far too long."

"Order up, Quinnie!" Brock calls from the kitchen. "You too, Anna."

She sighs. "Duty calls."

I load my orders on the tray and head out to deliver them on the floor. This is the most intimidating part of the job for me, carrying this heavy tray filled with food, but I'm becoming more comfortable with it.

I balance it carefully on the palm of my hand, praying I don't spill it. The second I pass by the bar my foot gets caught on something, and I stumble, losing my balance.

Everything feels like it happens in slow motion. The momentum of the tray moving forward is unstoppable, along with my fumbling steps. A collective gasp fills my ears, and I watch helplessly as the contents of the tray hit the floor and the plates shatter before both of my knees hit the ground.

It takes everything in me not to cry. Even though I know accidents happen, I feel like a failure. The sight of the broken plates confirms my earlier speculation that maybe I'm not so cut out for the real world after all.

"What the hell happened?" I glance up at Andy, who is sizing up the mess with a furrowed brow. "Are you hurt?"

"Are you kidding?" Alice snickers. "Her ass is fat enough to cushion her landing."

"Watch it, Alice," Quinn barks as she helps me up and asks, "Are you all right?"

"I'm fine." I dust off my knees and pause when I see the scarlet liquid on my fingertips.

Xavier pushes past my cousin and scans me from head to toe.

"You're bleeding." He scoops me up into his massive arms and shifts his gaze to Andy. "Where's your first aid kit?"

"On the wall in my office, through the kitchen," Andy replies, and Xavier takes off in that direction.

My eyes trace Xavier's concerned face. "I can walk, you know."

He shakes his head. "There could be glass in that cut. No walking until I look at it."

"I didn't know you were a doctor too," I tease.

He smirks. "Don't be a smartass. I just know a lot about fixing wounds."

Xavier sets me on Andy's desk and grabs the kit off the wall. Without any hint of hesitation he rifles through the box, searching for the correct supplies to treat my leg. His last words ring in my ears, reminding me there's so much about him I don't know about.

He brings over a bottle of peroxide and gauze and sets the open box next to me. He pours a capful of solution and opens one of the sterile bandages. "This won't hurt. I just need to clean it up." After I nod, he holds the gauze below the small cut on my knee and pours the peroxide into the wound. It bubbles and fizzes—flushing the germs out before he dumps another capful into it. His eyes inspects the cut, and I know the logical reaction would be for me to be worried about the pain, but all I can focus on are his large hands on my body. The tenderness of his touch causes my stomach to flip. "You don't appear to have any glass in there—looks like just a bad scrape."

He dabs some triple antibiotic ointment on a clean wad of gauze and applies it to the cut before covering it with a bandage. His skill amazes me. My father would never have been able to do that. Injuries like this were always handled by my mother, which makes me wonder why Xavier is so good at it. "Where did you learn how to do all this?"

He shrugs. "Just something I learned over time. I've always had to take care of myself, you know."

One corner of my mouth pulls down into a small frown. "Did your mom teach you?" I know the question is prying, and he's told me he doesn't talk about his family, but I can't help wondering what happened to him when he was a little boy.

Xavier blows a rush of air through his nostrils. "My mom died when I was a kid."

I gasp and instantly wish I could take back my nosy question. "I'm so sorry. That's terrible. How old were you?"

He swallows hard and tosses the open packages in the trash. "Eight."

My heart instantly crushes in my chest. I can't imagine losing someone as important as your mother at such an early age.

I place my hand on his, attempting to comfort him, but he jerks away and shakes his head. "This is exactly why I don't talk about my family. I hate pity. Don't feel sorry for me."

I flinch at the sudden change in tone. "I'm sorry, I just...I want you to know I'm here for you...if you ever want to talk about her."

He closes the box and latches it shut. "I've done just fine not talking about her for this long, and I'd prefer to keep it that way. She's dead. I'm over it."

I can tell by the pained expression on his face that's far from the truth. "It's okay to miss her—"

"Enough!" he snaps. "Damn it. Are you always this nosy?"

"Are you always this evasive?" I fire back, unable to stop myself.

He directs his stern blue eyes to me in what I'm sure is a look that's meant to get me to back off, but it doesn't scare me. Not one bit.

"I just think that if you talked about her—"

"That what? I'll suddenly be a better person. News flash, beautiful, that's not how shit works in the real world. Dragging up things from the past only fucks with people's heads more. It doesn't magically heal them. People don't talk about certain things for a reason, and believe me, I have mine."

"It's still not healthy. If you would just—"

"Why don't you follow your own advice, huh? I saw the bruises on your arm that first day. Why don't you tell me what made you really run away from home? What was so bad? Did your boyfriend beat you? Your father? Who?" The air whooshes from my lungs and he takes in my panicked expression. "It's not so easy to talk about something *you* don't want to, is it?"

Memories of the day I left home flood my mind. Thoughts of what I went through just to make it out of there cause a sob to rip out of me. Damn him for making me feel this way—for making me remember the hellish life I left behind.

"Damn it." Xavier closes his eyes and takes a deep breath before opening them and reaching out to embrace me. "I'm sorry, Anna. I shouldn't have...*fuck*."

I shake my head as guilt washes over me, finally understanding why he didn't want to talk about his past. The pain of my own past is hard to bear, and I can only imagine what he must feel like if his was worse than mine.

"I'm sorry too." I bury my face in his chest and continue to cry softly.

We stay like that for a few minutes—both quiet and unmoving. For a moment it feels like whatever wall Xavier has built around himself comes down a bit, allowing me to see inside, if only for a brief moment. The memories that haunt him aren't something he obviously wants to discuss, so I'll respect that, but I hope one day he'll trust me enough to let me in all the way.

Quinn clears her throat. "Everything all right in here?"

Xavier pushes away from me and takes in my tear-stained face. He grimaces, like the sight of me causes him physical pain, before stepping back. "I've got to go."

Panic fills me. He's pulling away just as I thought we were getting somewhere, and it scares me. I don't know him well enough to know whether I'll ever see him again, if he walks out this door right now. "Xavier...wait. Please."

He shakes his head. "I can't."

I swallow hard as he zips past Quinn in the doorway and possibly out of my life forever.

I bite down on my lip and try to force the tears of abandonment away. It's crazy to feel this way about him, but I can't help it. There's so much more to him than the tough persona he presents to the world. He's hurting, and I just wish I knew how to help him.

"What was all that about?" Quinn asks the moment Xavier is out of earshot. "You sure you two aren't sleeping together, because that felt fucking intense."

I sniff and grab a tissue from Andy's desk. "I think I just pushed him away."

She tilts her head. "How did you do that?"

"He told me that he doesn't talk about his family, and I couldn't stop myself from prying. He got upset. We both said some things...then apologized, and now I'm not sure where we stand." I wipe under my eyes, the black mascara staining the tissue. "I don't know if I'll ever see him again after this."

Admitting out loud that I might not see him again causes another sob to rip through me. My cousin is instantly at my side, hugging me.

I wrap my arms around her, and she sighs. "Oh shit. This is worse than I thought. You have feelings for him already, don't you?"

While it must be obvious that I do, saying it out loud makes it real, and I'm not sure I'm ready for that. But I have to give her something. Quinn won't stop pushing me for details unless I do.

I close my eyes, and tear rolls down my cheek. "I don't know what's going on between us. All I know is the idea of never seeing him again...it scares me."

She nods. "I completely understand. Things are still new between the two of you, and it's hard to dig into heavy issues at this stage, but you can't let him leave Detroit with this weight hanging between the two of you. You have to let him know you're here for him."

"What if he doesn't want to see me again?"

Quinn smiles. "He does. Trust me. You should go after him."

"Now?" I shake my head. "I can't. What would Andy say if I just left in the middle of my shift?"

She waves me off. "I'll tell him your leg hurt, and you needed to go home and rest. He'll be so worried over the worker's comp claim he won't bat an eye about you leaving. Here,"—she digs in her pocket—"take my car."

I furrow my brow. "Do you want me to come back and pick you up?"

"No." She grins. "Brock will give me a ride."

I raise my eyebrows. "I take it you two are getting along now?"

Her grin widens, and she licks her lips. "You could say that. We've been working on it the past two nights in the parking lot after work in the backseat of his car."

I laugh and hop off the desk with only a minor stinging pain on my knee. "You guys are too much. Call me if you need a ride, and I'll come back for you."

"Will do. Speaking of calling..." Quinn pauses for a beat. "Did you call Uncle Simon yet?"

"No," I whisper. "I'm still not ready to talk to him yet."

Quinn frowns. "Okay, but you should consider doing that soon. Ma says he's worried sick and been talking about flying out here so you'll talk to him. It's been a week, Anna. I don't know how much longer Ma can stall him."

I sigh. "I'll do it tomorrow."

That answer seems to satisfy her because she nods. "Good plan. Two overly emotional men in one night might be too much for you."

I roll my eyes. "Goodnight, cuz."

"Night. Don't do anything that I'd do." She winks.

"Isn't the saying don't do anything that I *wouldn't* do?"

"That's exactly my point. If you were like me, you'd fuck that man into submission. Your 'friends first' tactic seems to be working, so don't be like me," she teases before she struts by the two cooks, smacking Brock's ass as she passes by on her way to the dining room.

Brock stares after her and says to no one in particular in a dreamy voice, "I love to watch that girl go."

Sooner or later I'm going to have to get the scoop on those two.

The moment I lock myself into Quinn's Honda, I scroll through my phone to find Xavier's number. If he's on his bike he's not going to answer, so it's pointless calling right now. There's only one place that I know he likes to go, so I crank the engine alive and head in the direction of the diner.

Nerves jitter through me as I drive through the city. What in the hell am I suppose to say to him? Am I supposed to tell him that I'm sorry again, or do we drop it and move on? What if he sees me and walks away, angry that I didn't get the hint the first time?

I sigh and keep driving, because I have to at least try. I don't want our friendship to get crushed because I couldn't take a hint and back off a touchy subject.

I pull into the parking lot, and there's no sign of Xavier's bike. My shoulders sag as it occurs to me that I have no clue where he lives. We've only ever met in public places, so I don't even know how to attempt to find him. I pull out my cell and dial his number but it instantly connects to his voice mail. "It's Anna. Call me, please."

I drum my fingers on the wheel and debate my next move until I spot Nettie through the window, serving tables.

She'll know where I can find him.

I hop out of the car and shove my phone in my back pocket as I make my way toward the diner's entrance. It's then, in the distance, I hear a motorcycle rumble. I stop in my tracks and wrap my arms around myself as I stare in the direction of the sound.

Xavier pulls into view, and my eyes glue to him. His dark hair blows back while the dark sunglasses he's wearing hide his eyes from me. The material of his black t-shirt strains against the defined muscles in his chest and arms, and his jeans hug his powerful thighs perfectly. He's sexiness personified, and I can't tear my eyes away.

He parks next to me but because of his glasses I can't get a good read on his expression. Xavier flicks down the kickstand and swings his leg off the bike. "What are you doing here, Anna?"

I hug myself tighter. "I didn't like how we left things."

He leans back against his bike and crosses his arms over his chest, still hiding his eyes behind the dark plastic. "Don't sweat it. It's over. Let's not rehash the bullshit."

There's no doubt the small crack I broke through has now been bricked shut, and I've learned pushing him doesn't always end with the result that I want.

I readjust my arms and nod. "You're right. No need to discuss things we've dealt with."

His lips pull into a tight line. "Then why are you here?"

I take a step toward him, feeling the pull that connects us drawing me to him. "I wanted to make sure we're still all right."

"We're still friends. Nothing will change that." Coldness rings through his voice and it scares me. I don't want him to push me away.

I take another step, unable to stop myself from getting closer to him. He raises his eyebrows as I straddle one of his legs and place my hands on his sides. "*Nothing*?"

Xavier shakes his head. "No."

An overwhelming need to taste his lips flows through me, and I can no longer fight against it.

"Then I'm breaking rule number two of our friendship clause."

And with no clue what in the hell I'm doing, I lean in and press my lips to his.

His entire body tenses for a moment— muscles contracting beneath my touch before relaxing as he wraps his arms around me and pulls me against his hard chest. His tongue flicks across my lips, begging to be let in. The instant he thrusts his tongue into my mouth, he emits a low growl from the back of his throat. My sex clenches as I find myself more turned on by him than ever.

A wave of pure, unadulterated lust washes over me, and I curl my fingers into the fabric of his shirt, wanting to hold him next to me forever. Large fingers slide over my collarbone and up my neck before finally cradling my cheek, locking me in place. There's no going back now. I have most definitely crossed a line, but I don't care. I want this.

I want him.

He pulls away and leans his forehead against mine. "Spend the night with me."

I swallow hard and hope to God that I'm ready for this, and that I can handle the outcome of what all this will mean for me. What it will mean for us.

"Okay."

Xavier kisses me one last time before he orders, "Follow me."

The moment we pull apart, I shiver while my body craves the return of his warmth. I turn away, clenching my hands into fists as I head toward Quinn's car, and when I hear Xavier's bike fire up behind me, the gravity of what I just agreed to hits me. On one hand I can't believe I'm doing this, but on the other I'm so excited and turned on I can't stand it. This is soon. I know that—the little voice in my head that keeps repeating it over and over is pretty loud right now—and promiscuity isn't exactly something my conscience condones, but that voice needs to just shut up and allow my body to have its moment. It's been tortured by Xavier's close proximity long enough.

I follow Xavier on his bike, running through in my mind how I think this is going to go down. Do we sit in his living room and have drinks first like they do in the movies, or do we just get right to it the moment the door is shut?

I tap my thumb on the steering wheel as we come to a red light. I wish Quinn was here right now. She'd be able to give me some pretty solid advice since this is all new territory for me.

The moment the light turns green Xavier takes off again, but quickly slows down and pulls into a hotel parking lot.

Apparently he can't wait either.

After I park beside him, I kill the engine and take a deep breath, removing my seat belt in the process.

I can do this. He's not a stranger anymore, and I trust him. But my pep talk doesn't do much to settle my nerves. This is a huge step and will change *everything*.

Suddenly the door opens, and I gasp and clutch my chest. Xavier rests his arm on the top of the car and leans down so he can see my face. "You all right?"

"Yeah—yes. I'm good. I'm ready to do this," I say with confidence.

Xavier smirks. "You sound like you're trying to psyche yourself up. Is being alone with me really that scary?"

I swallow hard as I stare into the deep-blue pools of his irises. "I'm not afraid of you."

His eyes roam over my face, like he's searching for answers to some unspoken question that he has in his mind. "You know, just because we broke rule number two, it doesn't mean we *have* to go after number one next."

My mind suddenly goes blank. "Remind me what that one is again?"

Xavier's plump lips pull up into a devilish smile. "You—naked in my bed."

My eyes widen. "I, um..."

Oh my God. This man has me completely flabbergasted. If I can't even respond to him talking dirty now, how can I believe I'm ready to move on to the next level with him? Maybe he's right. Maybe I am rushing things.

I stare up at him, unsure of what to say.

He smiles and nods, like he understands my plight. "It's okay, beautiful. You don't have to explain, and you've always got the right to change your mind. How about we watch a movie at my place instead?"

Relief floods me, and instantly I'm thankful that he's not making a big deal about this. Most men would be pissed. "A movie sounds nice."

Xavier holds out his hand. "Come on."

I take his hand, and he leads me toward the hotel entrance. I furrow my brow as we walk through the door and right past the front desk. "When you asked me to come over to your place for a movie, a hotel isn't exactly what I had in mind," I tell him honestly, still a little confused as he presses the button for the elevator.

We step inside and Xavier presses the button for the twentieth floor. A number of things flow through my mind. If this city is his permanent place of residence, him staying in a hotel doesn't jive.

When we step onto our designated floor I can't stop myself from asking, "I thought you said you're from here."

He leads me down the hall. "I am from here."

"But you don't live in Detroit permanently?" I try to clarify.

"I do. I have a permanent address here," he answers.

I twist my lips as we stop at the last door. "Then how come you're staying in a hotel, instead of your own place?"

He sighs as he fishes his room key from his wallet and slips it into the slot. "The property I own is my family home, but it's not really a place I feel comfortable to actually stay in."

So many questions stem from his one simple statement. I want to know what about the place makes him feel that way, but I know from my experience that sometimes home isn't always a good place to be. I opt for a simpler approach. "Do you still have family living there?"

He holds the door open and motions for me to go inside. "Let's not talk about my family. Please?"

I tense instantly and wish I could take back being so nosy. We've fought about my prying enough for one night.

The hotel suite is amazing. I've never been in one that looks more like a small apartment before. The sitting room has a couch and two formal armchairs pointing at the flat-screen mounted on the wall. A small, high-end kitchen with dark wood cabinets and stainless steal appliances flows into the sitting room. "This is really nice."

He nods. "I stay here every time I'm in town."

I turn back toward him. "How often is that?"

"Not often—every couple of years."

My heart instantly sinks. "Who takes care of your house if you're gone so often?"

He shrugs. "I pay someone to look after it."

I sigh. "I can't believe you're leaving soon. Am I ever going to see you again?"

He leans against the wall and stares down at the floor. "It's probably better if you don't"

"Says who?"

His head jerks up, and he meets my stare. "Me."

I shake my head and step toward him. "If we're going to continue being friends, you have to stop with the self-loathing attitude. You aren't a bad person. If you were, I wouldn't be here right now."

Xavier reaches out and grabs me by the waist, effectively pulling me to him. "You don't know how badly I wish that where true."

Intensity radiates off him and my heart pounds against my ribs as he leans in to kiss me. My hands press against his chest, and I close my eyes, allowing my mouth to drift open as I wait for lips to meet mine.

"Well, *well*...what do we have here?" A distinctly female voice purrs behind me. "Are you going to be done playing with her soon or will she be joining us this evening? I'm lonely back here."

I turn just in time to spot Deena stride out from the bedroom, wearing a couple of red strings and pieces of fabric that I believe she considers to be lingerie. I can't help but stare at her. She's practically naked in front of me and seeing her undeniably killer body, I understand why she was unimpressed with me at the bar the other night. She belongs on a magazine cover.

How can I compete with that?

Xavier's muscles tense beneath my fingers. "What are you doing here, Deena?"

She shrugs as she runs her finger along the back of the couch slowly. "I figured since we had so much fun together the other night that you'd want to do it again. I know *I* do."

My stomach turns as the words the "other night" replay in my head. He slept with her after he'd spent the evening with me? I guess I'm nothing special to him after all. I shove away from him and shake my head.

"Anna..." He grabs for me, but I swat his hand away.

"Don't!" I snap. "You don't get to touch me while you still have her."

He grimaces. "What happened with her...it didn't mean anything."

The conversation we had about his relationship with Deena flashes through my mind. "That's right. The two of you have some weird sex arrangement that makes it okay to use her." I shake my head, disgusted at how he could share his body with someone who means nothing to him. I feel so...used...and stupid. How could I be so naïve?

He scrubs his hand over his face. "It's not like that. Damn it. I just...I can't go without sex for that long, and I knew you—"

"Wouldn't give it up, you little prude," Deena fires at me, and her words feel like a punch to the gut. "I, on the other hand, was only too happy to give him what he needed."

"Shut up, Deena!" His voice takes on a threatening tone and the smirk on her face immediately disappears as he glares at her.

It's then that I know what Deena is saying is true, and Xavier is obviously not happy with her for telling me. My heart instantly crumbles. "Has the last week meant nothing to you?" Tears threaten to expose how betrayed I feel. The walls of the spacious hotel room begin to close in on me. I can't stand here in the middle of this messed-up situation and pretend like I'm not hurting.

As I take a couple steps backward toward the door my feet falter, and I struggle to get my balance. Anger and embarrassment flow through my veins. I clutch my chest, wishing I could reach inside and hold my breaking heart together.

"Anna..." There's an almost pleading tone to his voice, but I refuse to allow myself to get hurt any more.

I knew he was bad, that this wouldn't end well, yet here I am—locked in his hotel room getting a huge reality check.

I lift my chin and feel grateful that we never became physical. That would've made walking away from him now that much harder.

"Thank you." My gaze flicks from Xavier to Deena. "To both of you, for teaching me a very valuable lesson. Some people can't be trusted, no matter how much you want to believe they can be."

All the color drops from Xavier's face, and he nods before shoving his hands in his pockets. "I warned you."

I bat away a tear that's rolling down my cheek. "You did. I just didn't listen. Goodbye, X."

He stands there, making no attempts to persuade me to stay, while I walk through the door and out of his life forever.

Chapter
TEN

I crouch under the coffee table of our small one bedroom apartment and pray she doesn't call for me again.

I hate it when she does that.

I don't like helping her.

Her footsteps shuffle across the floor, and I watch her take a seat at the small kitchen table with its mismatched chairs. It's gotten worse over the few weeks—the need to take her medication. It's becoming a daily thing, and when she doesn't have it there's always hell to pay.

"Xavier?" Mama calls. "I need your help, son."

My entire body tenses as I hold my breath, praying no sound comes out of me this time. Maybe she'll believe I'm not here.

"Come on, son. Mama needs your help."

I jerk my hand back as a cockroach crawls across the floor and the top of my head bumps the table. Instantly, I freeze.

Her head whips in my direction. It takes a couple of seconds, but her eyes finally zero in on me under the table. "There you are. Why didn't you answer me before? Come over here."

I slink back, refusing to answer her.

Her eyes narrow, and she demands, "Get your ass over here now!"

All the muscles in my body begin to tremble as I stand and take a hesitant step toward her. "Why do I always have to do it?"

She shoves her greasy brown hair away from her red, splotchy face and sniffs. "I'm not strong enough to get it tight. You, you're strong." She hands me the old black leather belt that's on the table. "Hurry up, baby. I need my medicine."

Tears stream down my face as I stare at the worn leather in my small hands. "Please, don't make me."

"You know I love you, right, baby? Help Mama out. If I don't get my medicine it'll make me upset. You remember what happens when I get upset, right?"

This is her way of threatening me—the way she always forces me to do what she says. Typically I do it just so she doesn't become violent, but she looks worse today and I'm afraid of what another dose will do to her. I stare at the ragged t-shirt she's wearing. It's the same one she sleeps in, and she's been so high she hasn't bothered changing at all this week. Stains speckle the front of it from where I've tried to keep food in her.

I refuse to help her hurt herself any more.

I square my shoulders. "No."

She narrows her blue eyes at me. "What'd you say to me?"

I lift my chin. "I said no."

Without warning she draws back to smack me in the face, but like she said, I'm strong, and I snatch a hold of her wrist before she can make contact. "You little fucker. I hate you! No one will ever love you. EVER! You're a selfish little bastard."

I know this is the addiction talking. The books I've gotten from the library taught me that much. She wasn't always like this. There have been some good times too, and those are the memories I try to hang on to. Thoughts of the woman I hope she'll be again one day, when she kicks this habit.

"No, Mama! I want you to stop!"

"Leave then, just like your father did. Leave me here all alone." She sobs as she comes undone, and my heart crushes. "No one ever wants to stay with me. I've made you hate me too."

I wrap my arms around her, instantly sorry I made her cry. "I'm sorry, Mama. I don't want to leave. I want you to get better."

She turns her tear-streaked face up at me. "Then help me. One last time, then I'll get better. I promise."

I stare down at the belt, thinking that maybe this time she means it.

"Okay."

She grins and holds her sleeve up as I loop the belt around her arm and synch it as tight as I can. "That's good, baby. Look at that big vein."

The glee in her voice makes me shiver. I turn my head the moment she pulls out the needle and jabs herself with it.

A couple of seconds later, her body visibly relaxes.

"Much better," she sighs as she drops the needle to the floor.

She reaches out to try and pat me, but she misses. "Thank you, baby."

I gasp as I sit up in bed and reevaluate where I am—alone in my hotel room.

Beads of sweat cover every inch of me. It's been a long time since I've had that dream. I was hoping my fucked-up brain had somehow blocked my childhood out, but I will never be that lucky.

It's probably because of all of Anna's poking around about my past. I know she believes she's helping, but some people should learn to let sleeping dogs lie. Talking about shit only makes it worse. Bringing up the past brings back the nightmares of shit I don't want to remember.

Nervous energy flows through me, and there's only one way I know how to get rid of it.

Working out.

After a couple quick stretches I get down on the floor and begin hammering out push-ups. Focusing on the burn in my muscles takes my mind off the pain of my emotions. This is one of the reasons I got so big to begin with. Nothing else compares to the way I feel when I work out.

Working out, and fucking women: the two things that completely take my mind off everything. And they're my two greatest addictions.

Well, if I'm being honest, I suppose that was true once, but not now. Being with Anna takes my mind off my shitty past too. That is, until she tries to bring it up.

I know she means well, but there's no way she can fathom how fucked up things were for me. Her life with her domineering father is child's play next to what I dealt with. At least her parents care enough to be involved in her life.

"One hundred and twelve," I count out loud as I keep pumping in a steady rhythm up and down, and my eyes fixate on the corner of the nightstand as I get lost in the burn.

I was doing just fine with avoiding my past, until lately. Walking away from Anna is the best thing to do. She's fucking with my head, making me want things I know I can't have.

I'm not normal. No mind as fucked up as mine could ever have a shot at a normal relationship. It's not fair to her to drag her into my world.

Maybe if I just fuck her--get it over with— we'd both be able to move on. I'm just afraid if I ever get a taste of that sweetness that I'll be a fucking goner.

I know me. Once I become addicted I won't be able to let go, and I'll drag her down with me. She doesn't deserve that. She deserves more.

She deserves so much better than me.

The goodness that pours out of her lights my world up like she's a goddamn angel. She shouldn't want anything to do with a demon like me because I'll taint her. What she saw tonight will most definitely cause her to hate me. I should be glad that she no longer wants anything to do with me.

But, I can't let her go.

Not yet.

Not that easily.

I'm too selfish to do the right thing and leave her alone. The expression on her face when she told me goodbye nearly killed me, and every time I think about it, there's a sharp pain in my chest.

I'd kick my own ass if I could. Better yet, I'd go back in time and refuse Deena the night she showed up begging to fuck me the first night we got here. That bitch is evil, and I've had enough of her attempting to sink her hooks into me.

Spending this week with Anna wasn't one of my brightest ideas, but I couldn't help myself. I couldn't stay away from her. She's not like any other woman I've ever met. The fact that she calls me out on my shit confirms her realness, and that's what I crave more than anything in this world.

I've got to see her one more time.

Chapter
ELEVEN

The tears have finally stopped, but my mind hasn't. I lie in my bed, replaying what went down at the hotel. I don't understand how I didn't see that coming? I've only known him a week, and I've already grown attached to him, but that doesn't mean I know everything about him. I mean, he was still sleeping with his old assistant and hadn't said a word to me about it. He led me to believe I might be special to him, but apparently I'm not.

I sigh again and shift restlessly, unable to find a comfortable spot.

"Anna, you going to tell me what happened, or do you prefer to keep us both awake all night with your longing sighs?" Quinn mumbles from her bed. "It's bad enough you've been a puddle of tears since I got home. What's up?"

I take a deep breath and sigh again. I don't want to annoy her any more than I already have. Maybe if I talk about it, I can calm down enough to sleep. "It's Xavier..."

"That much I figured. Want to talk about it?" The concern in her voice is almost enough to make me want to cry again.

"He's been sleeping with his assistant." I choke back a tear. "I know we aren't a couple—that we're just friends—but it hurt. I didn't know he was...seeing someone."

She turns on the lamp on her nightstand and leans up on her side to face me. "He *what?!* Are you kidding me right now? I'm going to kill him."

"He really didn't do anything wrong. I knew we are just friends. It's my fault for allowing myself to grow attached." I shake my head, and the tears burn my skin as they roll down my temples.

"Now you're just talking crazy." Quinn flings her feet over the side of her twin bed and focuses her gaze on me as I lie on the twin air mattress on her floor. "X is chasing you, Anna. Any idiot can see that. Seems to me that he's a selfish man who was having his cake and eating it too—that is until you found out. Don't you for one second put any blame on yourself for feeling something for him. X made it damn near impossible for you not to. The man is relentless in his pursuit."

She's right. From the moment I met him on the plane, he's been impossible for me to shake. Xavier has been a constant in my life since I got here. Maybe all the emotion I'm feeling for him is just an excuse my brain is making to cover up all the feelings I've been avoiding since I left home—ones I'm not ready to deal with just yet.

I wipe my eyes. "It all makes sense now, you know."

She tilts her head. "What does?"

"He kept telling me that he's a bad person and that I shouldn't trust him. I should've listened, huh?" The burn in my chest from my broken heart still lingers. "I guess I need to stop being so trusting and believing everyone is good."

Quinn shakes her head. "No, Anna. That's what makes you so special. You're one of the sweetest people I know. You're practically a saint compared to the rest of us. Don't allow one asshole to ruin that for you. One of these days, you'll find a guy who will appreciate you."

What if I messed up my one shot with a good guy already? The way I left Portland behind because I couldn't picture marrying a man who I didn't truly love flits through me. Jorge is sweet. Sure, he doesn't have that all-consuming effect on me like Xavier does, but at least he was safe, and he never made me feel like this. Ever.

"Maybe I already found him and let him go. Jorge wouldn't have treated me like this. Maybe coming out here was a mistake."

Quinn comes over and sits next to me—the air mattress sinking a little beneath her weight. She brushes my hair away from my face, and a sad smile plays on her lips.

"I know you don't mean that. Don't let being hurt by a man make you doubt your decision to be here. You came here to experience an unsheltered life, and while I don't promise life here won't come with its bumps and unexpected turns, I do promise it'll be an amazing and freeing ride. Promise me you won't let what X did make you throw away that chance to find yourself. Don't go running back to Jorge just because it's the 'safe' thing to do."

There's no mistaking the look of compassion in her eyes. If I turn tail and run back home, I would not only be letting myself down, but Quinn as well. And I don't want to do that. Besides, she's right. Deep down, I know she is. I need to take this as a lesson and learn from it while I stick it out here.

"I promise."

"Good." Quinn hugs me against her. "Our fun together is just getting started and I would hate it if you left now."

I smile at her. "We do need to hang out more. I'm sorry I've been so occupied lately. Xavier is a pretty consuming man."

"We're going to change that." Quinn pushes herself off the mattress and snuggles back down in her own bed. "Tomorrow night you and I are going out. Now that Mr. X is out of the picture, we'll start having girl's nights out."

In the silence of the room, my thoughts drift back to Xavier, and the events of the evening. The oddity of it all still puzzles me. Why doesn't he stay at his own house? Why a hotel? None of it makes any sense to me. I wish I could just stop thinking about him, but I can't. It would make forgetting him a whole lot easier.

"Quinn, can ask your opinion about something?" I ask.

"Shoot," she answers simply.

I go right for the one question that keeps lingering on my mind. "Do you think Xavier is married or something?"

She quiet for a moment as though she's contemplating her reply. "He better not be or, seriously, I will shank him. What makes you think he is?"

I shrug. "Tonight he said he has a house here in Detroit, but that he never stays there—that he actually *pays* people to take care of it while he stays at a hotel. Don't you think that's strange? Why wouldn't someone stay in their own home if they could?"

She nods and her eyes drift up to the ceiling like she's searching for answers. "Yes, but I don't think he's hiding a family or anything. There would be some trace of it on the Internet if he was."

"True. I just can't make any sense of it."

"Don't waste your time thinking about him anymore, Anna." She leans over and flips off the light. "He doesn't deserve it."

She's right—I know that—but how can I tune Xavier out when he's weaseled his way into my heart? Getting over him and his betrayal will take time. I can't stop thinking about him just because he's a big jerk.

I roll over and sigh, hoping a good night's sleep will help erase some of the good memories I have of Xavier, so I can start completely hating him and move on with my new life.

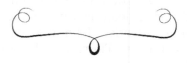

Being slammed at Larry's is a welcomed distraction. There's not much time to wallow in the fact that I'll never see Xavier again or mope about ending things on such a horrible note. As much as I want to hate him, I can't. It's not in me. Besides, he wasn't mine, so it wasn't like I had some sort of claim on him. I allowed things to get out of hand in my own head, believing there was more going on between us than the friendship we'd officially established.

"Something wrong, Anna?" Tyler asks as he slides table four's order over to me through the window.

I shake my head, breaking myself out of my own thoughts. "No, I'm great. Just a little tired, that's all."

He nods and a blond curl falls across his forehead. "Does your knee hurt?"

"My knee?" I glance down and remember falling with the tray yesterday. That feels like a lifetime ago. All my personal drama has steered my mind away from my little mishap at work yesterday. "Oh, no, it's fine. That's very sweet of you to ask."

Tyler smiles shyly. "Just wanted to make sure you're okay."

"I honestly don't see why you men fawn all over her. It was just a little fall," Alice says while sliding in next to me to enter her order into the computer. "She only got a damn scratch."

"Don't be a jealous bitch, Alice," Quinn warns, flanking my side. "I know it was you that tripped her yesterday. There's nothing else there that she could've tripped on."

Alice narrows her green eyes and shoves her red hair over her shoulder. "Prove it."

Quinn glares at her. "One of these days you're going to get fired, and I hope I'm there to laugh my ass off when you do."

Alice crosses her arms over her chest. "We'll see which one of us gets fired first."

I don't miss the ice in her voice as I detect her threat. I know Alice holds a lot of power around here, but would Andy seriously fire Quinn because Alice told him to? I hoped not, but like Quinn said, men seem to do almost anything for her.

"Ladies? Is there a problem?" Andy asks as appears next to Tyler in the kitchen.

Alice smiles sweetly at Andy, instantly making my stomach turn at just how fake she really is, while Quinn shakes her head. "No problem, Andy. Just a little girl talk. You know how we get."

Andy rolls his eyes and pops a couple antacids in his mouth. "Talk on your own time, then. Get back to work."

Quinn begins to turn away, but the moment Andy is out of earshot Alice growls, "This isn't over, bitch."

Quinn, never the one to back down from speaking her mind turns in her direction with a heated expression. "Bring it. Any. Time. I'm not scared of you."

With a huff, Alice spins away from us and returns to her position behind the bar, flirting with every male customer in sight.

"Are you the only person that ever stands up to her around here?" I ask Quinn, still feeling intimidated.

She shrugs. "I've been here longer. From day one I didn't tolerate her shit, and she's been threatening to have me fired since then."

"I thought you said Alice always gets her way?"

"Her bully tactics work on a lot of people, but I always stand up to her. I don't allow her to walk all over me. Threats from her mean very little to me anymore because as you can see...I'm still here." She winks at me before scurrying off to check on her tables.

I stop dead in my tracks on the way back to my section the moment I spot Xavier sitting at a table in my section. For a moment I debate running to hide in the kitchen and begging Quinn to take over my tables, but I know on a busy night like tonight she'd hunt me down if I tried to double her work.

Xavier is just as sexy as always. His hair, styled into a wild, sexy mess, frames his ruggedly handsome face while his tight black t-shirt and jeans hug his chiseled muscles, reminding me of how solid they felt beneath my fingers last night. He absently taps his thumbs on the tabletop as he waits for me.

I swallow hard and force my legs forward toward his table. I might as well face him and get it over with. He's here for a reason, so I need to find out why.

The moment our eyes meet, Xavier stiffens a bit in his seat. I can tell he's nervous and he's probably here to apologize, which is a start, but it doesn't change the fact that I've learned my lesson about him. We are friends, nothing more. Well, if we can salvage what's left of our friendship, that is.

I pull the order pad from the back pocket of my shorts as I approach him, planning to keep it strictly business. "Hey, what can I get you?"

Xavier frowns. "Can we talk?"

I sigh heavily and shake my head. "We're slammed tonight, and I just took my last break."

"Come on, Anna. Don't be like that. Talk to me, please?"

I don't get it. After last night, I thought I'd never see him again. He's leaving tonight to go back on the road, so rehashing the events from yesterday isn't something I thought I'd have to go through today. I'm not ready to have this conversation with him. It's hard to even look at him knowing that he's been with someone else. It hurts too much and I don't want to keep getting my heart broken. I have to push him away.

"I think we said enough last night, don't you?" I turn to walk away from him.

"Hey." He reaches out and grabs my wrist, halting me in place. "Stay. Talk. Hear me out."

I can't allow more lies to fill my head. There needs to be space between us. "No. As a matter of fact, I would appreciate you moving out of my section. I refuse to deal with this at work."

"Fine."

Xavier shoves himself out of the booth but doesn't head for the door like I expect. Instead he stalks off toward the bar. Alice dries her hands on a dishtowel and smirks at me as he sits down at the bar.

Damn him.

Alice leans across the bar to take Xavier's drink order. He makes no attempt to hide the fact that he's staring at her breasts as she gives him an eyeful with her v-neck, fitted t-shirt. A flirty smile plays along his lips as Alice reaches into the cooler and hands him a beer.

"Are you going to kill him, or should I?" I don't even realize I'm clenching my jaw and staring intently at the situation unfolding in front of me until Quinn snaps me out of my daze.

Anger continues to bubble through me as I witness Xavier blatantly flirt with Alice in front of me. "Ugh. He infuriates me."

Quinn puts her arms around my shoulders. "It's for the best, Anna. He's playing games and you don't need that. No more crying over him. Ignore him, and he'll eventually get the hint and leave."

I close my eyes and a couple of tears stream down my face. I bat them away and pray for the power to be strong in his presence. I just have to get through this shift and then I'll never have to see him again.

"You're right."

"That's my girl. Pretend he's one of Alice's regulars and steer clear. He'll get bored and be gone before you know it. Come on, we have orders waiting on us."

I follow Quinn to the pick-up window and without even turning around, I know Xavier is watching me. The weight of his stare sends a tingle down my spine and I question if I'll be able to really ignore him all night. The pull to him is still pretty damn strong.

Brock sets a couple more plates on the ledge and winks at Quinn. "Ladies."

A blush fills Quinn's cheeks, and it's so adorable, I can't help but smile.

I arrange the plates on my tray and turn around just in time to see Alice giggle at something Xavier said while resting her fingers on his forearm. The overwhelming desire to snatch her hand off him hits me, but I beat it away, remembering quickly that he's not mine. He made that very clear.

Xavier takes a long pull from his beer, and his eyes flit over to mine, halting me for a beat before I straighten by back and march past him.

Alice doesn't miss Xavier's attention on me either. Her icy glare would freeze me in place if I wasn't already so heated.

For the next hour or so things continue the same way—Xavier sitting at the bar drinking, while Alice does her best to entice him. All evening his eyes never leave me. Every time I glance in his direction, he's openly watching me.

On my way to enter a food order, Xavier reaches out and snags my wrist as I walk by. "You ready to stop ignoring me yet?"

I tilt my head to the side. "Why? Don't have enough company already?"

Out of the corner of my eye I see Alice cross her arms over her chest. She makes no attempt to pretend like she's not watching our little exchange intensely, which irks me. What's going on between me and Xavier is none of her business.

He doesn't take his eyes away from mine. "You mean the bitchy bartender? That's nothing. I'm sitting here killing time—waiting for you to get over yourself and talk to me."

Get over myself? Is he serious right now? I did nothing to him. He needs to remember the reason I'm not speaking to him.

"Just like Deena was nothing?" I fire back.

"Exactly," he says, his voice agitated. "Don't you get it? Other women don't mean a thing to me. You matter."

I furrow my brow, confused by how he can make such a statement about me when it became quite clear last night that we barely know each other.

"Why?"

He sighs. "You're sincere."

I shake my head. "You can't possibly know that about me. Not after a week."

"Sometimes time is irrelevant in understanding the beauty of another person's soul." He pulls closer until my hip touches his outstretched knee. "Can you get off early? I would really like to spend some time with you before I have to leave. I don't want us parting on bad terms. Your friendship means a lot to me. I don't want to ruin it."

Although I still don't forgive him for lying to me about Deena, it would be nice to salvage our friendship. He was my first real friend in Detroit, after all. "I wish I could, but we're still open for another two hours."

Xavier's lips push down into a frown, and he releases my wrist. "I understand."

He closes his eyes and grimaces just for a moment like he's in pain. The expression on his face almost makes me change my mind. I don't want to hurt him, but I have to protect myself. We need a clean break.

He stands and fishes his wallet out of his back pocket before laying down a hundred dollar bill on the bar. He wraps his arms around me without permission and kisses the top of my head. "Goodbye, beautiful. I'll miss you."

I can't bring myself to say the words. Telling him goodbye makes him leaving real...*final*. I'll never see him again, but even as hurt as I was about him sleeping with Deena, I'm just not ready to fully shut him out.

My heart squeezes as I stare after Xavier. The urge to stop him surges through me, but I know allowing him to walk away without a fight is what's best for both of us. I don't think I have it in me to ever trust him again, and no relationship can ever work without trust.

Chapter
TWELVE

Anna

The last two hours of work drag on. I know it's stupid, and we've said our goodbyes, but I still miss Xavier. Deep down under all those playboy ways, I know there's a good guy. I saw him peeking through during the little bit of time I spent with him and that makes it suck even more that he's leaving because maybe, given time, we could have fixed what is broken between us.

Quinn stacks her tray on top of mine. "I'm beat. Let's count out our drawers and be done. I want to go home and sleep."

Brock leans against the counter and pulls Quinn into his arms. "Sleep? I thought we had plans."

The intimate way he yanks her hips against his causes her to giggle. "I suppose we can go out for a little while." She reaches in her apron pocket and hands me her car keys. "You'll be all right driving home?"

"Yeah. I'll be fine." I take the keys and stuff them into my pocket before removing my apron and tossing it on the counter next to them. "Watch this while I go to the bathroom, will you?"

Quinn giggles as Brock nuzzles her neck and then whispers in her ear.

"Sure," she says as I head to take a short break before cashing out for the night.

Once I've used the bathroom, I move to the sink to wash my hands. I stare in the mirror at my green eyes, and even I can note the sadness that lies within them. It's going to take me a while to get over Xavier. Even in a week, he's left a lasting impression on me.

I readjust my dark ponytail and head back out to count my money from the shift with Andy so I can get out of here and be depressed at Aunt Dee's.

Andy's sitting at the bar with his logbook, ready to do final counts with the wait staff. I grab my apron off the counter and take a seat next to him.

I glance around as I toss my apron on the bar. Only Alice and I are left in the place. "Did Quinn count out already?"

Andy nods as he makes a note on the paper in front of him. "Yeah, she was first. She was anxious to get out of here tonight."

I roll my eyes and wonder if she and Brock made it out of the parking lot before they attacked one another.

"All right." Andy turns his attention to me and reaches for the apron. "You made three hundred seventy-two dollars and twenty-three cents. Cash total we need to have turned in is one hundred and fifty-two dollars and thirty six cents." He reaches in the pocket and searches around with his hand. After a few seconds he furrows his brow and scratches his balding scalp. "Do you have it somewhere else? These pockets are empty."

My heart leaps into my throat. "What?!"

I shoot off the stool and begin digging around in the pockets. "It was right here before I went to the restroom. I left it with Quinn."

Andy's lips twist, and he blows a rush of air through his nose. "Looks like we have a problem. One of two things happened. One: Quinn took the money when she left, which could be why she wanted out of here so quickly. Or two: you have it."

My mouth drops open, shocked. No one has ever accused me of stealing before. "Andy, I wouldn't steal from you."

He rubs his chin as he takes in my expression. "I'm leaning with option one then. I don't feel like you're lying to me. I usually can tell when someone's guilty." He shakes his head. "I hate to fire Quinn. She's been a good employee for the last year."

My eyes widen. "Fire Quinn? You can't. She loves this job."

"Love it or not"—Andy shrugs—"Larry's doesn't tolerate theft of any kind. If we suspect it, you're done. That's why we have you all sign that accountability contract when you start. It's our insurance that you all understand our zero tolerance policy."

Oh no! I know she wouldn't take the money. I can't allow her to lose her job. "Andy, please don't. Fire me instead."

Alice leans against the bar with a smirk on her face. "I told you not to trust them, Andy. They're not sweet like they claim to be—especially this one."

"Alice," he scolds. "That's enough."

She shrugs. "Just saying, I think she's your thief. You should fire her now before she robs you blind."

I narrow my eyes at her. "What's your problem with me? I've never done a thing to you."

She rolls her green eyes. "I just don't like you."

"It's because of Xavier, isn't it? You're jealous!" My voice raises an octave as the adrenaline flows through my veins.

I can't remember ever feeling this angry with someone.

Alice laughs and flips her hair over her shoulder. "Jealous? Honey, please, don't flatter yourself. If I wanted your man, I'd have him."

I clench my fists tighter. I've never been one for violence, but she's got me seeing speckles of red. I want to scream at her and call her a liar—tell her that he'd never touch her—but after last night I'm not so sure. I thought things between him and Deena were over the first night we met. I didn't even know she was still around, or worse still, competing for Xavier's attention. So how do I know he wouldn't be into a sex-only relationship with Alice too?

When I don't immediately retaliate, Alice smirks. "Fire her, Andy."

"Alice, I can't just get rid of her because you don't like her," he says and his shoulders sag.

She folds her arms. "Do it. She stole the money, and I don't want her around anymore."

I see the struggle in Andy's eyes, but I know he'll side with her eventually, so I'll make this easy for everyone. "I quit. Blame me for the money if you like, but I didn't take it, and Quinn wouldn't either. If you want to blame someone"—I point to Alice—"blame her. She's probably the one who took it just to get back at me for being jealous."

"That's absurd," she argues. "Don't listen to her, Andy."

He drags his eyes up to my face. "I think you'd better go, Anna."

Tears begin to burn my eyes. It's so hard to let this job go. The two things I've found comfort in since I got to Detroit are both no longer apart of my life. It hurts, but I'll do anything to keep from causing Quinn any problems.

I square my shoulders. "Not until you tell me that Quinn keeps her job, no questions asked."

She's done so much for me already. Ensuring her job is the least I can do.

Andy nods. "You got it."

"Thank you," I whisper, trying to keep it together until I get outside.

I turn my back and head toward the door when I hear Andy say, "Good luck, Anna."

That's when the first tear falls. I throw my hand up in a lame wave as I keep walking. I don't want them to see me break down. I don't want Alice to know just how weak I really am.

The moment the cool night air hits me, I dash toward Quinn's Honda. I open the door and flop down in driver's seat, allowing all the emotions I've kept bottled up to come crashing out as I sob hard.

What am I going to do?

Quinn was my ride to and from work. I can't expect her to be my chauffer when I find a new job. I grip the steering wheel and rest my head on my hands and cry harder as the feeling of overwhelming failure engulfs me.

I don't want to give up. Not after only one week. If I could find another job quickly, then I won't feel so bad when I explain what happened to Quinn and Aunt Dee. It will take some of the burden off.

I crank the engine alive and glance down at the clock. It's only nine thirty. Surely there are bars and restaurants still open so I can go and check out a couple of job prospects.

I drive around the city, looking for any restaurant I see with an open sign. After going into two, and being asked to come back tomorrow, my optimistic balloon deflates a little.

Looking for a job this late is a dumb idea.

I check the clock again and my stomach rumbles. With everything going on, I forgot to eat lunch and dinner today. I'm completely famished.

I begin keeping my eyes peeled for a drive-through when a familiar diner comes into view and I pull into the parking lot.

It feels strange coming here without Xavier, but I'm comfortable enough here to go in and eat alone. I know Nettie will keep me company.

Bells on the door chime the moment I step inside and Nettie glances up at my from behind the counter. "Lord, child. Come on in here and sit down."

She pats the counter in front of her. "You and I need to talk woman to woman."

"Oh...okay." Feeling completely uneasy, I take the seat in front of her, and she hands me a menu.

I study the menu and try to pretend Nettie isn't watching me like a hawk. My face is probably still a puffy mess where I've just been bawling in the car. It was a mistake coming here looking like this. Hopefully Nettie won't pry since Xavier isn't with me.

"I'll have the pancakes again and a water."

"You got it." She takes the menu from me and stares for a long second. "He fool around on you?"

I raise my eyebrows.

As much as I want to talk with someone who understands Xavier, I refuse to tell someone who's almost like his mother what happened yesterday. I'm sure my appearance screams that I'm hurting. I don't need to make it worse.

"No. I mean, we aren't together. We're just friends. He can *be* with whomever he wants."

Nettie leans against the counter and her mouth quirks. "The two of you still pretending you are just friends?"

"We *are* just friends," I say adamantly.

"Sure you are." She winks at me. "Like Carl and me. The sooner you learn to set your foot down with that boy, the better off you'll be."

"Xavier doesn't want a relationship with me."

She cocks her head and gives me the are-you-kidding-me-face. "Honey, you're the first girl I've ever seen him stick with for longer than a night. He cares for you, and I know that may be hard to believe, but I know my boy. Xavier was the most carefree I've ever seen him the nights he brought you in here. Give him a chance, he might surprise you."

I shake my head. "I don't know Nettie. He was...seeing someone else the entire week. How can I trust him after that?"

"That boy..." She shakes her head and clicks her tongue. "I was hoping he was finally settling down. He's a good man, Anna. Just had a rough life, is all. Poor kid was out on the streets at fifteen."

"*Fifteen*?" I repeat in disbelief. "Was his family that bad? He refuses to speak about them. The only thing he ever told me was his mother died when he was eight."

"Tragic, isn't it? When he came in here that first time, hungry, I could see in his eyes the boy was just desperate. Carl and I took him in, gave him a job and got him off the streets."

"So, when you say the streets—you mean homeless?"

Nettie frowns. "Yes and no. Xavier, like most runaways around here, found refuge with a local gang, but he was still very much on his own and didn't trust a soul. It took a long time for him to really believe Carl and I wanted to help him."

"Where was his father in all this? Didn't he care?" I question. I'm flabbergasted as to where all the support he should've had was. It breaks my heart.

"No clue. I know he lived with his grandmother until he headed out on his own."

I pull my lips into a tight line. "Was she so bad?"

The expression on Nettie's face tells me that she wants to tell me more, but she's reluctant.

"I've talked about his business enough. I best shut up. I'll grab Carl from the back and have him cook your pancakes." She gives me a sad smile as she heads to a wooden, swinging door and out of sight.

I rub my chin as I process everything I've just learned about Xavier Cold. It doesn't change that he fooled around with Deena behind my back, but I believe Nettie when she says he cares for me. It truly felt like he did when we were together. It doesn't matter if I could ever forgive him for that or not, the fact remains that he's gone, and any chance we had at ever becoming more than friends is over.

The diner door chimes behind me and before I even see him, I feel him.

I slowly turn and my jaw drops. Xavier stands there in a pair of dark wash jeans and a blue t-shirt staring straight at me. He shoves his dark hair away from his face, but a single strand falls across his forehead, and his blue eyes widen.

He clearly didn't expect to see me, just like I'm still in shock that he's standing here before me.

He licks his bottom lip and then grazes his teeth across it. "Anna? What are you doing here?"

I swallow hard. "I, um...I was hungry."

He takes a couple of hesitant steps toward me, and my heart flutters in my chest as that familiar pull hits me full force.

Once he's close enough, he reaches out and cups my cheek in his hand. "You didn't come here for me?"

I melt into his touch and close my eyes. The spicy scent of his cologne and soap lingers on his skin. I inhale deeply and then open my eyes to stare into the deep-blue pools of his irises.

There's no denying I feel something for him, I'm just not sure what. All I know right now is that I'm addicted to his touch.

"I thought you were already gone, so I didn't expect to see you here, but I'm glad you are."

"My flight was cancelled, and I realized I hadn't said goodbye to Nettie and Carl, so I came to see them before I leave in the morning."

He studies my face intently as we remain alone in the diner. "Why have you been crying? Remember what I said? I don't like seeing this beautiful face frown."

I blink slowly. "I was fired tonight."

"Why?" he immediately asks.

I sigh and Xavier takes a seat next to me and listens intently as I explain what happened at Larry's.

"So you stopped here while you were job hunting?" he asks as he puts all the pieces together. "Don't you find that an odd coincidence?"

"What do you mean?"

He shrugs. "You need a job, and I still need that personal assistant."

The mention of Deena's old job causes what happened to flash through my mind and it brings back the hurt I feel.

"You sure you don't want your old assistant back? The two of you seemed pretty *cozy* the last time I saw you together. I'm sure she'd be happy to have her job back."

He flinches and licks the corner of his mouth. "I deserve that. I hurt you, and for that I'm sorry. I wish I could take it back. She came over, stripped in front of me and I gave into a moment of weakness. You have to understand, Anna, I'm not used to all this." He motions between the two of us. "I'm going to fuck up from time to time. Being friends with me won't be easy, but I want you to give me another shot. Come work for me. Give me time to make it up to you."

The word *friends* slice through me. Our connection feels like so much more than just a friendship, but I know at this point neither of us are ready to move our relationship beyond that. Being his employee will create that boundary we need. Not to mention that I still desperately need a job.

"Xavier..."

"Sixty thousand dollars."

My eyes widen. "What?"

"I don't want you to say no. I will pay you sixty thousand dollars."

That's a lot of money to a fresh-from-college girl like me, but taking this job isn't about the compensation it will bring. It's about spending time with Xavier.

I shake my head. "You don't have to pay me more to make me take the job."

Xavier reaches over and takes my hand. "I want you to know how badly I want you."

The way he says it makes me believe he means as more than just as an employee. Maybe that's wishful thinking on my part, but the thought of him wanting me—in any way—makes my toes curl.

If I want to see what could possibly happen between Xavier and me, taking this job is the only way to get time with him.

"I'll do it," I say firmly.

He raises his eyebrows. "Really? You're not going to fight me on this?"

I shrug, attempting to play it off coolly. "I need a job."

"Is that the only reason?" His gaze remains glued to me, gauging my reaction.

I might as well be honest...to a degree. "No. It's not the only reason, but it's the best one I can give you for now."

He rubs the stubble along his jawline as he considers what I've said before a hint of a smile plays along his lips. "That's good enough for me."

Xavier pivots his butt on the barstool and places his feet at the counter, resting his elbows on the counter before calling out, "The service around here sucks!" loud enough for Nettie to hear clear in the back.

He glances over at me and winks before a cocky grin spreads across his face. I laugh and just like that, we fall back into our easy relationship. I forgot how easy it was to just "be" with him, like it was before all the crazy drama came between us.

Friendship with Xavier won't be easy, but I'll miss him too much not to try.

I throw the last of my things back into my suitcase and zip it up, glad that I packed light when I moved here.

Quinn stands beside me and sighs as she wraps her arm around my shoulders. "Are you sure you know what you're doing? I don't want to see you get hurt again, Anna."

I smile at her, touched that she cares about me so much. "I'll be fine, Quinn. Xavier and I are friends. We settled everything the other night."

She nods. "Yeah, yeah. I know that's what you said, but you forget that I saw how upset you were when he broke your heart."

"He didn't break my heart. We'd have to be dating for him to do that."

Quinn raises a perfect eyebrow. "That's what you keep saying, but he wants you and you want him. Both of you are playing with fire, and I don't want you to be the one to get burned."

I know she's right, but it's worth the risk. Xavier is like a drug I can't get enough of. The thought of never seeing him again sends panic through me and I refuse to pass up the opportunity to spend more time with him.

I pull the bag off the bed and set it on the floor.

Quinn pulls me into her and hugs me tight. "Call me every day, okay?"

A faint knock on Quinn's bedroom door catches my attention. Aunt Dee stands there, taking in our goodbye with her glistening eyes. Her dark hair is pulled into a loose bun, and she's wearing some ridiculous orange shirt with neon green yoga pants. I'll never get used to her odd taste in clothing.

"Are you all packed?" she asks as she steps into the room. "A black town car just pulled up out front, and I'm thinking it's for you?"

I pop the handle up on the large roller bag. "Yep. I've got everything."

I hold my breath as she embraces me to try and keep from crying. "You can come back here any time, you know that, right?"

I nod and close my eyes, inhaling the sweet scent of her perfume. Sadness washes through me because it's one thing to leave my parents' home to move in with family, but it's entirely different leaving everyone you know to run off with a man you've only known for a week.

For the first time in my life, I'll be one hundred percent on my own.

I pray I'm ready.

Aunt Dee pulls back and pushes my hair behind my shoulders. "Take care of yourself, yeah?"

"I will," I manage to squeak out just as there's a knock at the front door.

She pulls her lips into a tight line. "I'm sure that's for you."

Quinn steps over and wraps her arm around her mom as I head toward the front door. I take a deep breath and my heart skips a beat when it opens and my eyes land on Xavier there dressed in jeans and a t-shirt. How can one man make such simple dress attire appear so damn good? Sex appeal for him is effortless. It's not really fair to the rest of the men in the world.

His blue eyes brighten the moment he sees me. "Hey, beautiful. You ready?"

There's no mistaking his excitement, but I can't tell if it's because I'm coming along, or because he's excited to get back to the wrestling world he loves so much. Either way, it warms me to see him happy and not all dark and moody.

"Yeah, I pack pretty light. Everything I own is in these two bags." I roll the large suitcase out the door and readjust the backpack on my back.

He immediately takes the handle of the large bag and hooks his fingers under the strap of my backpack, slipping it off my shoulder. "That's good. We'll be traveling a lot. The less shit you carry around, the easier it is."

Xavier heads toward the car and the awaiting driver, who is standing by the open trunk. I trail behind him and the thought occurs to me that I never asked much about what kind of work schedule I'll be expected to keep.

"Will we be on the road a while? Do we not come back here often?"

He shakes his head as he hands my bags to the driver. "I don't ever come here if I can help it. The only reason I was here this week is because the company forced me to take time off."

"Why's that?"

He opens the door for me to get into the car. "Remember the guy from television? Assassin?"

The memory of the wrestler calling Xavier out on national TV hits me. How could I forget?

"Yes."

He curls his fingers around the top of the door. "Things between he and I were getting out of hand. Our matches in the ring were beginning to turn real, so they made me take a break. Told me to go home and reflect on everything I'll lose if I didn't settle my ass down and control my temper. Told me to take my mind off how much I dislike Assassin or else it could ruin my title shot."

I lean against the car and stare up at him. "Did coming here help clear your head?"

"You definitely occupy a lot of space in my brain right now. Not much else has been on my mind this week." He winks as me, and I immediately blush.

This is what confuses me so much—when he says things like that. People don't talk to their friends like that.

Do they?

Xavier chuckles, knowing he's flustered me, and motions for me to get in.

The tinted windows in the car, coupled with the black leather interior, make it dark in here. The moment I'm in the middle of the seat, Xavier slides in next to me and for a brief second our bodies touch. The close proximity of his skin next to mine causes a shiver to rush down my spine. Even though I wish it wouldn't, my body reacts to any little contact with him. Hopefully the more I'm around him, the more my body will realize we are better off as friends and stop urging me to attack him every opportunity I can.

My eyes drift up front and I notice Jimmy, Xavier's manager, sitting in the passenger seat.

Xavier catches my line of sight and says, "Anna, you remember Jimmy, right?"

Jimmy turns around to acknowledge me, wearing a pair of white sunglasses that are straight from the eighties and compliment his perfectly styled mullet.

I smile at him. "Of course. How are you?"

He pulls his sunglasses off, revealing his warm brown eyes. "Welcome to the team. When we get to the hotel, we'll go over the schedule for the next couple of months."

"Sounds good. Are we going to be on the road a lot?"

Jimmy nods. "A lot of the talent go home for the weekend after Thursday's show, but X just goes straight to the next city."

"Do you always stay wherever he is?"

Jimmy shakes his head and holds up his left hand and points to his ring finger. "My wife would kill me if I did that."

I tilt my head. "But you stayed here with him this week?"

Jimmy smirks. "Had to make sure my boy here stayed out of trouble. The company has very strict policies, so they sent me along with him. I've got to make sure he doesn't do something that'll cost us both our jobs."

I giggle at the thought of the small man in front of me having to keep an eye on the very intimidating Xavier. "So you're a like a babysitter."

Xavier grunts next to me, and Jimmy laughs. "I wouldn't call it that exactly. He's a grown man and can do whatever he wants. I'm strictly here for guidance and support, well, for the most part I'm just here to make sure he's being taken care of and not getting stiffed in the fine print of contracts."

I nod. "Understood. So what exactly is *my* job?"

Jimmy's lips pull into a tight line. "That's between you and X. I typically stay out of the relationships he has with other employees."

When Jimmy adds the "s" on the word employee it makes me wonder just how many personal assistants have come before me. I know what kind of relationship he had with Deena so it's very possible that he's had that same type of relationship with all of them.

Xavier says I'm different—that he doesn't want that type of arrangement with me—and in a small part of me, that hurts my feelings. It makes me jealous that these other women have had him, and I haven't. He believes I'm a good girl—too delicate to hurt.

That's the story of my life.

He's a player, and I know I'll be hurt by him again eventually, but it doesn't stop me from being attracted to him or wanting to experience unharnessed passion.

This relationship between us makes me question every moral I've ever been taught, and I can't help but think that one of these days I'm going to chuck them all out the window and just enjoy the "Phenomenal" ride.

Chapter
THIRTEEN

After a quick flight to Atlanta, we jump into an awaiting SUV that whisks us off to the hotel. Xavier and I made small talk on the plane, but there's no denying there's still some unresolved tension between us.

Things aren't as carefree as they once were. In large part that's due to me discovering the "Deena situation." It built a wall between us and made me trust him less. I've got my eyes and ears open now that my perfect bubble of what I thought Xavier is like popped.

Xavier readjusts in the seat. "Are you hungry?"

He's clearly searching for excuses to talk with me. "Yes."

"After we check in, we can find a restaurant."

I nod. "Sounds good."

The vehicle pulls up under the awning of the hotel, and Xavier opens the door, immediately turning around to offer me a hand. There's an undeniable zing that shocks my skin the moment we touch.

I wish he wasn't so damn good looking. It makes staying mad at him ridiculously difficult.

He releases me the moment I'm on the ground and heads to the rear of the vehicle to retrieve our bags.

Jimmy catches up with me and hands me a slip of paper. "Here's all my contact information. Save it all into your phone, in case you need me."

I take it and stuff it into my back pocket. "Thanks."

Jimmy grins and waggles his eyebrows above his sunglasses. "Good luck."

I frown, unsure of what I need luck for. Xavier's my friend. How hard can he possibly be to work for?

The trunk slams, and I jump a bit. I reach for my bags but he shakes his head and nods toward the door. "Let's go check in."

The automatic doors open and allow us access inside. The hotel is pretty standard. It's a basic, upscale chain with marble floors and a grand foyer with a pianist playing a light tune at the bar while the other guests mill about leisurely. I guess I'm a little surprised this is the hotel the super stars of wrestling stay in. Famous people are known for glamour and luxuries.

Xavier runs his fingers through his hair, shoving it away from his face as he steps up to the front desk. The petite, blond concierge's smile widens as she stares up at his face and sticks her chest out a little more.

"Hello, Mr. Cold. We've been expecting you." She slides his room card across the front desk in a hotel card. "Your room has been taken care of. If you need *anything* at all, please call me."

The blatant flirtation in her tone is unmistakable. I roll my eyes. Is this what he always has to deal with—women throwing themselves at him without any hesitation at all? No wonder he thought my behavior on the plane, when we first met, was refreshing.

Xavier takes the card and opens it. His eyebrows bunch together as he studies it. "There's only one room listed here. My manager was supposed to arrange for two."

The blond clears her throat. "I'm sorry about that, sir. Let me check our availability for another room."

After a few quick taps on her keyboard, she twists her lips. "I'm afraid we are completely booked. Whenever large events are in town, we fill up rather fast."

Xavier sighs as he glances down at me. "We're going to have to share a room. Deena typically roomed with a female wrestler she's friends with, so we didn't book an extra room for you ahead of time."

I gnaw on the inside of my lower lip. The thought of sharing a hotel room with Xavier creates butterflies in my stomach. Being in such close proximity together all night is really going to test our control, but what choice do we have?

"It's fine. We're friends, right. One night won't hurt," I say, attempting to make it feel less awkward.

"It might be more than one night."

I tilt my head. "Why's that?"

He taps the card on the desk. "We stay in hotels all the time. Our rooms are booked months in advance. There's a good chance we're going to run into this problem in each city we visit."

One night I can handle, maybe even two...but weeks? My resolve won't last that long. I've never been attracted to a man like I am Xavier. The way he walks, talks, and even smiles is a turn on.

How can I resist all that wrapped up in one sexy, tattooed package?

There has to be another way.

"What about the roommate Deena stayed with? Do you think she'll allow me to bunk with her?"

Xavier shakes his head. "Star isn't exactly a *friendly* person. She won't allow just anyone to stay in her room. Besides, she and Deena have become tight. It wouldn't be a good situation to put you in."

Sharing a room with a woman who hates me because I'm with the man her friend wants probably wouldn't be best. Especially if she's a female wrestler.

I may end up strangled in my sleep.

"Understood. Lead the way, roomie." I try to continue to play it off, but under the cool façade I'm sporting, I'm freaking out—a lot.

He chuckles and motions for me to go ahead. "Ladies first."

I roll my eyes and head toward the guest elevators, and once I press the up button, we stand there in silence.

Hotel rooms are generally pretty small, but I might end up sleeping on the floor anyway because even the *thought* of sleeping in bed with Xavier while he's shirtless next to me nearly makes my mouth water.

I wish he wasn't so sexy. My stupid body can't control its hormones around him.

I glance over at him and notice the little grin on his face.

Oh boy. I can only imagine what he's thinking. If it's anywhere near the thought that just flickered through my mind, we're in trouble.

The doors open and once again he motions for me to go first while he follows behind with our entire group of luggage.

Who says chivalry is dead?

"What floor?" I ask.

He glances down at the card to double check the room number. "Fifth."

It's a painfully slow ride, and I beat back the urge to shout out a silly line like "How about those Dodgers." Awkwardness is very uncomfortable for me—as I would imagine it would be for anyone. It's extra hard for me, because I've never been in the position where I've had to share a room with a man.

Before I go any further, I'm not saying I've never seen a man naked. I'm no virgin. Jorge and I did it once out of curiosity, but he quickly put a halt to ever doing it again, claiming it was a sin against God for us to have sex before we were married. He made me feel guilty for having...urges, like I was a horrible person.

But that was more than a year ago. He never touched me again after that. The most I could ever hope for was a kiss with tongue, which didn't do a thing to settle my hormones.

Not once has Xavier made me feel like I was dirty or wrong for being attracted to him. He read me and knew that I was a good girl—that I *am* a good girl. Which is why he's kept his distance. Apparently he has too much respect for me to use me.

I still don't understand his commitment issues. If he cares so much for me, why doesn't he want to attempt to have a real relationship with me? Am I not good enough? Not sexy enough?

I wrap my arms around my torso, suddenly super aware of how overly curvy my body is next to someone like Deena. My breasts aren't fake like hers either. Mine are small, but perky.

Xavier notices my shift in body language and touches the back of my arm. "You okay?"

"Fine," I answer instantly in a clipped tone.

"I told you, you don't have to be worried about sharing a room with me. I'll even sleep on the floor if it makes you more comfortable."

"Don't be silly. You need to rest up for the match."

The elevator stops, and the door opens on our floor. We both exit, and I follow Xavier to our room. After swiping the key card, he flips on the lights and motions for me to go first.

The massive king-size bed occupies most of the space, and while sleeping in the same bed with Xavier scares me, it won't be like we're shoulder to shoulder.

The mattress gives a little under the weight of my backpack as he sets it down. "You still want to go eat?"

I shove my hands in my back pockets. "Yeah."

"Let's go then. There should be a restaurant downstairs."

Xavier closes the door behind us, and I follow him down the hall. The second I come to a stop next to him in front of the elevators, he reaches down and curls his fingers around mine.

A tingle rushes up my arm from the point where our skin touches. I should pull away and set boundaries, letting him know right off the bat that this is a business relationship only, but I can't do it. I like it when he touches me. My body craves more.

We're playing with fire, and one of us is bound to get burned.

At the soft ding of the elevator, we step inside the awaiting car. Xavier tugs me inside with him, and we ride down to the lobby.

The buzz from the crowd of people assaults my ears as the doors open, and there's a shriek and a bunch of camera flashes in my face as Xavier pulls us through the throng of people.

The chants of his name echo throughout the lobby, but he keeps walking, tucking me close to his side. The crowd is excited to get a glimpse of him, but he doesn't stop. He's like a man on a mission, determined to get us to the restaurant in one piece.

A boy around the age of ten, wearing a shirt with Xavier's face on it, waves his hands wildly, and it reminds me of the two boys in front of me on the plane.

Xavier spots the kid too and glances back at me. "Do you mind?"

"Of course not."

He smiles and then kneels down in front of the child, taking the poster and sharpie from his small hands. I smile as Xavier signs the poster and says a few words of encouragement about staying in school and going to college, the child nodding enthusiastically while hanging on his every word.

After the boy's mother snaps a picture of the two of them, Xavier ruffles the kid's hair and tells him goodbye.

My heart instantly melts at his interaction with his miniature fan.

Xavier notices the sappy expression on my face and takes my hand. "Come on, beautiful."

I wave goodbye to the little boy as we pass by and cut down a hallway. Thankfully security halts the rabid fans from following us, informing them that the restaurant is reserved for a private party, and that was as far as they were allowed.

I sigh, relieved to be away from all that madness. "Is it always like that for you?"

He shakes his head. "No. We try to keep where we are staying secret, but sometimes it slips out and fans get a little overzealous."

"That was sweet, what you did back there."

He glances down at me. "I always take time out for the kids. It's crazy to me that, to some of them, I'm their hero."

I squeeze his fingers between mine. "No, it's not. You're a great role model. Look at how much you've had to overcome to get where you are."

He swallows hard. "I've done a lot of bad shit too, Anna. I don't think I'm exactly role model material."

"Let's agree to disagree. I'm not saying you're perfect, but professionally you've done amazing. You should be proud of that."

He smiles and squeezes my hand back. "Thank you."

We round the corner and my eyes widen. Sitting in the hotel restaurant are some of the largest men and women I've ever seen—all of them buff, tall, and tanned. Xavier doesn't stand out as much in this crowd, but he certainly doesn't go unnoticed because the moment we walk in, most of the eyes in the place zero in on us.

I try to pull my hand out of from his grasp—I'm not sure how to explain our relationship to his coworkers just yet—but he only tightens his grip, refusing to allow me to pull away.

"Relax," he says in my ear, and I take a deep breath. "It's going to be okay. You're just a new face."

"Okay."

Curiosity. I can handle that.

Xavier leads me to a table in the back corner, where another muscle-bound man sits. His long, dark hair is pulled back into a low ponytail, and his dark eyes twinkle with intrigue the moment our gazes lock.

The man's eyes flit from me to Xavier, and he grins as one of his thick eyebrows quirk. "Fresh meat?"

Xavier laughs and bumps fists with the man before pulling out a chair for me to sit in. "Brian "Razor" Rollins, this is Anna, my new assistant."

Brian stretches his arm across the table. "Nice to meet you."

I shake his hand. "Likewise."

Brian turns his attention from me back to Xavier. "Deena's history then?"

"Ancient," Xavier replies while taking the menu from the server who approached our table the moment we sat down.

Brian clears his throat and tilts his head to the left. "And she knows that, right?"

Both Xavier and I glance to the other side of the restaurant.

Oh, crap.

Deena glares back at us from where she sits, which is next to a rather built female who I can only assume is Star—the friend Xavier warned me about.

My heart races in my chest. For some reason I believed that night in the hotel would be the last time I ever had to lay eyes on this woman. I certainly didn't expect her to be here.

The muscle under Xavier's jaw works beneath his skin. "What the fuck is she doing here?"

"She came in here with Rex. We all were wondering what was going on when you weren't with her. Is she working for him now?" Brian asks as he cuts into the huge steak on the plate in front of him.

The name Rex instantly rings a bell. That's the guy who is Xavier's rival for the championship belt. Why would she do that to Xavier, especially if she had a relationship with him?

Xavier sighs. "That bitch is vindictive as fuck."

Brian chuckles. "I warned you, brother. That woman has evil written all over her. I just hope she doesn't come after your new tail here."

My eyes widen. "Whoa. We're just—"

"Friends?" Brian cuts me off and winks with an ornery smile. "I know."

I'm not sure I like his implied tone, and the concern I had once before resurfaces. Exactly how many other women have been in my position? That unnerves me. I'm not used to being just another woman in an absurdly long line.

After Xavier orders the biggest steak they have, I give my order and glance around the restaurant. All the muscle-type men in here seem to be eating like Xavier. It must be part of their training to get all those muscles.

"So, you good now? Ready for tomorrow?" Brian asks Xavier.

"Yeah. I'm good."

Brian nods. "Good. You know it's important to have your head on straight. No more fucking around. Rex means business and he's going to do his best to make you eat mat to prove he's the ultimate contender for the belt. He's been gathering backing while you've been gone. He's got one of the writers in his pocket now."

Xavier leans back in the chair and rolls his ripped shoulders. "Let him try. I've been dying to really put a whipping on that fucker. He runs his mouth far too much for my taste. Someone needs to shut him the fuck up."

"While I'd love nothing more than to witness you doing that very thing, you have to be smart about it. He's going to try and antagonize you."

Xavier sighs. "I don't understand why he can't do his job like the rest of us. He takes things too far, makes shit personal, and that really pisses me off. I'll hit him harder than called for, every chance I get."

"He's got a death wish, X. He's going to fight dirty."

"I thought everything was choreographed? Why does he have to get personal?" I ask.

Brian turns his attention to me. "The man is afraid of X. We all know it, but he's hell bent on getting that belt, so he's going to try to exploit and pick at every weakness he can find so he doesn't have to fight him directly to get it."

"Deena," Without meaning to say her name out loud, it slips from my lips.

"Exactly," Brian agrees. "And you, now that you're in the mix."

Xavier rubs his face. "Shit."

Brian nods. "You walking in here hand in hand...my guess is he'll try to get to Anna just to press your buttons."

His brow flinches for a brief second. "She's too smart for that. She won't fall for his shit."

"She might not, but it won't stop him from trying."

Brian glances down at his phone. "Got to run, brother. Time to check in with the wifey." He stands and smiles at me. "Anna, good luck keeping my man on track. You've got your work cut out for you. This stubborn ass is pretty set in his ways."

I laugh as Xavier rolls his eyes. "Thanks."

The moment Brian walks away, I say, "I like him. He seems fun."

The waiter sets our food down in front of us, and Xavier cuts into his steak. "Brian is a good guy, and the only real friend I've got in this business."

"That's hard to believe, what with that charming, outgoing personality you have." I bump my shoulder into his and Xavier chuckles.

"Keep it up, beautiful. Insubordination will get you punished."

The water glass pressed to my lips, I stare at him over it and raise my eyebrow. "You don't scare me."

He licks his lips slowly as he glances down at my mouth for a brief second. "I should, but I'm glad I don't."

The tension between us is driving me crazy. While I know what he's saying isn't sexual in any way, my mind instantly takes it to the gutter. It's the main complication I'll face, working for a man I find insanely attractive.

I need to refocus and remember the reason I'm here. Maybe that'll occupy my brain and make me stop thinking of my new boss as an object of desire.

"So when are you going to tell me what my duties are?"

His jaw works around as he chews while considering my question.

After a moment he swallows and asks, "What would you like them to be?"

I shake my head. "That's not how this works. You're supposed to give me direction."

"Direction..." he mumbles. "Okay, the first thing you need to do is stay away from Rex. He bothers you, talks to you—whatever—you let me know."

"After the conversation I just heard, that goes without saying. What else?"

"Deena used to keep my schedule in order. She'd tell me where I had to be and when. That actually really helped. With everything I have going on, I lose track of interviews and promo shoots."

"I can do that. Do you have your calendar?"

"It's on my phone. Text me your email, and I'll send it over to you."

Now we're getting somewhere, and this feels more like a real job. "Anything else?"

"No," he says flatly. "I prefer to take care of everything else myself. Jimmy deals with all my business affairs, so things are pretty well-handled."

I probably shouldn't say this, but I'm going to anyway. "I know this puts my job in jeopardy, but I really don't think you need me if that's all the work you're going to give me. I at least want to feel useful."

"Just you just being here helps more than you'll ever know. It's nice to have someone around to talk to who's not cutthroat like the rest of these motherfuckers around here."

"So what you're saying is that you basically hired me as your companion?" I freak a little inside, suddenly needing to clear up exactly what this job *doesn't* entail. "I'm not a paid escort, Xavier, if that's why you brought me along."

He furrows his brow. "I know that."

"Do you? I'm just making it clear that I'm not like Deena."

"Beautiful, you couldn't be any more different if you tried." He takes my hand into his on the top of the table. "You're more woman than she can ever dream of being."

"I..." I swallow hard, completely lost for words.

It's moments like this that make me forget all the rough patches we've been through since I've known him. With just a few simple words, he has the power to make me believe that I'm the most special person in the world.

"I like you, Anna. I know I've got a fucked up way of showing it sometimes, but I do."

"I like you too," I whisper.

Xavier lips pull into a huge smile. "Good. Then try to look past all the bullshit and be my friend."

There's that pesky 'F' word again—the word that's going to drive me straight out of my mind one of these days. My hormones can only take rejection so many times before they shut down from disappointment.

But if a friend is what he wants from me, then a friend is what he shall have.

"I'm here for you. Always. You would never have had to pay me for that."

He brings my hand up to his mouth and presses his lips to my knuckles. My toes instantly curl and I chew on the corner of my lip. Heat rises up my neck and I know my cheeks are flushed.

I glance around the room, not many people are paying any attention to our little interaction. Only one person is watching us intently.

Deena glares at me from across the room, her slender arms crossed over her chest. If I had to guess, I'd say she's plotting how to kill me this very second in order to get me out of the picture.

I've made more enemies since leaving home a little over a week ago than I've had in my entire life. I guess this is all a part of living free and breaking rules.

I just hope I can make it through this unscathed.

Xavier

The show travels from town to town so often, I don't ever bother to unpack. I just live out of my suitcase, so to speak. It makes things so much easier.

I dig through my bag looking for a pair of clean underwear to sleep in when I notice Anna out of the corner of my eye. "Do you want to shower first, or is it okay if I do?"

She sits on the bed next to my suitcase. "I prefer to take mine in the morning."

The thought of her naked and wet, only a room away from me, causes my cock to jerk in my jeans. I'll have to make damn sure I'm out the door before that happens in the morning. God knows I'll never be able to resist her if I'm here for all that.

Fuck me.

I need a distraction before I go to the shower to jerk off while thinking about her.

I force my mind to think about my upcoming match, and after a couple of seconds my dick calms down and I'm able to function like a normal human being again.

"I won't be long. You can take the bed. I'll make a spot on the floor."

She shakes her head. "Don't be ridiculous. You have a match tomorrow, you need your rest. I'll take the floor."

"Anna," I warn. "There's no way in hell I'll allow you to sleep on the floor."

She sighs, knowing I won't give in on this. "Fine. We're both adults—we can share the bed."

I raise my eyebrows. "You're okay with that?"

"Of course I am, silly. We're friends, and I trust you." She tries to play it off as a joke to make it seem like sleeping in the same bed with me isn't a big deal, but I know her better than that.

I want her to know she can trust me. "You don't have to—"

"No arguing. It's a king-size bed, so it won't be an issue."

"You sure?" I quiz her.

"I trust you. I wouldn't be here if I didn't."

"Okay then."

I'm pretty sure I break the record for the fastest shower known to man. The idea of lying inches away from her all night sends a thrill through me. I roll my eyes at myself as I realize that I'm thinking like a fucking teenage girl excited about the possibility of touching someone I have a crush on. I scrub my hands down my face and attempt to convince myself to chill the fuck out.

I've got to get a handle on this thing because if this keeps up, I'm going to scare her off with my psycho obsession.

If she could ever see inside my head, she'd surely run away screaming.

Chapter
FIFTEEN

As quickly as I can, I strip out of my clothes and climb into the thin nightgown I wear for bed. The sheets are cool as I slide between them, but they do nothing to calm my flushed body down. I close my eyes and quietly tell myself, "Quit being a scaredy-cat. You can do this."

Xavier's deep laugh reverberates on the other side of the bathroom door. "Psyching yourself up again?"

Shit. How the hell did he hear me?

"N—no. That had nothing to do with you," I say trying to muster some confidence.

The door opens and he steps out wearing nothing but a towel and a smile.

Water drips from his hair onto his broad shoulders as he approaches the bed. I glance over to his side of the bed, and I notice his underwear is laying there.

He's going to change right in front of me?

My heart thunders in my chest. I should look away, but I can't help myself. I want to look at him.

Sins of the flesh really do carry some meaning. Father would be proud that I actually still remember some of the scripture.

I take a deep breath and search for a distraction. I grab the one paperback novel I brought with me off the nightstand and open it in front of my face.

It's a romance novel, and so far the love story is very angsty and intense—which reminds me a whole lot of the relationship I have with Xavier.

"Is that a good one?" he asks.

I turn toward him to answer just as he drops the towel and grabs his underwear off the bed.

"Ohmigod!" I shriek and immediately cover my eyes. "I'm sorry I didn't mean to—"

"Look?" Xavier chuckles.

"Yes," I whisper, completely mortified.

"It's okay, Anna. I'm sure what I've got isn't anything you haven't seen before. You were an engaged woman once. I'm sure you're experienced in that region."

I squeeze my eyelids tighter.

If he only knew just how lacking I am in that department, he would probably tease me relentlessly, so I don't reply.

Once he's dressed, Xavier pulls back the blankets and slides in next to me. I expect him to stay on his side of the bed, but he doesn't, scooting close enough to me that our arms touch as he leans over and tilts my book up so he can read the title.

"*Rock My Bed*? That sounds dirty. I never pegged you for the type to read smutty books," he teases.

I shake my head. "It's not smut, it's a romance. The woman is trying to help the broken man heal and see that he's a good person, even though the hero denies that he is for most of the book. "

Xavier leans back against the pillow and tucks one arm behind his head. Even though I shouldn't, I allow my gaze to wander down the toned muscles of his bicep and chest. He's so beautiful, it's hard not to stare at the work of art that is his body.

"That's the problem with women in fiction. It's always the man who needs fixing. Why can't it be the chick who's fucked up for a change?"

"There are lots of great works out there about that very thing," I reply.

"Not as many as men with problems," he fires back. "All you women read those books and pray to find a 'fixer-upper' who you can 'heal' when the reality is that most men don't talk about their issues for a reason. It's best to leave the past in the past than dig old shit up."

Instantly, it hits me that he's talking about more than just fictional characters. He never wants to talk about his family for a reason.

"That may work for a little while, but surely you don't believe avoidance is the best way to handle problems."

He shakes his head. "Of course I don't think that. Sometimes an ass-kicking works just as well for people who have it coming."

I sit up and face him. Now might be a good time to try and get him to open up to me. "You're talking current events though. I'm talking more along the lines of old problems you can't necessarily fight your way out of."

He turns those intense blue eyes on me, and my heart races. "I know what you're trying to do, Anna, but it's not going to work."

Busted.

"I don't know what you're talking about."

Xavier shoves himself up and off the bed before walking toward his suitcase. He rifles through his clothes, pulling out a pair of jeans, socks, and a t-shirt.

Every time I feel like I'm starting to get somewhere, he shuts me down and runs away. "Where are you going? We're talking."

After he quickly dresses, he shoves his feet into his boots. "I've told you before, I don't talk about my past."

"Why?" I ask, confused and curious as to what could possibly be so bad that he won't tell me anything about his past.

"My problems aren't like one of your books, Anna. There's no fucking formula to fix me. My shit—it's fucking real. It's not all in my head. The things I've lived through, the things I've done—" He cuts himself off and squeezes his eyes shut, like it pains him to even think about it. "I should be in prison right now, but instead, I'm sitting here with you. Don't think for one second that I'm not a monster, because I am. I can't change who or what I am. I hate to disappoint you, but I'm not a hero. I'm the fucking villain in this story."

"That's not what I'm not trying to do!" I argue, even though deep down I know he's right. From the moment I met him, I have tried to size him up and justify my feelings for him.

"Yes, you are. You've got it into your head that I've got some redeemable quality that I just haven't uncovered yet. Do you know how insane that sounds? I'm not like you, Anna. Growing up, I didn't have the luxury of getting lost in some fictional world. I didn't have time to have a fucking imagination, or dreams. All I worried about was staying alive and surviving—something you wouldn't have the first clue about."

"You think I've had it easy? My father *hates* me." Tears burn my eyes, but I refuse to allow them to fall. "Do you know what that's like?"

Xavier runs his fingers through his hair and drops his head to stare at the floor for a moment before returning his icy blue stare to me. "More than you'll ever know."

The words bounce around in my brain, and they anger me. "And I'll never know because you won't tell me a damn thing about you. You give me bits and pieces, but you never tell me anything real. How am I supposed to be a friend and help you if you refuse to open up to me?"

"Don't push this, Anna. Let it go." He raises his voice, and I flinch.

I'm pissing him off? Well good, because I'm pissed off now too. "No!"

He narrows his eyes at me and grabs his keys off the table. "I don't need this shit."

He storms toward the door, running away yet again. But this time I'm not letting it go. "We aren't done with this conversation."

The muscle in his jaw works beneath his skin as he turns around to face me. "We are now."

It takes every inch of my willpower not to reach out and grab his arm to force him to stay here with me and finish this.

"Where are you going?"

"Out," is all he says, before turning back around and pushing through the door.

My body jerks when the door slams shut behind him, and I don't even get so much as a second look.

If I keep pushing like this, I will lose him— I know that. But I also can't have a friendship with someone who refuses to hide vital parts of themselves from me.

I flop back onto the bed and stare up at the white ceiling. I owe him an apology. I have no right to pry, forcing him to tell me things he doesn't want to, but I'm greedy. I want all of him.

I lay awake staring at the alarm clock on the nightstand. It's nearly two in the morning and Xavier still hasn't come back yet.

This isn't good.

He needs his rest. Tomorrow is Tuesday, and I know *Tension* is a live televised event and Xavier has a match. Being out like this won't be good for his performance.

I pick up my phone, debating whether to call him or not when I notice a new text has arrived from Father. I clutch the phone to my chest. I've been avoiding him now for over a week, but he's been relentless with his messages.

As always, my curiosity wins out. I raise the phone up and flick my finger across the screen. My breath catches. What I read is such a different tone than what I'd been receiving. Most of the week Father's words have been angry and demeaning—pointing out all my faults, and telling me how leaving everything behind was a huge mistake. How I wasn't being smart. How if I didn't come back, I should forget I even have a family.

That one hurt the most.

It was the last one I read before this new one, which blows my mind.

Father: I need to know where you are and that you're safe. At least give me that. I sigh as I read his words. He's worried. I can tell. The least I can do is let him know where I am. I quickly tap out a message in reply.

I'm safe. I'm in Atlanta. Working for a wrestler who's on TV.

It's not an exact location, but it should be enough information to appease him. As hard as it may be to believe, I do love my father, but he's too controlling and I need distance from him.

I'm my own person with my own will—desperate to make my own choices. And the choices will be mine, and I will be happy making the wrong ones because at least the mistakes will be my own.

Speaking of wrong choices, I need to talk to my 'possible wrong decision' and apologize. Make him come back and get some sleep.

I scroll down through my contacts and my thumb hovers over Xavier's name just as the door opens and he creeps through the door. I squint, as the light from the hallway fills in around him.

The second the door closes, we're wrapped in darkness. It takes a moment for my eyes to adjust, but finally they do, and I see Xavier standing beside the bed, staring down at me frowning, his hands shoved deep in his pockets.

He's quiet for a few long, torturous seconds, but finally he sighs and sits on the bed. "I'm sorry I kept you awake."

I sit up and reach for his hand. "Don't. It's me who should be apologizing. We've had this talk before and I know you don't like to—"

Xavier presses his index finger to my lips. "I've had some time to think about all that. It's not fair of me to blow up when you ask simple questions about my family. You're curious about me, I get that. Maybe someday I'll be able to talk about them, but right now, I just can't. I hope you can understand that."

I nod.

"There are things about me, Anna, that I don't want anyone to know—especially not you. My family...they weren't good people, but they were all I knew. I thought the things they did were normal for so long. It wasn't until I met Nettie and Carl that I discovered differently. I don't want you to pity me. That would kill me more than anything. I have to be strong. Don't you see?"

I stare into his eyes and trace the scruff along his jawline. "It's okay to be vulnerable sometimes, Xavier. You can be that with me. The past is just that—the past. I base how I feel about you on the man I know you are today. You're protective and strong, and above all else, you have an amazing heart."

He closes his eyes and leans into my touch. "You don't know what you're asking for. I'm so fucked up, Anna."

I bite my lip and cradle his face in my hands. "You're not. I wish you could see what I do."

I know we've had problems, and our relationship is nowhere near perfect, but right now I don't care about any of that. Every inch of me craves him. I want him to know that he matters to me—that I'm not going anywhere.

I lean in closer to him, and he closes his eyes again before resting his forehead against mine, resisting my kiss. "If we smash these fucking friendship rules there's no going back. Once I have you—that's it, you're mine. I won't allow another man to take what's mine. Do you understand?"

My mouth drifts open and I whisper, "Yes."

He presses his lips lightly against mine, teasing me. "I've wanted you from the moment I saw you, Anna. All this waiting has been driving me out of my fucking mind."

Xavier's hand slides up my stomach, teasing me with his slow touch. He continues going up until he reaches my breast. The thin fabric of my nightgown is all that separates his hand from my bare skin, and I'm tempted to tear it away myself, just to feel him.

His touch is so much better than I ever imagined. I close my eyes and get lost in how good it makes me feel. Never has a man turned me on like this before.

It's almost like an out-of-body experience. Never have I been this wild and carefree. Never have I acted on something I've wanted so badly.

And it feels amazing.

My head falls back a bit, and I moan before he threads his fingers in my hair and pulls it back up. His mouth crushes into mine, and I throw my hands into that sexy hair of his.

"I'll be a good man to you, Anna," he says against my lips. "I swear it."

"You're already a good man," I whisper.

He crushes his mouth against mine again. His tongue searching and probing my mouth like it's too excited to behave. This kiss feels so different. It's primal and demanding, like he's marking me as his.

Xavier's nose skims my cheek before he nips on my earlobe.

"I need to feel you."

He pulls back the blanket and slides his hand up my thigh until his fingers reach the edge of my nightgown. With one quick swoop, it's over my head, and my breasts are fully exposed. Goosebumps pepper my naked flesh, and I dip my head as he appraises me.

His index finger slides under my chin, and he lifts my head so he can gaze into my eyes. "So fucking beautiful."

My heart pounds with excitement. All my daydreams about what this would be like are being surpassed already. I can't even explain what I'm feeling. All I know is that I want him. My body actually aches for him to touch me more.

The warmth of his mouth, licking and teasing the sensitive skin below my ear, causes an ache between my legs so intense I actually squirm.

Xavier chuckles. "Patience, baby. I'm going to make you feel so good."

My hand slips under the hem of his shirt and I run my nails across the deep ripples in his abdomen. I'm so ready to feel his body of perfection pressed against me. He grabs the back of his shirt and drags it over his head, making his hair wild and sexy.

His defined muscles tense as I lean in and kiss a trail along his broad shoulders. He closes his eyes when I reach his neck and press my lips against his flesh. The salty taste of his skin coats my tongue as taste him.

I pull back and his eyes flash down to mine. "Change your mind?"

I shake my head. "I want you."

That simple phrase triggers something because I'm instantly on my back beneath him as he kisses his way down my chest, pausing to swirl his tongue around my taut nipple. He grazes his teeth against it, teasing me even more.

"Oh God," is all I can manage to breath out.

He pushes himself up off the bed and makes quick work of unzipping his jeans and kicking off his boots. I watch openly as he shoves his boxers and pants down around his hips before allowing them to drop to the floor. His cock springs free, and my mouth drops open. It's quite impressive.

Staring at his sizeable length, I have the desire to do something I've never done before. I crawl toward him and run my hands up his muscular thighs. His breath catches the moment I tease the tip of his length with my mouth.

"Christ," he mumbles before tangling his fingers into my hair as I continue my assault on him. I gag a bit when his head touches the back of my throat and I pull back a bit but keep going.

Xavier moans. "Fuck. You keep that up, and I'll come in that pretty mouth of yours."

I don't want that to happen—not today anyway. I want to feel him inside me, moving, pushing me to my limits. He emits a low growl, and I pull away.

His hooded eyes stare into mine. "Now it's my turn to taste you."

He bends down and flicks his tongue across my bottom lip as he grabs the waistband of my panties and tugs them off my body. Xavier kneels down at the edge of the bed and grabs my hips, flipping me onto my back and dragging my ass to the edge of the bed. A thrill of the unknown shoots through me as I lie here, stripped bare before him.

"Spread your legs," he orders, and I comply without hesitation.

A rush of cold air hits my most sensitive flesh before it's immediately replaced with warmth. Xavier's dips his tongue and drags it between my folds. He licks rapid circles over my clit, and I cry out with the tingling build of pleasure I've never known before.

My entire body shakes as an orgasm rips through me, and I scream out his name.

Once I've calmed down, Xavier kisses the mound above my pussy and begins kissing a path up my stomach, chest, and neck. "That was so fucking hot. I nearly came just watching you get off."

The weight of his body on top of mine feels heavenly as I stare into his eyes. "I'm going to fuck you now. I want to feel that tight little pussy around me, milking me."

One of his hands grips my thigh and hooks it around his waist. "Is this pussy ready for me?"

I suck in a quick breath as he slides his cock against my wet folds. I don't know how much more teasing I can take. "Yesssss."

"Then I want to hear you say it." He kisses my lips, and I taste myself on him. "Tell me, baby. I want to know you're mine, and that you know you belong to me."

I arch my back against him and run my hands down his back.

Every inch of me craves him, and usually I'd be too embarrassed to talk like this, but if I don't voice what he wants to hear he's not going to give me what I need. "I'm yours."

"Don't you fucking forget it, either," he growls and pushes inside me.

I dig my nails into his back and whimper. I should've warned him that I'd only had sex one other time.

He furrows his brow. "Jesus. Are you all right?"

I relax around him, and the burn begins to fade away as I get used to his length. "I'm fine. It's just been a while."

He brushes my hair back from my face. "How long is a while?"

I swallow hard. "Over a year, but I've only done it one other time."

He squeezes his eyes tight. "Fuck. You're probably not on the pill either. I should've asked."

I shake my head, and he begins to pull himself out of me. "Please. Don't stop. I need this. I need you."

I can see the conflict in his eyes and for a moment I'm afraid he's going to tell me no, but then he begins moving inside me.

He buries his face into my hair and whispers, "I'm not going to come in you. I'll have to pull out before then."

I nod, understanding. "Okay."

I close my eyes and bite my lip, as he pumps into me at a deliciously slow pace. When I open them, he's hovering over me, watching my face as he takes me.

A small bead of sweat forms his upper lip and I lean up and lick it. The salty taste washes over my tongue as he begins to pant.

"Damn it. I can't believe I'm this close already. It's you, knowing I'm inside you has me so fucking turned on. It's too fucking hard to hold back."

I shudder as his mouth covers my shoulder. "Your pussy is like fucking paradise."

He growls and lightly bites my shoulder, sliding his cock into me again and again.

I cry out his name followed by a "Yes." I can't believe this is finally happening. I feel the same tingle return, and I can tell I'm getting close myself. "You feel so good."

"Our bodies were made for each other."

The distinct slaps echo around the hotel room as his thrusts pick up pace.

My core clenches around him greedily, trying to hold him deep inside. "Xavier..."

"Hold on, baby. I want to come with you." Xavier pulls out of me and begins sliding his cock against my clit. "Fuck."

The repetitive attention to my clit sends me over the edge just as Xavier groans in my ear and comes on the outside of my folds, slicking my sensitive skin.

Xavier presses his lips to mine. "That was the most amazing thing I've ever experienced."

And I smile at him.

Because I feel the exact same way.

Chapter
SIXTEEN

Xavier

I stare up at the clock and panic washes through me. It's almost time for her to return. If she comes back and finds this, it won't be good.

I shake Mama's shoulders, desperate for her to wake from the deep sleep she's put herself into once again. "Please, Mama. Wake up. Grandmother will be home any minute. Please."

Even I can hear the pleading in my voice as I attempt to choke back tears. "She can't find you like this."

I yank until I'm finally able to pull her fragile body up a bit. The bones in her shoulders press against my small arms as I cradle her against me. Mama's head lolls from side to side as I continue to shake her.

Footsteps on the porch cause my heart to leap up into my throat.

It's too late now.

Keys jingle as the lock turns and the door is pressed open. I glance around my grandmother's living room, hoping to find an escape route, but I know that even if I find one, it won't do me any good.

I've got no place to go.

Grandmother's eyes lock onto me the moment she shuts the door behind her. The flowered dress she always wears to church on Sundays still appears perfectly pressed. I can't look her in the eye. It scares me too much. There's nothing but hatred for me in them, so I do my best to look everywhere—anywhere—but directly into her eyes.

I concentrate on a wisp of dark hair poking out from her low-set bun under her hat as I attempt to explain myself. "I'm sorry. She just—I couldn't stop her."

Grandmother sets her purse down on the coffee table and approaches the spot in the middle of the floor where I'm still clinging to my unresponsive mother. The moment she begins smacking the bible she carried in against her hand, a chill runs down my spine.

"I told you to watch her. Is that so hard?" she asks while she begins circling around me. "You had one job, and you couldn't even do that right."

My entire body jolts when she lands the first unexpected blow to the back of my head with the book. Instinctively, I throw up my hands up to protect myself. "I'm...mmm...ssss...sorry."

"Listen to that stutter. Every time I touch you with the holy word you do that. You know why, boy?" she taunts before she hits me with it again on the side of the face.

I close my eyes and silently beg for Mama to wake up. She's the only one who can stop this now.

"Answer me!" Grandmother shouts.

"Because I'm evil," I whisper, knowing that's what she wants to hear.

She shoves the hard spine of the book into the back of my head, pushing it forward. "That's right, you little demon spawn. Look at how you poisoned my baby. She wasn't like this until she ran off and got pregnant with you, by that *monster*."

The mention of the father I've never known hurts worse than the physical abuse she's inflicting on me. I've asked Mama about him, but all she's ever said was that he wasn't from around here, and she only spent one day with him, before he left town, and was never heard from again.

It would be amazing to just have a name.

"Pick her up," Grandmother orders.

I stare down at my mother, who is much bigger than I am. To lift her would be an impossible task. She's not going to like my answer.

"I can't."

Whack!

A gasp leaves my mouth as she smacks me hard across my face. The metallic taste of blood coats my tongue, alerting me to the fact that she's just getting warmed up.

"I'm only eight, Grandmother. I'm not strong enough."

Her mouth twists as she levels her icy blue stare on me. With one hand, she grabs my shirt collar and yanks me to my feet, causing me to drop my mother on the floor with a loud thud in the process.

Her fingers thread into my shaggy hair, and she yanks my head back so she can gaze upon my face. "You better call on the devil to help you lift her, because if you don't, I will kill you."

She lets go and pushes me away from her. "Now, lift!"

I let out a shaky breath and squat down next to my mother. I hook my arm under her knees and the other around her shoulders. My shoulders tense as I yank with all my might. Relief floods me the second I'm able to pull Mama up off the floor. My fingers dig into her chilled flesh as I hold on with all my might.

"Put her on the couch. She needs to sleep it off."

I take a staggering step forward, followed by another, amazed at my own strength and my ability to carry her. Even though my arms burn under her weight, I refuse to let go. The pain is a welcome distraction from the beating I know I'm about to endure.

I lay her down gently and readjust the pillow under her head, pushing a lock of her dark hair away from her face. She looks so peaceful, it's easy to forget everything she's done to me when she's like this. The worry that she won't wake up far outranks any anger I feel toward her.

I'm jerked away from her by a firm grasp and shoved to the floor. "Keep your filthy hands off her!"

I hook my arms under my knees and remind myself to stay strong as Grandmother draws the bible in her hand back, ready to hit me yet again.

I close my eyes and hold my breath the moment she begins to swing.

A gasp so loud comes out of me it wakes me from my own sleep as throw my hands up to shield myself from the blow that isn't real. My hands shake as I push my hair back from my face and attempt to calm my breathing. Sweat pours off me as I grip my head in my hands.

Why won't these fucking dreams go away?

Anna sits up next to me, and even in the darkness I can see the concern in her eyes. She slowly reaches out her hand and touches my back and I flinch.

I can't have her touching me—not now—not after having a nightmare like that.

I shove off the bed and instantly drop down on the floor. Push-ups come easy to me, but the burn I crave doesn't come to me until I've counted at least fifty.

Anna scoots to the edge of the bed and gazes down at me. "Do you want to talk about it?"

"Seventy-two. No. Seventy-three..." I continue on the only way I know how to get rid of the demons that lie in wait in my mind. Punishing my own body to near breaking point, just so I won't feel anything else, usually provides relief.

I hate what remembering the past does to me.

It makes me a crazy fucking freak.

Anna throws her legs over the bed and lowers herself onto the floor next to me. She watches me intently for a moment before reaching over to lay her hand on mine as I continue doing push-ups.

The little gesture causes me to lose count, and I turn to stare at her as I continue. She doesn't say anything. She doesn't have to in order for me to understand that she cares about me. The small act of sticking by my side while I work my own shit out is enough.

This girl is special. I can see that now with certain clarity. But the problem still remains—I don't deserve her. She's too good for me. It's only a matter of time before she realizes that, too, and leaves me. When that happens...it will kill me. I know it will.

I'm so fucking addicted. This will not end well for either of us, because I won't know how to let her go.

Chapter
SEVENTEEN

Xavier has been quiet today. He doesn't seem upset or anything, just cautious around me. I'm sure what I witnessed last night wasn't something he wanted me to see, but Lord knows I'm not going to force him to tell me what upset him. The last time I tried that, things got crazy.

I just don't like seeing him hurting.

The car comes to a stop, and Jimmy hops out first, opening the door for Xavier and me to get out. I stare up at the huge brick arena that we're about to enter. It reminds me a bit of a coliseum, and Xavier's powerful presence imitates that of a gladiator about to enter for battle.

My eyes drift over to him. His dark hair is pushed back from his face while glasses shield his eyes from the evening sun. Xavier threads his fingers through mine as the security guards open the rear entrance doors for us.

A large black man with a completely bald head nods at Xavier. "What up, X. You ready for tonight, man?"

Xavier grins. "Razor won't know what hit him, Freddy."

Freddy laughs. "Funny, he just told me the same thing." He marks something off the clipboard he's carrying and jerks his head inside. "Come on. I'll show you where the dressing room is."

"Stick close to me in here. Backstage is chaotic, and I don't want to lose track of you," Xavier says as tightens his grip on my hand and leads me inside.

I smile at him, wanting nothing more than to reassure him that he has nothing to worry about. "It's going to be fine. Focus on your match. I'm not going anywhere."

He nods and focuses straight ahead as we pass by a few men wearing *Tension* t-shirts with the word "crew" stitched onto them.

A few of the guys call out to Xavier as we head down a long white hallway. The crewmen zip around us, carrying assorted pieces of equipment and props, and even as an onlooker I can tell that every employee is under a time-crunch to make tonight's show go off without a hitch.

The beefy security officer escorting us down the hall stops at the last door on the right. "You can wait in here with the other wives, miss."

Xavier shakes his head. "No fucking way. Anna stays with me. I'm not throwing her into that snake pit alone, Freddy."

Freddy sighs. "What did you expect, X? She can't go back into the dressing room. The guys would flip their fucking shit."

Xavier pulls his lips into a tight line as he stares into the room where all the wives are waiting. I follow his line of sight and spot Deena, wearing a slinky, red mini dress and one of the most evil grins I've ever seen.

I don't like the idea of being alone with this woman, but I can't allow Xavier to worry about that. He doesn't need another problem in his life to deal with. I want to help him, not be a hindrance.

I squeeze his fingers. "I'll be fine."

His gaze snaps down to me. "Are you sure? I can have Jimmy—"

I shake my head. "Don't worry, I can handle her. Go, do your thing. I'll wait right here for you."

"You're sure?"

"Positive. Now, go." I nudge his arm.

Xavier bends down and presses his lips to mine. "Call me if there's *any* problem."

I stay in the doorway and allow my eyes to appreciate the view of his phenomenal ass. No longer do I have to wonder what having him would be like because now I know he really does earn the first part of his stage name.

"It's nice, isn't it?" Deena questions as she slithers up beside me. "He can make you feel so special while he's using you. He's so good, it's easy to fall for the lie that he might actually care for you. That you're special to him."

I roll my eyes. "Give it up, Deena. He doesn't want you anymore."

Her blue eyes trail over my face as she appraises me. "That's right because the two of you have a connection now? Is that what you think?"

I know I shouldn't let her bother me—that she's playing games with my head—but damn if that doesn't sting. It's like she knows exactly what to say in order to get to me.

"I almost feel sorry for you."

I lift my chin. "You shouldn't waste your time."

She quirks an eyebrow. "Why's that?"

"You're the one that needs to get over it and move on. He's done with you and your…'relationship.' It meant nothing to him. Get that through your head and butt out of our business."

She narrows her eyes. "In a month from now, don't say I didn't warn you. I came over here to offer you some friendly advice—woman to woman."

I fold my arms over my chest. "What's that?"

She smirks. "Make friends with the other wrestlers, because maybe when he's through with you, one of them might take you on, if you're lucky. They're all loaded."

I curl my lip. "You disgust me."

She laughs. "The innocent card works for you. Keep it up. It's a great cover. I might have to actually use that one myself."

Maybe I need to be more direct?

"Stay away from me."

"I'll stay away from you all right, but I can't promise the same for your boyfriend. He has a hard time turning me down…as you well know." She winks at me.

Blood boils in my veins. I'm not usually one to condone violence of any sort, but I would like nothing more than to throttle her. Pulling her hair and smacking that cocky look off her face would make me so happy, but I refuse to sink to her level.

I won't allow her taunts to incite the reaction she wants.

When I don't say a word, she laughs in my face and turns to walk into the hallway where the man I recognize from television as Xavier's nemesis awaits. Assassin grins as he wraps his arm around Deena's waist and kisses the side of her head. It's almost like he's pleased that she's just been in here, pushing my buttons.

I take a deep breath and walk into the room. The walls are white, just like the hallway, and there are several tables set up with women and children sitting around them. Babies sit on their mother's laps and bang their toys onto the blue tabletops while their mothers attempt to feed them.

There's an empty seat next to one of the ladies with a toddler on her lap, and I make my way toward it. My fingers curl around the back of the chair, and the woman glances up at me with warm chocolate eyes and a kind smile, and for some reason I automatically feel at ease with her. The three other tables are filled with women chatting amongst themselves, but for some reason, this lady is alone like they are excluding her.

"Is this seat taken?" I ask.

"No." She gestures toward the seat. "Have a seat."

I return her smile with a polite one of my own. "Thank you. I'm Anna."

She nods and lays down the spoon she was just feeding her daughter with before extending her hand to me. "I've heard about you. I'm Liv, Brian's wife."

I take her hand, curious as to exactly what she's heard when remnants of her child's lunch rub off onto my fingertips.

Liv grimaces. "Sorry about that. Here." She hands me a napkin. "Do you have any?"

I take the napkin and begin to wipe the spaghetti sauce from my fingers. "Children? No. I'm not even married yet."

Liv laughs and tosses her brown hair over her shoulder. "I wasn't either, until last month."

My eyebrows flick up in quick surprise. I know that having babies out of wedlock is a common practice these days, I've just never known anyone who's done it.

"Is she…" Damn. How do I ask this question without sounding completely rude?

Fortunately, I don't have to because she finishes for me. "Brian's?"

I nod.

"Yes." She hugs the little blond-haired child tighter against her and kisses the top of her head. "Acts just like him too. Ornery."

"Anna meet Kami. Kami can you say hello to Miss Anna?"

Kami stares up at me with the same dark eyes that her mother has, but I can see a lot of Brian in her as well. "Helwo."

"Good job," Liv praises her.

The little girl giggles and squirms as her mom tickles her ribs before setting her down so she can play around on the floor with a couple of other small kids.

"She's adorable," I say as I watch the children play.

"Thanks. She can be a handful most days, but I wouldn't trade it for anything." Liv begins cleaning up the mess in front of her. "So you and X…are you all a couple? Brian wasn't sure."

My lips twist for a brief second. Xavier hasn't come right out and said he's my boyfriend or anything, but we've been attached at the hip for a little while now. I believe that would qualify us as an item. "Yes."

"That's good news. I was so excited when I heard he ditched Deena. She wasn't the one for X, but she wouldn't give up trying to sink her claws into him."

I can't help snickering. "Wow. Not a fan, huh?"

"Definitely not. It's girls like her that give women in general a bad name. This room is full of them." She gives me a pointed look, and I glance over at the other tables filled with women dressed a lot like Deena. "No matter how clear X made it that he didn't want a relationship with Deena, she still tagged along with him, hoping he would give in and she'd find a way to weasel into his pocket."

My thoughts automatically revert to Alice and what Quinn said about her. "I know another girl like her. She's a bitch too. It must be a genetic trait with gold-diggers."

Liv grins. "I like you. It's about time X had someone like you. Being around a genuine woman will be good for him."

"Thanks. I hope so."

"I'm sure things will work out."

At that second Kami begins to cry and Liv hops out of her seat to scoop the child into her arms. Liv cradles her little girl to her chest and speaks softly into her ear attempting to console her. She's a good mother. I've only known her a few minutes, but there's no mistaking how much she adores the little girl.

My cell phone buzzes in my back pocket. Quickly I dig it out and check the screen.

Crap.

With everything going on last night I forgot to call Quinn to let her know I made it to the hotel safe. She won't be pleased with me.

I answer on the third ring, and Quinn immediately starts in on me. "What's up with not calling, Hookerbot? How am I supposed to know you're safe if you don't check in?"

I furrow my brow. "Hooker-what?"

"It's my new slang word, but don't go and try to distract me from being pissed at you. Call me every day—ring a bell?"

I sigh. "I'm sorry. Things were a busy last night."

"Uh-huh. I bet they were. You slept with Mr. Sexy, didn't you?"

A blush creeps over my face, and I can ever feel my ears burn from all the blood rushing to my face. I could deny it and keep it private, but I don't want to. I want her to know. "Yes."

She shrieks. "Anna Cortez! You little slut."

"Quinn!" I scold. "It's not like that."

"Oh, I know it's not. You two are way past random fucking now. You're moving into the 'when's the wedding' phase."

I shake my head and roll my eyes. "Trust me, we aren't anywhere near *that*."

"But you screwed his brains out anyway? I'm so proud." I hear her mock sniff on the other end of the line. "So, how does it feel to be out in the big world all on your own?"

I grin. "It's so freeing. I don't think I've ever been this happy."

"Do you miss home at all?"

I sigh. "No. There's nothing in Portland for me anymore."

"I'm so happy for you, cuz. But I think you need to call Uncle Simon. He's been hounding Mom to death about you."

"I texted him this morning."

"Did you tell him where you are?"

"Not exactly, but I did tell him what city we were in, and that I was working for a wrestler. That's it. Why?"

She's quiet for a moment, and my pulse picks up speed as I wonder what's going on.

Finally she answers, "Uncle Simon has been threatening to come get you and take you back home. He's convinced that you're screwing up your life, and he needs to intervene."

I sit up a little straighter in my seat. "Do you think he'll come here?"

"I don't know...maybe? You know how he is."

I swallow hard and glance down at my forearm, remembering the last time I saw Father, and the bruises he left there when he was trying to force me to stay in Portland.

I don't want to see him. Not here. I'm not ready.

Liv approaches the table. "Quinn, I've got to go. Thanks for the heads-up. I'll call you soon."

"Okay. Love you."

"Love you too."

She joins me back at the table holding Kami. "Sorry. I didn't mean to interrupt. Your mom?"

"Cousin," I correct as I stuff my phone back in my pocket. "She's like my sister though."

She nods and checks the time on her cell phone. "Are you going to watch the match tonight? Brian really enjoys the nights he and X get to go at it."

"Yes. I'd love to. I've never seen Xavier perform yet."

"Oh, in that case, we have to go out into the arena tonight. There are seats reserved for family near the entry ramp. You'll be able to get the 'extreme fan' experience there."

"Sounds great," I say enthusiastically, genuinely excited to watch Xavier do something I know he loves so much.

Liv stands, picks up Kami and gathers her bags. "I'll find you just before they go on, and we'll go out on the floor together. They should be the last event. I've got to go back to the hotel for a bit and put her down for a nap otherwise she'll never make it tonight."

"Okay, see you then." I wave to her as they leave, and I catch myself smiling.

Liv is the type of person I can imagine being friends with. She took me under her wing—no questions asked. There's not much kindness like that in the world nowadays.

Sitting along at the table, I fiddle with my phone. None of the other women in the room approach me, although every now and then I catch one of them staring openly at me, judging me with their eyes, only to quickly turn away once they realize I've seen them.

It's nearly an hour before Xavier returns. He's dressed in camouflaged cargo pants and a plain black tank top that puts his defined body on display. I swear some of the other women in the room sigh as he approaches me, and I resist sticking my tongue out at them to rub in the fact that he's mine.

He pulls out the chair next to me and sits down. "Sorry I was gone so long. We always have a meeting with the writers ahead of time to find out what we need to do for the show."

"Because it's all scripted, right?"

He nods. "Yeah, but we get to improvise a little too. Brian and I are the best at that."

I lean my elbow on the table and rest my chin in my hand. "So you already know who's winning the match between you?"

"Yeah."

I bat my eyes. "Care to share?"

He smirks. "Really? Like there's even a chance it wouldn't be me."

"My, my. Cocky, aren't we?"

"It's not cocky when you're that damn good." He winks at me.

I roll my eyes and laugh. "So, what do we do now?"

"The show starts in an hour. I'm going to go do some cardio to get ready, and you're going to watch."

"You want me to sit there while you work out?"

He nods. "You don't want to?"

My eyes trail down his cut biceps and chest, and I allow my mind to wander back to last night when he was doing push-ups. Even though he was in a bad place mentally, while he was doing it, he still looked damn fine.

I could watch that man work up a sweat any day.

"Of course I do." I smile. "I love watching you."

He grins and leans in and kisses my lips. "The feeling's mutual."

A shiver flutters through my entire body, and if we weren't in a room full of children, I might be tempted to jump his bones. I'm so ready to go another round with him in bed.

He chuckles. "Come on, beautiful. We've got a busy night ahead."

A little while later I find myself sitting on a metal folding chair in my shorts and t-shirt observing a room full of beefy men working out before it's time for them to go on. While sitting here I've learned the guys who are just getting their foot in the door, so to speak, go on first—as opening acts, if you will—while the more popular superstars go on later in the show.

To each man, their match is serious. It's scripted and all that, but watching exactly how much physical pain some of them are in when they return backstage alerts me to the fact that the physicality of their job is very real. Someone can really get hurt if control isn't maintained at all times.

Most of the men are focused on their on pre-game routine. All but one, that is.

Rex "Assassin" Risen has been intently staring at me every time Xavier's back is turned. Like right now.

Xavier stands in front of me alternating lifts with fifty-pound dumbbells, while Assassin leans against the wall, his arms folded over his chest, watching us with a mixed expression of curiosity and amusement.

It's almost as if he's planning something devious, and I don't like that thought one bit.

I debate whether or not to alert Xavier to the situation, but decide against it so he can remain focused on his match. If his head isn't on right, he could get hurt out there. I can't have him out there worried about this guy, who is obviously a jerk. After the match is over—when I know he'll be able to handle it without getting himself hurt—I'll tell him.

The short man, wearing a baseball cap and headphones with a mic attached, who has been alerting the men when their match is up pops into the room. "Assassin, you're on deck, man."

Assassin pushes himself off the wall and strides past us. Xavier's body stiffens, as if it takes all of his self-control to allow him to pass without saying a word to him. I know exactly how he feels. It's the same feeling I get when Deena is around.

The area goes nuts when Assassin's entrance music plays, and his name is announced. The cheers from the crowd are unmistakable, and I wonder if they would love him as much if they knew that he was a grade-A asshole?

Xavier sets his weights down and begins to stretch. "I'm up next. You can watch from the monitors by the wrestler's entrance into the arena, if you want."

I stand. "Actually, I've got other plans."

He tilts his head. "You're not going to watch me?"

"I am, but Liv is going to take me out on the floor so I get the 'extreme fan' experience."

He laughs and wraps an arm around my waist, pulling me against his chest. "I also plan on giving you a phenomenal experience again, tonight."

I giggle as he kisses my lips.

"All right, that's enough, lovebirds," Brian says as he approaches us with one arm around Liv, holding Kami in the other.

My eyes instantly widen as I take in the shiny, gold belt around Brian's waist. "You're the champ?"

Kami pats his chest. "Daddy champ!"

Brian smiles at us. "She really isn't a fan, is she, X?"

Xavier laughs. "Told you."

I shrug, feeling embarrassed that I didn't know.

Liv takes Kami from Brian's arms and then gives him a quick kiss. "Have a good match, babe." She turns to me. "Let's hurry and get our seats."

Xavier pats my butt after I pull away. "I expect extra loud cheering from your section when I come out."

I laugh. "You got it."

Liv leads me down the hall and waves at the security guards, addressing them by name. She turns to me and hands me a laminated pass. "Here, keep this on. You'll need it until the guys get to know you. The show's on a commercial break, so outside the door will be packed. Stick with me so I can get us to our seats."

I nod and do as she instructed while following her through a door leading out into the public concession area. People mill about in every direction, and their chatter is deafening. We head through a tunnel into the arena, and I'm awed by the bright lights and sold-out crowd.

We bob and weave through the fans, and I spot a few 'Phenomenal X' t-shirts along the way. *I need one of those*, I think to myself, and laugh at the thought of always having him so close to me.

Finally, we arrive at our section, and Liv walks all the way over to last seat near the barricade. "You sit here. They'll come down that ramp to get to the ring."

The metal stage is backlit by millions of mini bulbs and a monstrous screen. There are several men running around, checking things before the show resumes, and the excitement in the air is so thick I can nearly taste it. An overhead announcement is made alerting people to take their seats.

"Thirty seconds."

"Are you excited?" Liv asks me, balancing Kami on her hip.

"Yes! This is amazing. It's one thing to watch videos and stuff, but it's another to be here in the moment."

A man in a dark suit steps into the ring, microphone in hand and my whole body jitters with excitement.

The lights dim and the crowd roars the moment Xavier's entrance music, *X Gon' Give It To Ya*, blares throughout the arena. My eyes flit to the huge screen, ecstatic to be out here watching him in all his glory. Twenty-five thousand spectators are on their feet going wild. Banners and posters pepper the stands with the words 'Phenomenal X' written across them.

"Keep your eyes on the black curtain. He'll come through that." Liv adjusts the noise canceling headphones on Kami's little head. "It'll get crazy when the crowd spots him."

I grip the railing and lean against it for a better look around the slew of fans, who are already waving their arms like mad. Smoke wafts around the stage, and the lights in the entire arena shut off. Red flashes speckle the stage, drawing everyone's attention. The camera crew line themselves up on the ramp, ready to catch all the action for the millions of viewers at home.

The moment Xavier steps through the curtains I swear the noise in the place amplifies ten decibels. My eyes rake over him as he stands there staring out at the crowd, his chiseled arms are on full display, and the fabric of the black tank top he's wearing straining against his toned chest.

There's no hint of emotion on his face as red lights shine on him. The intense expression on his face causes my heart to flutter. It's intimidating, and reminds me a lot of the time in the bar when he went after that man who put something in my drink.

Xavier crouches down, and I jump as fireworks shoot up from the stage surrounding him. More smoke clouds around him as he jumps up and throws his shoulders and head back as a loud howl erupts from his mouth.

My God.

My breath catches. He looks like a warrior ready for battle, not a guy about to take on a friend in the ring. Xavier is one hell of an actor, because even I believe him.

He struts down the ramp and makes his way over to the side of the aisle I'm standing on. Rowdy fans pat his shoulders as he walks by them, heading right toward me.

His dark hair appears even darker because it's wet. He must have poured water over his head backstage at some point. Water speckles his shoulders as he stops in front of me and leans in over the railing to kiss my cheek for a second, allowing the camera crew to get a good shot of our brief moment of intimacy before he continues his march to the ring.

"The following match is scheduled for one fall," the man in the ring announces. "Making his way to the ring, from Detroit, Michigan, weighing two hundred and sixty-five pounds, he is...Phenomenal X!"

I scream at the top of my lungs as Xavier pulls himself onto the ring and slips through the red ropes.

Liv elbows me. "Listen to that crowd. They love him."

"I can see why. He's amazing," I say in a dreamy tone as I watch Xavier climb up the turnbuckles of the ring and flex his arms and howl.

There isn't a whole lot of time between Xavier's music and another song being played. It's song with a very thick Latino sound, and the heavy bass beat pounds around the arena.

Brian pushes through the curtain, and Liv cheers and encourages Kami to do the same for her daddy as he flexes his pectoral muscles, making them bounce to the beat. The championship belt gleams against the flash of the stage lights, and it's hard to miss the charisma of this man. I laugh as he makes his way down the ramp and winks in Liv's direction.

The announcer introduces Xavier's opponent. "Making his way to the ring, from Miami, Florida, weighing two hundred and forty pounds, he is...Brian 'Razor' Rollins!"

Pandemonium erupts as Brian's playful expression turns serious the moment he steps into the ring with Xavier and then holds the belt in the air. Both men stare each other down, making the crowd believe that they hate each other.

Bright lights flick back on overhead and a bell rings. Xavier and Brian circle each other, and I hold my breath. I don't like the idea of the two of them hurting each other. I know it's their job, but that doesn't make it easy to watch.

Brian and Xavier step toward each other at the same time and lock up. It appears pretty evenly matched until Brian twists around and catches Xavier in a headlock.

Brian grabs his other wrist and grunts as he pulls his arm tighter around Xavier's neck. Xavier's arms flail about wildly for a second, but then he punches Brian in the ribs. Brian's grasp loosens, and Xavier turns around in time to clothesline his opponent.

A collective, "Ohh," echoes through the massive room as Brian falls down to the mat. Xavier doesn't waste any time climbing to the top of the corner rope, standing tall as he towers over the ring. Cameras flashes go crazy as Xavier stretches his arms out and sends his body flying toward Brian.

Brian kicks his leg in the air just as Xavier comes down on him, landing against the left side of Xavier's jaw.

Xavier grunts and lands on the mat next to Brian. Both men remain motionless for a moment, and then Brian begins to crawl toward Xavier, ready to cover him for the pin.

Brian hooks his elbow around Xavier's leg the referee falls down to the mat, and smacking it as he counts.

"One!" the crowd chants along with the referee.

"Two!"

The count is interrupted as Assassin flies through the crowd, hopping over the barricade and sliding into the ring. As soon as Rex is able to stand, he begins attacking Brian, ripping him off Xavier.

Liv gasps beside me and covers her mouth as the bell from the ring begins sounds, signaling the end of the match.

"What is it?" I question, thoroughly confused as to why she's upset. "Isn't everything choreographed?"

"This isn't a part of the show. That asshole, Rex, has gone rogue."

My eyes widen as I direct my attention back to the ring. The moment Xavier realizes what's happening, he jumps to his feet.

Rex wastes no time sliding back out of the ring and walking backwards up the ramp while Xavier stares him down.

There's a cocky smile on Rex's face like he's just rained on Xavier's parade and enjoyed it immensely.

"Winner of this match due to disqualification, and *still* the heavy-weight champion...Brian *'Razor'* Rollins!" the same announcer calls out.

"I don't understand. What just happened?"

Liv frowns. "Xavier was supposed to win the belt from Brian tonight."

I gasp as my eyes flick back up to the ring where Xavier is kneeling beside Brian talking to him along with a doctor.

"Can Assassin do that?"

Liv shrugs. "He just did. Now the shit is gonna hit the fan. That asshole had better not have hurt Brian. We need to get backstage so I can check on him when he goes back there."

I follow Liv to the backstage area and instantly we're surrounded by loud chatter as the other wrestlers are trying to figure out what in the hell just happened. Rex is nowhere to be seen, but his is the name on everyone's lips.

What will all this mean for Xavier? I know how much he wanted to win that belt. I don't know who Rex thinks he is, but he just started a war—and Xavier isn't the type to back down.

Chapter
EIGHTEEN

Anna

I lean against the brick wall and chew on my thumbnail as I wait for Xavier to come out of the locker room. As yet, there's no word on how Brian is doing or if any damage was done.

The door across from me opens, and Rex comes strolling out. His dark hair is slicked back, and the t-shirt he's wearing appears three sizes too small as the fabric strains against his chest. A huge grin spreads across his face the moment he spots me.

I shake my head. This man is a disgusting human being. I don't understand how someone can be so happy after hurting someone like that.

"Hi."

There's a slick tone in Rex's voice that reminds me of a slithering snake. It's enough to make my skin crawl.

Rex leans his shoulder against the wall so he faces my side. I fold my arms across my chest and turn my head the other way, doing my best to pretend he's not there.

"I've seen you around today. You're the new X girl, right?"

I flinch. I don't like that he's implying I'm just some passing fad for Xavier. "Leave me alone."

Rex chuckles darkly. "I can see Deena was right about you."

I whip my head in his direction and stare at him while wrinkling my nose. "She knows nothing about me."

He shrugs. "Maybe so, but she does know X and his track record when it comes to women. She says you're not seeing your relationship with him for what it really is."

I roll my eyes. "She knows nothing about our relationship. What Xavier and I have is—"

"Special?" I don't appreciate the smirk on his face. "Don't you think he makes all his women feel that way?"

"He doesn't have women," I fire back. "There's only me."

He shakes his head and sighs. "When he breaks your heart, Princess, you can come to me." He leans in, but I move further away to keep him from actually touching me. "I don't mind X's sloppy seconds. He's got great taste in whores."

Before I can stop myself, I smack Rex across the face with as much power as I can muster. "Screw you. Don't ever call me that."

He grins as he rubs his face, completely unfazed by my actions.

I turn on my heel and storm away from him, refusing to stand there and listen to any more of his ridiculous attempts to get under my skin. A few feet away, I spot Xavier coming down the hallway toward me.

I run to him and throw my arms around him, willing myself not to cry.

He wraps his arms around my waist and pulls back to gaze at my face. "Everything okay?"

I shake my head. "I just smacked Rex across the face for calling me one of your 'whores.'"

Xavier's eyes darken. "Where is he?"

I grip his arms, attempting to hold him in place. I shouldn't have told him, and had it not been for him catching me while I was still heated over the situation, I probably would've opted to tell him later, when Rex wasn't around.

"Let it go, Xavier. I handled it."

He shakes his head. "The fucker has it coming."

He steps back, peeling me off of him in the process, and heads in the direction I just came from. I trail behind him, but his legs are so damn long it takes me twice as many steps to keep up.

Rex is still leaning against the wall in the same spot he was in when I left him, only now he's talking on his cell phone. Xavier doesn't say a word as he charges Rex and grabs him by the shirt, pulling him away from the wall and then slamming him back, causing Rex to let out a grunt. Rex's phone falls to the concrete floor and shatters next to his feet.

Rex laughs darkly. "Do it, knock yourself out of your title shot—for the second time tonight."

"That's not what this is about," Xavier growls.

Rex's eyes flick over to me and then back to Xavier. "*Her*? She's what's got you so riled? This isn't like you, X. That pussy must be something else."

My mouth drops open, and my heart pounds against my ribs. Rex has no clue what he's asking for.

Xavier rolls his fingers tighter into Rex's shirt as he draws his fist back. Rex's eyes widen as the growl emanating from Xavier's throat echoes down the hall. Before Xavier can deliver the blow, Freddy comes up behind him and hooks his arms under Xavier's, halting him from swinging, and yanks back.

"Don't do it, X. He's not worth it, bro. Settle it in the ring," Freddy says trying to calm Xavier down. "Pull your shit together. Think about your fucking job."

Xavier's chest moves rapidly as he sucks in air through flared nostrils, his murderous stare fixed on Rex.

Rex shoves himself off the wall and pulls at his shirt casually, adjusting it back into place. "Yes, X, we'll settle this in the ring. I've already had a chat with the writers. They're going to make it happen. Save all that rage to give the fans a good show, yeah?"

"I don't give a fuck about the about the show," Xavier growls while fighting against Freddy's hold.

"Then do us all a favor and quit. You know I'm the rightful champ."

"You're fucking delusional," Xavier retorts.

"You're the one who can't see the big picture around here, friend. Throwing everything you've worked for away on a piece of ass...*that's* delusional." Rex laughs as he turns and stalks down the hallway, not giving Xavier any chance to reply this time.

Xavier fights even harder against Freddy, attempting to go free so he can go after Rex, but Freddy doesn't loosen his grip. "Chill the fuck out or I'm not letting go."

I take in the nearly seven-foot man who, even with arms the size of most people's thighs, is struggling to keep Xavier still. There's no way I would've been able to break up a fight between those two. I'm glad he came along when he did.

Xavier closes his eyes and takes a deep breath, trying to calm himself down. "All right. I'm good."

"You sure?"

Xavier holds his hands up in surrender. "Yes."

Freddy slowly releases Xavier and then stands, blocking the hallway in the direction Rex retreated while Xavier readjusts his shirt.

Freddy points his gaze at me. "Get him out of here before he does something he will regret. This company isn't big on second chances."

I take Xavier's hand, and his eyes soften a bit when he glances down at me.

"Let's get out of here."

As I pull him toward the exit, he doesn't resist me like I expect. Outside, there is a driver standing by the open door of an awaiting car. Fans scream from the other side of the fence the moment they catch a glimpse of Xavier, and he waves without smiling before following behind me into the vehicle.

He's quiet on the way back to the hotel. I keep glancing in his direction, but his face remains unreadable. I imagine he's trying to decompress after all that, so I sit silently at his side and reach over and take his hand. I want him to know I'm here for him no matter what.

His blue eyes cut in my direction as he threads his fingers through mine.

I turn and stare out the window and replay the action of what just went down. Freddy's words reverberate in my skull. I know Xavier was trying to defend me against Rex, but he has to stop trying to fight every guy who bothers me. It's not worth putting his career in jeopardy.

Finally we make it to the hotel and Xavier wastes no time getting us up to our room. The bed is freshly made, erasing the crumpled of sheets we'd left after sleeping together last night.

I sit on the edge of the bed. "You're going to have to stop doing that, you know."

Xavier shoves his hair away from his face. "Doing what?"

"Defending me every time some jerk says something to me. Fighting them all isn't worth putting your career on the line for."

"Anna, when it comes to you, nothing else matters. No one will speak to you like that and get away with it. It's not going to happen."

I reach out and take his hand. "Don't you see, that's exactly what Rex wants. He wants you to lose your head. He's threatened by you and would like nothing better than to see you destroy things yourself."

I tug on his hand, and he resists for a moment before he finally sits down next to me. The mattress sinks under his weight.

"You're right. That's why he interfered tonight. In our pre-show meeting the writers informed us all that I would be winning the belt, and then I would have to give Rex a shot at winning it."

I nod. Everything begins to make since. "He'd rather go up against Brian than you?"

"Yeah. Which is crazy because Brian is a strong motherfucker."

I lay my other hand on top of his. "But he's nowhere near as intimidating as you."

His mouth pulls up into a cheeky grin. "You think I'm *intimidating*?"

I smile. "Have you seen *you*? You make grown men shake in their boots with one look."

Xavier pushes a lock of hair back behind my ear. "That's funny."

I tilt my head. "Why?"

He stares into my eyes. "I don't feel very threatening when a five-foot-five girl scares the shit out of me."

"M—me? *I* scare *you*?" I stumble over my words while trying to figure that one out.

His finger traces my jaw and his lips follow along the same path with feathery kisses. "Mmhmm. I've never felt this way about a woman before."

I close my eyes and lean my head back as he licks the sensitive skin below my ear. "And how do you feel about me?"

I know I shouldn't press him, but I'm curious and want to hear him say he's beginning to feel something just like I am. I want what's growing inside my heart for him validated.

"You're special to me, Anna, and I want to keep you forever," he whispers.

Every muscle in my body trembles with need for him. Him admitting he feels *something* is a start. We've gone from him not wanting a real relationship, to wanting to make what's happening between us last forever. Right now, that's enough.

I stare into his eyes. "I'm not going anywhere."

"Promises like that are what worry me." He presses his lips to mine. "Someday you might. When you see what I'm capable of, you'll leave, and never look back."

I shake my head. "Nothing will change how I feel about you."

He leans his forehead against mine. "Promise?"

"Yes," I whisper.

He crushes his lips against mine and works his hand underneath my shirt. His eyes are hooded with desire and there's no mistaking what's on his mind.

"We have to use a rubber this time. We've been cutting it too close with me pulling out. That doesn't always work."

I sigh and twirl a lock of his hair around my finger. "True, but I read online there's only a few days a month a woman can actually get pregnant, and that's shortly after her period. I'm due for mine in a few days, so I think we're safe."

He kisses my neck. "I want you to know that I don't bareback with other women."

I tilt my head. "Bareback?"

"Fuck raw—sex without a condom," he clarifies. "I've only ever done that with you. I wasn't expecting that first time to happen, and once I was in the moment all I wanted was to feel you. I wanted you wrapped around me with nothing between us. I know it's stupid, but coming on you was my way of marking you."

"Mark me? That sounds all caveman-ish," I tease.

He shrugs. "Call it what you want. I wanted to leave my fucking mark on that pussy of yours. It's mine. I know it, and so do you."

I laugh at his Neanderthal ways but don't disagree with him. "I have to admit, I like knowing you're the only man who's ever done that to me."

Xavier grazes his top teeth over his bottom lip in a slow, deliberately sexy manner. "How about you let me do it again, since we're official."

My heart does a double thump in my chest. "*Official*? Are you saying that I'm your girlfriend?"

"Yes. I don't want anyone else. Only you."

The biggest smile known to man spreads across my face, and I wrap my arms around his neck. "You don't know what that means to me."

He kisses me again. "Yes, I do, because it means the same thing to me. What's happening between us—this shit is fucking permanent. You're never getting rid of me now."

"I'll never want to."

I giggle as he pulls me down on top of him, and I'm more than ready for our next round. I can't get enough of this man.

Both of his hands settle on my hips as my entire body rests on top of him. Xavier's playful smile disappears as things become very serious while his eyes search mine.

"You're so fucking sexy, do you know that?" His tongue darts out and he licks my bottom lip, causing my toes to curl. "You're my addiction."

His words play through my mind, and I smile as he presses his lips to mine. I feel his fingers slide under my shirt, caressing my skin.

My mouth drifts open as he unhooks my bra and then in one quick movement, he whips my shirt over my head, exposing my naked flesh.

He quickly sits up, leaving me straddling him, while he kisses and licks his way down to my taut nipples. Heat from his mouth on my skin causes a shiver of pleasure to pulsate down my spine.

He unbuttons my shorts and unzips them slowly. "I need you naked."

I pop up on my knees, allowing him to help me remove the rest of my clothes. I then grabbed the hem of Xavier's shirt and pulled it over his head. My eyes roam over his chiseled chest contoured to perfection. All the time he spends working on his body clearly shows.

As my eyes roam, the tip of his thick finger slides against my slick folds. "You're so ready for me."

Xavier kisses my lips as he flicks my clit. "You want me?"

I throw my head back and moan, focusing on how good his touch feels. "Xavier..."

"Tell me you want me, and I'll give you what you need," he whispers against my lips.

"Oh, God." My eyes roll back as he increases the pressure. "I want you, Xavier. So much."

"Good girl," he encourages me as his finger moves faster and faster, bringing me to the edge.

My entire body shakes as I come hard against his hand. I grip his shoulders and dig my nails into his skin as I ride the wave of euphoria.

Every muscle in my body relaxes as I float down from the high, and he chuckles. "We're just getting started, beautiful."

He flips me onto my back before standing over me. Xavier unzips his pants before shoving them, along with his underwear, down his legs before kicking them the rest of the way off, like he can't stand them between us anymore.

He leans over me and yanks my hips to the edge of the bed. Xavier spreads my thighs further apart as he pushes between them. He grabs the base of his shaft and rubs it against my most sensitive skin. A long moan escapes from my mouth. I'm so ready for him.

He growls as he slips the head of his cock inside me.

"Oh, God." My pussy stretches around him, accepting all of him, as he plunges balls deep.

He closes his eyes. "So fucking amazing. I'll never get enough of your pussy."

Xavier grips my hips as he begins to pump into me with a steady rhythm. Sweat beads form all over his body as he drives into me desperate to find his release.

I can't tear my eyes away from his face as he rocks into me again and again. A strand of his dark hair falls across his forehead as he glances down, watching his cock work in and out of me.

His eyes glaze over and I can tell he's enjoying every minute of this just as much as I am.

"Fuck, Anna." He bites his bottom lip as he closes his eyes. "Shit. It's hard to hold back when I'm inside you. I need to stop."

A familiar tingle starts to roll through me. I'm so close again. "Don't stop."

He bites his bottom lip as his entire body tenses. A string of curses pour from his mouth as he keeps pumping into me. He digs his fingers into me as he comes hard inside me.

The sight of him lost in his own pleasure pushes me over the edge right behind him and we get lost in ecstasy together.

Chapter
NINETEEN

Xavier

The show must go on, isn't that how the old adage goes? It's been two days since I've seen Rex, but that doesn't mean jack. I'm still as heated as ever.

We caravanned with Brian and Liv down here to Orlando on Wednesday for Thursday's live televised event, *Thursday Tension*. Anna and Liv seem to be hitting it off well, and I love watching her around Kami. It allows me to see her tenderness on full display.

I rub my face as thoughts of what having my own family with Anna might be like cross my mind. Shit. I have to stop thinking like this—I'm poison, and no kid deserves to have a father who will eventually taint them.

It runs in my blood to fuck up lives, which is what I'll probably end up doing to Anna, but I'm too much of a selfish prick to walk away from her.

Anna sits on the bench across from me as I lift some free weights, gazing into my eyes. "You okay?"

"Fine. Just focusing on the match," I bite out between rep counts, trying to shield her from what's really on my mind. I don't need her knowing that she's got my head all twisted up with ideas of things I can never have.

Hell, before her, I never wanted a family, or a wife either.

I continue my reps when I notice Rex across the gym, staring at Anna intently. My first instinct is to run over there and poke his eyeballs out with my fingers so he can never look at her again, but I restrain myself, because Anna's right. I have to learn to control my shit, or else Rex is going to get exactly what he wants—me out of the company.

Anna's face twists as she glances down at her phone.

I don't like seeing her sad. "What's the frown for, beautiful?"

She shakes her head. "I checked my bank balance. It looks pretty scary."

I pause for a brief second. I told Jimmy to wire some money to her account yesterday. It better be in there.

"What's it say?"

"It says I have over thirty thousand dollars, that can't be right. I'm going to have to call the bank."

I set the dumbbells onto the rack. "That's no mistake. I had the money wired to your account."

Her shoulders drop and she frowns. "Xavier, I can't accept that."

I wipe my face with a towel. "Yes, you can."

"Xavier...it doesn't feel right to take money from you. Not now. Not after we..."

I set my eyes sternly on hers so she knows this isn't up for discussion. "You're mine. I take care of what's mine. End of story."

She opens her mouth in what I expect to be another protest, but when I raise my eyebrow she closes it and sighs. "There's no fighting you on this, is there?"

"Nope," I say, popping my lips on the "p" sound.

"Fine, but no more deposits. That's enough money to last me a year."

I chuckle and shake my head. "I'm not agreeing to that."

Anna rolls her eyes, but I know I've won. She can't fight me too hard when all I want to do is take care of her.

I turn around to stretch to get ready for my match, and I notice that fucker Rex is still staring at my girl. I don't know how much longer I'm going to be able to go without saying anything. It's not like me to hold back, and it's taking a lot of fucking willpower to do it right now.

The stage manager walks in and points at me. "X, you're up."

I nod. "Thanks."

I grab a bottle of water off the rack, and I glance over at Rex. His eyes meet mine and the fucker has the nerve to smirk. He knows the minute I walk out of this room there won't be anyone around to defend Anna.

I can't leave her alone back here.

I grab her hand and pull her up. "Come on. You're going with me."

Her brow furrows. "Where?"

"To the ring," I tell her. "I won't be able to focus, because I'll be too worried about what's going on back here. I need you where I can see you. You can stand in my corner ringside during the match."

I pull her with me down the hall toward the backstage curtain, not giving her a chance to argue.

"I can't go out there like this," she complains.

I glance down at the jean shorts and tank top that has my face plastered across it. Her brown hair falls over her shoulders in soft waves, and I find myself instantly confused as to why she thinks there's anything wrong with her.

"Stop. You look fucking amazing," I tell her honestly.

She bites her lip, and I groan. She has no clue how sexy she is when she does that. It makes me want to nip that pouty lip of hers. Little shit like that drives me fucking crazy.

My entrance music starts, and Anna tenses next to me.

I lean over and whisper in her ear, "Stick with me. You're going to be fine."

I kiss her cheek and then pull her through the black curtain with me.

Tonight's sold-out crowd is insane. There are faces in every direction I turn. I love this. This is where I thrive. I feel the fucking love these people have for me, and it pumps me up to work hard to keep their approval. It's a high that cannot be duplicated.

Smoke wafts around me and I pull Anna to the center. "Stay here so you're clear of the pyro."

She nods, and I kneel down in front of her as the fireworks explode around us and I leap to my feet and toss my arms out to my side, straining every muscle within me as I howl. The crowd joins in and while I wear my predatory face for the masses, inside, I'm smiling.

I grab Anna's hand and pull her down to the ring. I'm going to catch hell from the company for this when the match is over, but it'll be worth it to have her by my side.

"Making his way to the ring, from Detroit, Michigan, weighing two hundred and sixty-five pounds, he is...Phenomenal X!" the announcer says as we walk down the ramp to my already waiting opponent.

"Stay here." I kiss Anna's cheek and leave her in the corner, standing on the floor, before jumping up onto the ring and slipping through the ropes.

My opponent, Dexter, is young and hungry, but he's no real match for me. He's about three inches shorter than my six-foot-four stature and I've got at least thirty pounds on him. The writers instructed me to make this match seem like a challenge because they have big plans to move this young man up in the biz, and they need the crowd on his side.

I stare down the blond-haired man and turn my head from side to side. The crowd loves these intense showdowns, and it makes them cheer for me even harder. The sound of them chanting my name echoes around the arena and gets my adrenaline pumping.

We begin circling one another, and the kid impresses me by making the first move. We hook up with our arms in a test of strength. At first I allow him to push me a bit to sell it to the crowd, but then he gets cocky and tries to move me into an armbar.

Time to teach this motherfucker who's boss in this ring. No one attempts to overpower me and get away with it. Company or not, I'm teaching this prick a quick lesson in pain.

I laugh and shove him back hard against the ropes. His eyes widen as I bring a big forearm across his chest and knock the wind out of him, only to pin him against the ropes and say just loud enough for him to hear, "Welcome to *my* house."

I hit him one more time before he falls down with a hard thud. His chest rises and falls rapidly as he stares up at the lights burning down on us from overhead.

I reach down and grab a handful of his hair, forcing him to get up. "No time to rest, chump."

When he stands, I kick him in the shin with my boot and then ram an elbow hard into his gut. He groans and grabs his midsection. The second he bends over, I seize my opportunity and hook an arm around his leg and hoist him up on my shoulders.

The crowd gets to their feet as I fall backwards, slamming Dexter's back against the mat so hard the entire ring shakes. A collective sound of the crowd empathizing with his pain fills the arena and I know this match is about to end. The kid can't take much more.

I roll over and pin his shoulders without any resistance and the referee falls to the ground and begins to count.

"One...two...three."

The place erupts, and I'm unsure how it doesn't physically blow the roof off the place with the energy radiating off the crowd. I raise my arms in victory as my music plays.

"Winner of this contest is...Phenomenal X!" the announcer calls out, and I smirk at the crowd as if it were even a contest at all.

I strut over to the corner and before I climb up the turnbuckles for my trademark moves after winning a battle, I reach through the ropes. I want to share this moment with her.

Anna stares at my hand with wide green eyes. "Come celebrate with me."

She takes my hand, and I sit on the rope, widening it for her to get inside as the crowd begins to catcall. My woman is damn fine, and I'm ready for the world to know she's mine.

Anna sets foot inside the ring with me, and I pull her into my arms, and kiss her square on the mouth for the world to see before I climb the ropes and howl again, suddenly thankful for this amazing life I've been given.

The crowd continues to go crazy as they celebrate with me.

After I finish my portion of the show, I help Anna back out of the ring, and we walk hand in hand up the ramp to get backstage.

The moment we pass through the curtain, I pull her into my arms, and she giggles. "That was amazing, Xavier. What a rush!"

I kiss her lips. "I loved having you out there with me."

"Good," a cold voice says, interrupting our intimate moment. "From now on she's a part of the show."

My gaze jerks over to my boss, who is standing there openly watching us, wearing his silver suit that matches his hair and name with a scowl on his face. I raise my eyebrows and instantly know I'm in deep shit. Mr. Silverman never speaks to the staff unless he's promoting or firing one of us.

"Come again, sir?" I ask.

He shoves his hand into his jacket pocket. "You took your lady friend out to the ring, inadvertently making her a part of the show. Her contract is being written up as we speak. We can't run the risk of having you take her out there again without one. I don't like lawsuits, Mr. Cold."

I hadn't thought about that, but I like the idea of her being in my corner every time. "Will she need to sign today?"

"Take her to legal and then hit the showers. I want this taken care of before you leave tonight."

"Yes, sir," I reply as he turns to walk away.

Mr. Silverman pauses mid-stride and pivots on his heel. "One more thing. When the writers tell you to do something, you do it. I'm very disappointed that you didn't give the fans a longer match."

Fuck.

"It won't happen again, sir."

He nods. "See that it doesn't. I want you following the script to a 'T', if you expect to keep your job here."

"I will. You can count on that."

That answer seems to appease him, because he smiles before he leaves us. Mr. Silverman never smiles, so it takes me back a bit. That man is always so fucking serious.

I squeeze Anna in my arms. "This is great news. Now you can be in my corner every match and get paid for it."

She raises her eyebrows. "Really? That's a dream job."

I sigh. "It is, until they want you to do something physical. That's where I'm going to draw the line, beautiful. I won't have you getting hurt on my watch. If they ask you to do that, I want you to quit."

She nods. "Okay, but I'll still be able to come with you backstage, right?"

"Of course, but you won't be able to go ringside any longer."

"Seems fair."

I can't believe, for the first time in my life, things are actually working out in my favor. I have a career I love, and the woman I adore at my side. Life can't get any fucking sweeter.

Anna and I walk into the hotel holding hands. I like that we are always touching. It's nice to feel so connected to her.

A small crowd of about ten people loiter in the lobby. No matter where we go, fans are tipped off as to where we're staying, Not that I'm not complaining. Fans coming to shows and buying shirts with my face on them go toward my paycheck, so I have no problem giving them a few minutes of my day.

The crowd swarms us instantly, and I begin posing for pictures and signing autographs. Anna steps back and allows the fans to have their moment with me. A small boy around the age of ten sits in a wheelchair, wearing a baseball cap with my stage name across it.

I kneel down beside him and take the poster and marker he's holding. "What's your name, little man?"

"Xavier!" he giggles. "Just like you."

The short, curvy brunette wearing glasses nudges his arm. "It is not, Johnny." Her eyes flick to mine. "Sorry. You're his hero, and he always wants to be just like you."

I smile and wink at the kid. "Johnny's a pretty awesome name too."

"You think so?" Johnny's eyes gleam with excited.

"I do. Here you go." I hand him back his things with my autograph.

"Thank you so much, Mr. Cold. This will mean so much to him. Ever since his mother died, he's really locked himself into a shell. The only time he's happy is when he's watching you on TV," the woman with him tells me.

My lips pull into a tight line. I wish I had some encouraging words to tell the kid, like the pain gets easier with time, but then I'd be a fucking liar and I don't want to do that. So I give a very generic response.

"Happy to help." I wave to the rest of the crowd. "I have to get going. Nice to meet you all."

Panic sets in when I don't spot Anna right away. My eyes scan the lobby for her, and I quickly spot her talking to an older Latino man in the corner of the room.

I flex my fingers as I stalk toward them. I don't allow anyone to bother Anna.

She doesn't see me when I step up behind her, but the man glowers over her shoulder at me.

Pops better pipe down and wipe that expression off his face, before I do it for him.

"Is *he* why you ran away from home?" The man's lip curls up. "This is so unlike you, Anna."

Oh shit. This is her father—the father who she says hates her.

My entire body stiffens. Father or not, I won't allow him to lay a finger on her again.

Anna glances back at me then returns her gaze to her father. "You don't know anything about me, or what I want."

"You're my daughter, I know what's best for you." He grabs her elbow. "Jorge said he'll take you back. When we get back you can fix things between the two of you."

Without thinking, I shove his hand off her.

"Don't fucking touch her," I growl. "I saw what you did when you laid your hands on her last time. You will not put another goddamn bruise on her again."

He narrows his eyes at me. "I don't like your tone, or what you're implying. I'll have you know I'm a Christian man. I only inflict physical punishment when necessary. It's my right as her father."

My nostrils flair, and my blood boils beneath my skin. "That's fucking bullshit. Going to church does not justify beating another person. You'll never get another chance to touch Anna, I fucking promise you that."

Her father has the same look in his eye that most men do when I threaten them.

Fear.

I lift my chin and stare down at him, letting him know he's not taking her anywhere.

Her father shakes his head and points at me. "This? You left your entire family for him? This tattooed punk."

His words don't bother me. I've been called far worse in my life.

"Don't talk about him like that," Anna fires back.

"The man's a low-life. He will do nothing but destroy your life." He grabs her arm again and rage fills me.

Before I can shove him off her again, Anna yanks her arm away. "I love him, and I'm not leaving with you."

My breath catches at the same time as her father drops his mouth in shock.

She loves me? How is that fucking possible? The only person I ever loved in my life—the person I would have done anything for—used my love against me.

I can't go through that again.

I won't go through that again.

It's wrong for her to love me. I don't deserve it. She doesn't deserve what loving someone like me will do to her.

Her father's right. I will destroy her.

But I refuse to allow him to take her. He could hurt her, and I promised that I wouldn't allow anyone to do that.

I stiffen next to her.

"You can't possibly love him. You haven't known him long enough." Her father stares at her through narrowed eyes. "If you don't come home with me right now, forget about ever coming back."

Anna folds her arms over her chest. "Consider it already forgotten."

"Unbelievable," he mutters to himself. "You'll regret this, Anna, when he doesn't want you anymore."

Her father doesn't say another word before he pivots on his heel and storms toward the exit.

Anna stands with her back to me and takes a deep breath. "I'm sorry about that. He's angry with me, and he took it out on you. I'm sorry for the hurtful things he said."

I grip her shoulders and pull her back against my chest as I kiss the top of her head. "I've got pretty thick skin, beautiful. I'll admit what you said shocked the hell out of me, though."

She turns in my arms so she can peer up at me. "I know that wasn't the best way for you to find out how I feel about you, but I couldn't help telling him how much you mean to me."

"Anna...I—" She shoves her fingers against my lips, effectively cutting me off.

"Don't," she says. "You don't have to say anything. I know it probably scares you that I love you. It scares me too, but I can't help the way I feel. So, please, don't shut this down yet."

I swallow hard. In only a couple of weeks this girl knows me pretty well. I should tell her that her father was right, and that she should've listened to me when I warned her off when we first met, but damn if I don't want to. I'm a selfish bastard, and I'm not ready to give up what I feel when I'm around her. From the very beginning I've relished being surrounded by the goodness that's in her, and now that I know she loves me, the monster inside me that craves that emotion will never allow me to let her go, even if that's what's best for her.

She removes her fingers and presses a soft kiss against my lips.

"Take me upstairs."

I nod and grab her hand, unable to deny her sweet request, because more than anything else, I need to feel her against me. I need to know she's *real*. I've never deserved love—my grandmother made sure to pound that into my thick skull—and I most certainly don't deserve Anna's, but by God I'm going to fucking take it and hold onto it as long as I can.

Because I know she's the only person in the world who's ever felt this way about me.

The front door opens and closes. I hold my breath as I lie in the corner of the living room on the hardwood floor, beneath the one blanket that Grandmother gave me to sleep with.

Mom stumbles in and locks the door behind her. She stares up the steps like she's debating on whether or not she can make it to the top without falling. Today is the fourth day she has been gone, and her coming back now means she's either out of money, or the drug source she found for the last few days has run dry.

Mom grips the railing of the step and sighs before she shoves herself away and heads my direction.

She plops down on the couch and rubs her face. The soft glow of the streetlights outside slip through the curtains and illuminate her face. Her hair is matted and there's dirt all over her face. I don't know where she's been but from the looks of her, she's been living hard outside somewhere. Leaves cling to the flannel shirt she's wearing, and her blue eyes appear lost and tired.

She blinks slowly a few times before she pivots on the couch and makes eye contact with me.

"Xavier? Baby, why are you sleeping on the floor?" she questions with a slight gravel in her voice, like she's nearly lost her voice.

I clutch the blanket against my chest. "Grandmother told me to sleep here until you got home."

She raises her hand slowly like it's taking a lot of effort and then pats the cushion next to her. "That's silly. You come up here and sleep with me."

"Mama, I'm eight now. I'm big. We won't both fit," I say, wishing that we could.

"Don't be silly," she says in that dreamy tone she always has when she's high. "Come snuggle with your mama. I've missed you."

I push my body up and drag my blanket along with me. I sit next to my mother before she pulls me down with her as she covers us up with the blanket. She smells of vomit, body odor, and cigarette smoke, but I don't care. She's my safe haven, and the only person in this world I love.

"Xavier, promise me you'll always be at this house. I want to always be able to find you here," Mama whispers as she strokes my hair.

I close my eyes, relishing in the moment. "I'll wait here forever for you, Mama."

She pats my head. "That's my good boy. I love you."

For the first time in a long time, I feel peace wash over me. Maybe tomorrow will be the day she decides to stop living life on the edge and clean herself up.

Nothing would be better than that.

Sleep comes easy because tonight, unlike most nights, I'm completely relaxed, feeling safe in her arms.

I don't move an inch all night, and the sound of birds chirping outside wakes me. For a moment I forget where I am. I'm not used to sleeping on something soft—my bed is always on the floor—and I don't remember sleeping with something cold beside me.

My eyes pop open, and my breath catches in my chest as I find myself still wrapped in my mama's arms.

Her cold, lifeless arms.

I freeze and panic engulfs me.

"No. No. No." I shake my head and nudge her. "Mama? Mama, please!"

If Grandmother finds out that I allowed this to happen to her, she'll kill me.

I sit up and shake her. "Come on, wake up."

My mind flashes to something I saw on television once, and I quickly press my lips to her chilled ones. I blow a puff of air into her mouth, but nothing seems to be happening, so I try again.

Tears flow down my cheeks.

This can't be real. The one person I love in this world can't be gone.

I refuse to give up. I'll keep putting air into her as long as it takes.

The next thing I know I'm being jerked back by the hair on my head.

"Get back, you little beast! Look what you've done!" Grandmother wails.

She falls to her knees beside the couch and throws herself across mama's body and sobs. "Gina. My sweet, Gina. Why did you allow a demon inside you?"

I attempt to slink off the couch. Maybe if I can hide somewhere good, she won't hit me today.

The cushion underneath me moves a bit and the couch creaks. Grandmother's eyes flash to me, and they narrow instantly.

"You! You did this to my baby!"

For an older woman she's fast. She jumps to her feet and wraps her hands around my neck, squeezing hard.

I gasp for air, but everything around me begins fading in and out of view.

"If she'd never loved you, she'd still be alive. You ruined her life. You're the one who should be dead. Not her! Not my Gina!" she shrieks and tightens her grip.

The darkness flows over my eyes, and for the first time, I welcome death.

Hands shake me vigorously. "Xavier, wake up. Please. You're scaring me."

My eyes open at the sound of Anna's sweet voice, and I scramble back against the headboard of the bed to get away from her touch. My chest heaves as I stare at her with wide eyes.

Dreams like that are so fucking real. They take me right back to the place in my life I try so desperately to shut out.

Sweat rolls down my chest and onto the sheet wrapped around my body. I need to get my mind off this shit. I have to forget.

I jump off the bed and fall to the floor on my stomach. I begin doing push-ups as fast as I can, needing the burn. I wish Anna wasn't here to see this. I don't need her to know how weak I am inside—how broken I am.

Just like before, she sits next to me on the floor and watches me. After a few moments her hand reaches out to mine in an attempt to comfort me.

I close my eyes. That little bit of contact with her feels so good.

"Will you talk to me about what happens when you're like this?" she asks, her voice soft.

I keep working. How can I tell her the man that she loves is bad news?

When I don't answer, she tries again. "Please, Xavier. You can trust me."

The sincerity in her voice makes me want to tell her. I've never talked about my childhood with anyone. It's too hard.

"Whatever it is, we'll get through it together. Let me in. I want to know all of you— good and bad." She's on her knees beside me now, wrapping her arms around my shoulders, attempting to calm me down.

I lie down on the ground so I don't hurt her by accident, and she rests her chest against my back.

She smoothes my hair back and kisses the side of my head.

"I'm here to listen."

I nod, not knowing what else to say to her.

"Do you want to tell me what you were dreaming about?"

I take a deep breath and stare straight ahead at the nightstand in front of me. "My mother died with her arms around me, and sometimes my nightmares take me back there."

She's quiet, allowing me to take as much time as I need. I still can't look at her though. I don't want to risk seeing pity in her eyes.

I debate ending my story there, but there's a pressure in my chest, and for some crazy reason it feels like everything I've ever bottled up is fighting to climb out of me. Maybe Anna should know everything about me. She's the first person who's loved me since my mother. She needs to know what she's in for.

"My mother was a drug addict. It was just her and me until her addiction became the main focus of her life. We were evicted from our apartment when I was eight. Mom ended up loving drugs more than anything else, and we lost everything."

Anna squeezes my shoulders in encouragement but remains quiet.

I lick my dry lips and taste the salt on my upper lip that still lingers from my vigorous workout. "We moved in with my grandmother a few months before Mom died. My grandmother was a religious woman, but she was filled with so much rage toward me. She was convinced I was an evil seed, planted in her daughter, making her an addict. The blame was always placed on me and she took it out on me, physically. My mother's love for her demon seed is what ruined her life, because she refused to give me up."

I shake my head and bite back the emotion I feel creeping up on me. "That's why I can't love you back, Anna. My love will destroy you."

Anna leans in and kisses my cheek. "You know that's not true, right. No child is to blame for their parent's sins, and what happened with your mom, that'll never happen between us."

"I don't want to hurt you," I whisper. "It would kill me if I did."

She lies down beside me and gazes up at me, and for the first time in a long time I feel safe again—safe, because this amazing woman loves me.

"It will kill *me* if I don't get the chance to love you," she says as she strokes my face. "I love you, Xavier. We can make this work. We can fight our demons together. You don't have to be afraid of what we feel for one another."

I close my eyes and lean into her touch. "I'll try."

I'm sure that's not the answer she was looking for, but it's the best I can give until I can wrap my head around this and make sure I can keep her safe from those demons.

Even if the demon she needs protection from is me.

Anna

The third time backstage is a little easier, and I'm beginning to learn the ropes here quickly, just like I did at Larry's. There are people back here who are best to avoid, while others, like Liv, are an absolute joy to be around.

In the catering room, I find myself sitting next to Liv and Kami. The other women stay clear of the two of us, like they have the past couple of times I've been in here.

Deena curls her lip in disgust at me as she passes by our table. I have the feeling as long as I'm with Xavier, she's going to hold a grudge against me.

"She's a treat, isn't she?" Liv says next to me. "She's just like the rest of them over there—conceited and stuck on their own appearances. That, and how much money their man spends on them."

I shake my head. "That's so superficial."

Liv smiles. "That's why I like you, Anna. You're nothing like them. I have a feeling that's how X feels too. The good ones get tired of that type sooner or later and look for quality."

The mention of Xavier's name makes me smile. Ever since he opened up to me the other night, I feel like we've grown so much closer. He's yet to tell me he loves me back, but he seems to enjoy when I tell him how I feel about him, and that's okay. After what he's gone through, I'm amazed at the man he's become today. Most people aren't strong enough to overcome a past like that, and it gets the best of them, dragging them to low places they can never pull themselves out of.

I'm glad he trusts me enough to tell me what he went through. I firmly believe talking about things in your past is the first step to healing.

My cell buzzes in my pocket, and I pull it out to see Quinn's name flash across my screen. "Sorry, Liv. I have to take this."

I stand and walk into the hallway for some privacy. "Hello."

"Hey, hot mama! I saw you on television the other night. You looked great. How's things going?" Quinn asks.

"Good." I sigh. "Xavier has worked it out so I get to go out to the ring with him every time he has a match." I pause and think about how much I could use her with me here. I need her guidance. "I miss you, already."

"Aww, I miss you too, but I'm so happy you're out in the world, living your own life."

I shove my hair back from my face. "My father came here, demanding that I go back to Portland with him."

She gasps. "He didn't? I take it you told him no? How'd that go?"

"It was intense. Father grabbed me, and Xavier shoved his hand away. I was worried for a minute for my father because Xavier can get crazy when he's angry."

"Girl, I know that's the truth. Uncle Simon should know better than to try and lay his hands on you with your bodyguard around."

I pick at my nails as I lean against the wall. "He knows now, I think. He left without much of a fight."

"Honey, I know he's your dad, but I have to say, I think you're better off away from him. He's too controlling. I don't know why he always focuses on you and says nothing to your little brother."

"Armando does everything he should. He does exactly what Father wants without question— I did too when I was his age. Once he gets out of high school, I think things will change for him."

"Agreed," she says. "You know, Anna, speaking of change, I have *major* news for you."

I raise my eyebrows, completely curious as to what she's itching to get out. "Oh? Do tell."

"You'll never guess who Andy fired last night..."

I stand a little straighter as I ask, "Who?"

"Alice," she says with a snicker.

My eyes widen. "No way! Why?"

"Andy's inventory was off on a lot of things. Apparently Alice was helping herself to bottles of liquor whenever she felt the need to take one home with her. Andy installed a surveillance system when none of us were in the restaurant because at first he didn't know who was doing it, but then he saw Alice stealing, clear as day."

Quinn takes a deep breath and sighs happily into the phone like Alice getting canned is the best news ever. "Andy says he knows now that it was probably Alice who took the money out of your apron pocket, and he wants you to know he's sorry."

Karma has a way of coming around and making everything right in the world. Alice is a cruel person, and I'm elated that her wicked ways caught up with her. Too bad it didn't happen before I got fired for something she did. But, hindsight is twenty-twenty. If I hadn't lost my job, I would never have taken Xavier up on his offer, and we wouldn't be where we are now, working on our relationship.

"Tell him I accept his apology, but things happen for a reason. I'm happy where I'm at," I tell her honestly.

"I'm glad things are going well for you."

"Me too." A thought crosses my mind. "How are things with you and Brock?"

"Well..." she giggles. "That's actually the other thing I wanted to tell you. Brock and I are getting married."

My mouth drops. "Oh, my! Really?"

"Yes!" she squeals. "I can't believe it. I know it's crazy, but I love him and I know he's the one."

"Wow! Have you told Aunt Dee yet?"

"Ma met him a few days ago, and she adores him. He was so sweet to Ma, Anna. I feel really lucky to have found him."

"That's great, Quinn."

A short man with a buzz cut wearing a *Tuesday Tension* shirt approaches me and whispers, "Anna, the writers need to see you."

I cover the receiver on the phone. "Okay."

I move my hand. "Quinn, I have to go. We'll talk soon."

"Love you, Anna. Have fun with Mr. Sexy."

I giggle and shake my head as I tell her goodbye.

I turn toward the man. "Lead the way."

I follow behind him, unsure of what the writers could possibly want from me. It doesn't seem like standing ringside to support Xavier requires too much guidance, but I'm sure this is just protocol. I know Xavier meets with them before every show, so I'm sure it's nothing.

He leads me to a room and opens the door. "They're waiting for you."

"Thanks," I say as I step inside.

The room has two large folding tables pushed against each other with four laptops set atop them. Three men and one woman type furiously, and I go completely unnoticed by them. I scan the rest of the room, unsure of who I'm here to see. My gaze flicks into the corner, and I take a step back.

Rex sits with a smirk on his face and pats the empty chair next to him. "Saved you a seat, Princess."

The female writer looks up from her computer. "Hi, Anna, have a seat. We'll be with you in just a moment."

I do as requested, but I choose the seat on the other side of the empty one next to Rex. My entire body stiffens, every inch of me on edge. I don't like having him so close, especially without Xavier knowing where I am.

The female writer finally spins around in her chair and faces me. She's pretty, in that librarian kind of way, her dark hair pulled back in a low-set bun and her glasses resting low on the bridge of her nose.

The kind smile on her face relaxes me a bit. "Anna, I'm Vicky, the head writer of *Tension*. I wanted to meet with you to go over a couple of ideas I have for your character."

I furrow my brow. "My character?"

"Yes, dear. Now that you're a full-fledged member of our crew we've written a storyline for you. Your stage name is Anna Sweets, and you are Phenomenal X's love girlfriend."

I smile. I like that title. It's fitting considering we're official now. "Sounds good. Is that all?"

Vicky shakes her head. "You haven't heard the best part yet. Rex approached me with an idea that will solidify the rivalry between him and Xavier. Something that will really get the fans involved."

I readjust in my seat. Any idea of Rex's cannot be good—especially when it involves Xavier. "So what's the story?"

"You're going to love this, Princess." Rex winks at me, and my skin crawls.

"You are going to have an affair with Rex. It will drive Xavier into a jealous rage. Fans will love the intensity it brings," Vicky says.

I shake my head. "No. No way will I agree to that."

Vicky removes her glasses and carefully folds them before leveling her gaze on me. "You signed a contract, Anna, and this isn't up for negotiation."

I don't like being backed into a corner.

"What if I refuse?"

"Then we fire you and escort you off the property. You won't be allowed back into the vicinity at any of our shows."

I attempt to clarify as my stomach clenches. "So, if I don't agree to go along with this, I can no longer be backstage to support Xavier, in any manner?"

"Correct."

I sigh and shove my hair back from my face. This will send Xavier over the edge, but what choice do I have? If I don't go along with this, there's no point of me being on the road with Xavier.

I hate it, but I don't see any other way around it. Xavier will understand that it would all be an act, wouldn't he. Wouldn't it be worth it for me to be able to stay backstage with him?

I hope he sees it that way.

I stare at Vicky and do my best to pretend that Rex's eyes aren't boring into me. "I'll do whatever you want, as long as Xavier gets to keep his job. He won't allow all this to go down without a fight. I know him."

Vicky smirks. "Mr. Cold doesn't run things around here. If he tries to fight this, we'll fire him. Everyone in this business is replaceable."

"Including you?"

My snarky question leaves my mouth before I can stop it.

Vicky raises one perfectly manicured eyebrow. "Yes, even me. Now, if those are all the questions you have, we're done here. Get ready. Your first kiss with Rex in the ring is tonight when he faces Xavier."

"Fine, but it'll be Rex's funeral," I say with my eyes leveled with hers.

Before I can say anything else, Vicky turns back around in her seat and begins typing again. Rex sits with a smirk on his face.

"We could practice that kiss first, if you'd like?"

He waggles his eyebrows at me, and my stomach turns.

"Dream on."

I shove out of my chair and head for the door without a backwards glance.

Once I'm out in the hallway, I rub my forehead vigorously. How am I going to tell Xavier? He'll lose his mind.

I head into the weight room—the one place I know I can count finding Xavier. The man loves to push his body to the limits. Never in my life have I known a man as strong as him.

Xavier holds a bar in his hands, three large weights on each side, and his shoulders tweak up and down. I've learned during my time with him in here that this kind of training works his shoulders.

I sit on the bench in front of him, watching him work. After he finishes his reps, he sets the bar down and steps over it.

He plants his lips on mine. "Hey, beautiful, where were you?"

"With the writers," I tell him honestly.

He twists his lips. "What did they want?"

I take a deep breath. "They gave me a character name."

Xavier chuckles as he sits next to me and wipes his face with a towel. "What is it?"

I roll my eyes. "Anna Sweets."

He laughs. "That's fitting. Is that all they wanted?"

I shake my head and frown.

He slides his index finger under my chin and gazes into my eyes. "What did I say about frowning?"

My frown deepens. I can't help it. I don't want to tell him the truth, but I know I have to. It's not like I can exactly keep this from him. "They wrote a storyline for me...and it involves a love triangle with Rex."

"What?!" The roar in his voice is unmistakable, and I jump.

Instantly, he's on his feet and although I grab his wrist, attempting to calm him down, it's no use. I see the rage building in his eyes. "Please, calm down. Is there anyway we can get out of this?"

"You told them no, right?"

My mouth instantly goes dry. "I couldn't."

Pain flickers across his face. "Couldn't, or *wouldn't*?"

"Xavier...how...? I didn't...do you think I want Rex?" I ask, flabbergasted that he could ever think that about me.

"It wouldn't be the first time I've been used by a woman, just to get ahead around here." The coldness in his voice is unmistakable.

"Whether you believe it or not, I mean it when I tell you that I love you. I love you so much that it kills me to even think about being away from you. That's why I agreed. Vicky told me that if I didn't I would be fired and banned from coming backstage with you." My voice shakes as my emotions threaten to get the best of me.

Xavier runs his hand through his hair. "This is horse shit!"

Before I can say anything else he darts out of the room.

By the time I get to the door, the hallway is empty. I head to the right and search every single room. After about ten minutes of searching I turn around and head in the opposite direction.

Five minutes later I find myself back at the catering room. I glance inside and start to turn away when out of the corner of my eyes I spot Xavier, only he isn't alone.

Xavier stands beside the wall while Deena leans against it. My stomach clenches as I take in their seemingly intimate stance with one another.

Deena peers over Xavier's shoulder and notices me standing there watching. To add salt in the wound she runs her hand down his bicep.

Xavier's eyes widen as soon as he spots me.

Before I can stop myself, I storm over there and fling Deena's hand off of him. "Keep your filthy slut fingers off of him!"

Deena raises her hands in surrender. "I'm not fighting you. I'm with the next champion now. You can have X for all I care."

"Then remember that, and stay the hell away from him," I say through gritted teeth. "Leave."

Deena's stare meet the challenge in my eyes. Finally, she huffs and then practically runs out of the room without a fight.

I've never been jealous like this before. I guess I don't share well either.

I begin backing away from him, and he reaches for me, but I quickly swat his hand away.

"Anna! Wait!"

I don't want to hear his explanation. I know what I saw.

I storm down the hall toward the exit, but he catches my wrist and spins me to face him before I can make it outside.

"Leave me alone, Xavier!" I order.

"No," he says sternly.

"How *could* you?"

Xavier catches me in his arms, halting my escape.

"Leave me alone," I demand again and shove against his chest.

His jaw muscle flexes beneath his skin as he attempts to hide the emotion in his face. "Don't you see that I can't?"

"Why?" I plead.

Can't he see I just need to get away?

I can't deal with him...this...the entire situation.

He grips my shoulders, and his gaze locks with mine. "You're the one, Anna. The dream I've always been chasing. You make me feel whole. I'm addicted to your light. Please—" There's a noticeable break in his voice. "*Please*, don't take that away from me. You're the best thing that's ever happened to me. You give me hope that I can be a better man, because I see myself through your eyes. Give me a chance to be that man."

I close my eyes and allow the tears to streak down my cheeks. "You promised, no other women...just you and me."

Thick fingers slide under my chin and tilt my face up. His magnetic blue eyes hold mine. "I didn't break that promise. There's no one else. I swear to God, it wasn't what it looked like. No other woman holds me like you do. You're *it* for me."

Every fiber in my being wants to believe that what he's saying is the truth.

"You swear?"

"On my fucking life," he whispers. "I went to talk to Deena because I was trying to con her into asking Rex to put an end to the storyline. I won't allow him to touch you. It's not in me. I won't be able to hold back."

"I love you," I say so softly that I barely hear my own voice.

He cradles my face in his hands and rests his forehead against mine.

"Anna..." Xavier's warm breath falls across my lips.

The moment our lips meet everything else fades away. There's only me and him—no one else in this entire, crazy world. Even if he can't bring himself to tell me he loves me back yet, I know he does. I can feel it in his kiss.

And I'll wait patiently until he's ready.

Chapter
TWENTY ONE

Standing behind the curtain while Rex's entrance music plays throughout the arena turns my stomach. I'm not sure what's going to happen, but I know it's not going to be good.

Xavier pours half a bottle of water over the top of his head to help keep him cool during his match. Water soaks his trademark tank top and speckles his camouflage pants.

Rex approaches us to get to the stage with a smirk on his face.

I squeeze Xavier's hand in mine and wrap my other hand around his wrist. It won't keep him from attacking Rex if he really wants, but I hope my presence is a reminder for him to keep a cool head because his job depends on it.

Rex grabs the back fabric, ready to head out to start the show, and says, "See you out there, Princess."

"Screw you!" I retort.

Xavier tenses and I tighten my grip as Rex laughs and winks at us before disappearing into the arena.

My heart pounds in my chest. This is going to be worse than I thought. I have to stop this.

"Please, Xavier. Don't go out there," I beg.

"Don't worry, Anna. I'll be fine," Xavier says with a growl.

"You're not going out there like this. Forget what he said—he's not worth it!" I plead with him, attempting to calm him down.

He shakes his head and water drips from the tips of his hair onto his bare shoulders. "When are you going to finally hear me? You're everything to me. I'd trade my very soul to protect you, because *you're* worth it. I'll never let anyone hurt you, *ever*, and no one is going to take you away from me. No. One."

My heart squeezes in my chest. I can't remember the last time anyone has ever cared about me this much. He's trying to save me, I know, but all I worry about is saving him from himself—his own self-destruction. I run my fingers along his scruffy cheek. "Please, don't do this. Don't throw everything away for me."

He flexes his jaw while pure intensity shines in his blue eyes. "I have to. This ends now, Anna."

His trademark entrance song, *X Gon' Give It To Ya*, blares throughout the arena and my breath catches. Xavier's temper is uncontrollable. Pushing him into the ring with Rex now will not end well. This could ruin everything he's worked for. I have to try and stop him. I refuse to be the cause of his undoing.

"Please. Don't."

I know it's a lame attempt, but just begging him to not do anything stupid is the only thing I can think of. It's not like I can overpower him and force him to stay with me.

He cradles my face in his large hands. "It's too late. The show has to go on—you know that. I want you to stay back here. I won't be able to focus on him if I know he can get to you."

Xavier crashes his lips to mine quickly before pulling away and heading for the black curtain to give the fans the showdown they crave. The moment he steps into the spotlight the roof on the building nearly blows off with the force of the crowd's screams. I turn toward the monitor and stare, mesmerized by the pure determination on his face. I swallow hard as nervous energy flows through my body.

It's like a train wreck—I shouldn't watch, but I can't tear my eyes away.

He marches down the ramp and jumps up onto the platform before slipping through the ropes and into the ring. The rumble of the crowd pumps even more energy into the air. So much so even I can taste it. Xavier and Rex stare at each other from opposite corners. A chill runs down my spine as I take in Xavier's cold expression. It's murderous, and I really don't like what that might mean.

They circle each other for a moment before wrapping each other up in holds. They fall to the mat grappling, and Rex says something into Xavier's ear, but only loud enough for Xavier to hear. Xavier's eyes grow wild, and he slips out of Rex's hold with ease and rolls him onto his back. Xavier straddles Rex and lands a hard right punch to the side of Rex's face.

I cover my mouth. Shit just got very real. I've seen enough matches to know that they never really hit each other like that in the ring. Xavier is losing it—and on national television.

I have to stop him.

Before he destroys everything he's worked so hard for.

Chapter
TWENTY TWO

Xavier

On the mat, putting on a show for the crowd, is really fucking hard. All I want to do is pound the ever-loving shit out of Rex. He's run his mouth for far too long but fucking with Anna is the last fucking straw. I want nothing more than to end him. Holding back for the sake of my job is testing my sanity.

Rex wraps his arms around my neck and jerks my head toward his face and growls in my ear, "I can't wait to find out what Anna's sweet little pussy tastes like."

A cloak of red covers my vision, and that's all I can see.

I grab his shoulders and flip him onto his back, and the only thing I want to do is inflict pain. I draw my fist back and slam it into the side of Rex's face, and he grunts in pain.

I pull back my left and hit him just as hard and follow it up with another right hook.

Rex bucks his hips, and I fall off him. Crimson flows from Rex's nose and I stare down at my hands covered in the same slick liquid. I've hurt him, but it's not enough.

I roll off the ring and force a man sitting ringside off the metal chair he's sitting on. I grab the cold steel and toss it into the ring.

Rex pulls himself up the ropes so he can stand as I slip back into the ring. I grab the chair and as Rex turns to face me I smack him across the face with it as hard as I can. An audible crack echoes around the arena.

Rex falls down to the mat. He rolls side-to-side, groaning and clutching his face.

If he's still moving, he hasn't had enough.

I throw the chair down and grab him by the hair of his head and yank, forcing him back to his feet. Rex wobbles in front of me, and I'm tempted to ask him where the fuck his cocky-ass smirk is now, but I resist. I'd rather just focus on showing him who the king of this fucking ring is.

I draw back and land a hard right square into his nose. The bone breaks easily against my knuckles, and the delight is such that I actually smile.

It feels good to release all the anger I've been keeping bottled up inside. The animal inside me has been caged for far too long. Being under contract gave me something to lose if I lost my head and fought against the world. That's probably one of the reasons why the nightmares have been coming so frequently.

My mind flashes with visions of Rex's constant taunts...Grandmother beating me...Mom, dying in my arms.

The last one stings the most. I couldn't save her, but I can surely save Anna. I'll never allow anything bad to happen to her. No one will ever hurt her, including me.

Never again will anyone mess with *my* Anna, least of all this fuckin' cockroach. I'll see to that by breaking his fucking jaw.

I slam my fist into his jaw and Rex's mouth snaps open awkwardly as he falls to his knees before me. He stares up at me with hazed eyes, and I draw back one more time.

A large arm hooks around my elbow, and I find myself being yanked back. A roar that rivals an angry lion's rips from my throat. I'm still hungry to finish what I've started and it pisses me off someone that is preventing that.

I yank and pull and scream, "Get the fuck off me!"

"Chill, man. You've got to chill. They'll arrest your ass if you don't."

Freddy's voice cuts through the haze in my brain.

My vision swirls and when my eyes finally focus, I'm brought back to the harsh reality of what I've done. I stare down at Rex's uncharacteristically still body on the mat, surrounded by a medical team.

Oh God. I fucking did that.

Shit.

My legs give out below me, and Freddy, along with two other members of the security team, allow me sink to my knees. I grab my hair in my fists and squeeze.

This isn't happening. All I've ever wanted is to leave all my violence in the past, but no matter how fucking hard I try, I can't always contain my rage.

I press my hands against the mat and drop my head.

I fucked up. I'm going to lose everything.

I close my eyes and just focus on breathing. The fans in the arena mumble as the doctors work on Rex. Everyone's waiting to see if he's going to be okay.

"Brian, let me go!"

Anna's voice cuts though the noise, and I glance up just in time to watch her push away from Brian and dash across the ring, sinking down to her knees beside me. She wraps her arms around my shoulders and kisses my cheek.

"Are you okay?"

I peer into her concerned eyes. Tears flow down her cheeks, and I know that I don't want to live without her. I need her by my side always.

She needs to know how I feel about her.

I cradle her face in my hands and wish so badly we were alone in a room somewhere—anywhere—rather than being watched by millions of people while I'm still covered in another man's blood, but this might be my only chance.

"I love you, Anna, no matter what happens next," I whisper. "And I always will."

Tears continue to flow from her beautiful green eyes, but she gives a slight smile. "I'll love you forever."

I press my lips to hers in a soft kiss. Anna means the world to me and I'll do anything to protect her.

Police officers begin to circle me, and I know I've royally fucked up. I close my eyes and tighten my arms around Anna, trying to memorize the way this moment feels.

"On your feet. Xavier Cold, you're under arrest," an authoritative voice says.

I glance up at the officer in front of me as he pulls handcuffs from his waistband. My eyes drift back to Anna's face, and she shakes her head.

"No! You are not taking him!" she yells at the officer.

"Ma'am, I'm going to need you to step away from him," the cop orders.

Anna clings even tighter to me, and as much as it pains me, she needs to do as he asks.

I kiss her forehead. "You're going to have to let me go, baby. I don't want them putting their hands on you. I'll lose my shit."

She swallows hard and sniffs. "I don't want to be without you."

I cup her face in my hands, and I fight back all the emotion from my face. I can't let her see how this is breaking me.

"You have to be strong." I don't know if this is more for her benefit or my own.

Tears flow down her cheeks, and she reluctantly nods. "Okay."

"Good," I whisper, and before I get a chance to kiss her again, a cuff is locked around one of my wrists.

"You have the right to remain silent. Anything you say can and will be held against you..." Two officers yank me to my feet as they continue to read me my rights and pull both of my arms behind my back so they can finish linking both of my wrists together.

They begin leading me away, and I turn back to look at Anna. She's still kneeling on the mat clutching her chest while she sobs. More than anything I want to break out of these shackles and hold her. That frown on her face is killing me, and I hate knowing I'm the one who put it there. I close my eyes and pray I haven't just done something that will destroy us forever now that I've finally found my heart.

Turn the page to read the first four chapters of
Rock the Heart (Black Falcon Series, Book One)

Rock the Heart
(Black Falcon Series, Book One)

By Michelle A. Valentine

Chapter 1

This is the most uncomfortable seat in the entire world. The stiff leather chair nearly swallows me whole with its high back, and the bare skin on my legs stick to the seat. It's also stifling in here. If I didn't know better, I would say someone left the heat on in the middle of July. A bead of sweat trickles down my spine and I reach across the table to pour a glass of water.

I can't believe I'm this nervous. It's only a board meeting for crying out loud.

The glass meets my lips and I gulp down a drink.

My best friend of four years, Aubrey, reaches over and pats my wrist. "Sweetie, it's fine. This is no biggie."

I muster up a smile and nod. Of course it's no big deal to her. She's been through countless marketing meetings. This is my very first one. Sure, I'm only an intern, but proving myself will earn me a spot at Center Stage Marketing. Something I've wanted since my freshman year in college.

Aubrey and I both earned degrees from the University of Texas and she somehow landed an assistant position to one of the top executives in the company. They actually pay her to be here, while I'm just the annoying tag along in training.

Diana Swagger, one of the most respected female marketing executives and the president of the firm, strides in and takes her seat at the head of the long table, which fills most of the room. She's put together from head to toe—not one red hair out of place on her well groomed head. Her black suit screams money and respect, and from what I've heard about her in the staff lounge, she's a no nonsense type.

Aubrey clicks her pen next to me, ready to jot notes for her boss. Even though I'm only here to observe, I mimic her actions and do my best to pretend like I belong.

"Can anyone read the goals we discussed two weeks ago?" Diana asks while she unbuttons her jacket.

A middle-aged man, to Diana's right, rattles off a list of topics that might as well be said in a foreign language. None of the projects Center Stage currently has going are products or companies I'm familiar with, but I keep my eyes trained on him like he's the most interesting person in the world.

"...And we received the go ahead from Black Falcon's people to proceed with the children's campaign," he says.

This automatically catches my attention. Black Falcon hits a little too close to home. Most people know them for their music, but I know them because of their front man, Noel Falcon. The star-studded rocker is a huge part of my past. There isn't one childhood memory that he's not in.

Diana makes a note on her yellow, legal paper. "Good. Now we need a volunteer to go down and wine and dine Noel Falcon for a few days. We need him to know we are serious about his charity."

Everyone at the table quickly busies themselves with their paperwork in front of them. All of them avoiding Diana's stare.

Diana peers around the table. "No one is interested in this? Harold?"

The man to Diana's right looks up at her and adjusts his glasses. "Sorry, Diana. Rock stars aren't well known for working well with us boring ad types. Last time I personally tried working with one, he blew me off, then became irate that his marketing wasn't what he had envisioned. No offense, but this isn't the type of account I'm willing to take on again. It's a time suck."

Diana leans back in her chair, steeples her fingers together, and presses them to her lips. "Is no one interested?" Her eyes scan her employees one more time—all of them avoiding her stare— before they land on me. "How about you? You seem to be the only other one interested in this account."

Shit. Eye contact is a pain in the ass.

I swallow hard and my hand clutches my throat. "M—me?"

She leans forward in her seat. "I'm sure Mr. Falcon would surely give a young, pretty thing like you the time of day. All you would have to do is get him to spend some time with you and then find out exactly what his vision is for the children's charity Black Falcon is heading up."

My throat suddenly goes dry. How can I face Noel again? I want to scream at the top of my lungs I can't, but I know if I want a job at Center Stage I need to be a yes woman until I get my foot planted firmly inside this door.

I can do this—talk with an old friend on a very professional level. This might be a piece of cake.

I take another huge gulp of water, trying to calm my nerves, while Diana stares expectantly at me. If I let my history with Noel slip out she might yank this opportunity away, and I can't let that happen. Not after I'm so close to landing my dream job.

Aubrey nudges my leg under the table. She knows I'm stalling. She's heard the stories about Noel.

I set the glass down, deciding it's best to keep my relationship with him private, and nod my head. "I would love to take on this job for you."

Diana smiles and leans back in her chair. "At least someone is willing to go the distance for this company. What did you say your name was again?"

"Lanie...Lanie Vance."

Diana makes another note on the paper in front of her. "Does anyone have Black Falcon's tour schedule? We need to get Ms. Vance to their next show and get things rolling on this."

Harold types something into his tablet and quickly says, "Black Falcon's next show is tomorrow night in Houston Texas, then it appears they have a break until Rock on the Range in Columbus, Ohio a few days later."

Tomorrow? I scrunch my nose. That's a hell of a lot sooner than I expected. When I volunteered for this, I figured I would at least have a few days to mentally prepare myself. What in the hell am I going to say to Noel? Sorry for stomping on your heart four years ago? Oh and by the way I'm only here to land my dream job.

I resist the urge to bury my face in my hands. What have I just gotten myself into?

No, I have to look on the bright side. Houston is only about thirty minutes from my hometown. At least it'll be a free trip home for the weekend. It's been a couple months since I've seen my mom, and I miss her like crazy. New York is a hard place to get away from.

I can do this, right?

"Someone schedule this girl a flight for tomorrow immediately and give her the run down on this charity, so she'll know what information we need from the band," Diana says.

When I open my mouth to tell Diana I've changed my mind, Aubrey says, "Ms. Swagger, I would like to volunteer to go with Lanie. She's only an intern, and I would love to go along with her and show her the ropes on navigating clients."

Ms. Swagger nods. "Okay then, I'll allow that. Go ahead and book a flight for yourself and one for Ms. Vance and then report back to me on Monday after the initial meeting."

I slump back in the chair.

This may be the worst decision of my life.

Aubrey leads me into the hallway after the meeting is over. Every nerve in my body zings with adrenaline. This is it, my big break to show Ms. Swagger I deserve a job in her company, that I'm a marketing slave. The only problem is facing Noel.

Aubrey grabs my wrist and yanks me into the supply closet. "Oh. My. God." She shakes her head and her auburn curls bounce around her shoulders. "I don't even know what to say. On one hand, I'm thrilled you'll have the chance to show these stuffy assholes around here some of those mad marketing skills, but on the other I'm freaked the fuck out. Noel Falcon, Lanie?"

I sigh. "I know, I know, but what was I suppose to do? Tell Diana no because I have a painful history with the lead singer of Black Falcon? There's no way I could admit that to her. This opportunity just fell into my lap. I'd be crazy not to jump all over it."

Aubrey grabs my hands and squeezes them. "You're right. You can get through this. It's only Noel Falcon. We go down there and take him to dinner. You'll be fine because I'll be there the entire time for moral support."

I wrap my arms around her slender frame. "Thank you for doing this with me."

She pulls away and pushes my dark hair back before resting her hands on my shoulders. Her emerald eyes stare at me. "You're welcome, sweetie. Now there's only one thing left to do..." Her lips twist and she picks at my shirt.

I raise an eyebrow at the mischievous look on her face. "Oh, no. I know that look."

Aubrey's grin broadens. "Where's the closest mall? I can't wait to see Noel's jaw hit the floor when he sees you."

I roll my eyes and do my best to look displeased, but deep down I can't wait to see that either.

Chapter 2

The last chord of the song still hums in my ears. I can't believe I'm out here in this blistering heat. The sun beats down on my back and I just know my fair skin is going to scream at me later. But I have to be here, even if it is the last place I ever wanted to be—front row of my high school boyfriend's concert. God knows where he gets the inspiration for his music from.

The lead singer from the opening act, Embrace the Darkness, walks back on stage in his tight, black, leather pants and ripped up t-shirt. The crowd behind me is predominantly women because my old boyfriend is a rock-sex icon now. They scream even louder when the rocker grabs the microphone off the stand.

Two fights broke out behind me during the last band's set, so I'm a bit nervous to find out what's going to happen when the main act goes on, but I'm not leaving this spot. I've waited out here since the gates opened at noon to get center stage. I want the best view possible to lay my eyes on the first boy I ever really kissed.

"You guys are awesome. Thank you so much." The singer smiles and the rampant crowd of horny women shove against one another even harder to get closer to the stage. "Are you ladies ready to drop your panties for Black Falcon!?"

That gets them pumped up again. I look behind me and watch the waves of people scream and yell in excitement.

My ears ring, but I don't want to look like a total wuss and stuff my fingers in them in the midst of all these hard-core rocker chicks. That might get my ass kicked.

The middle aged woman behind me screams out Noel's name followed by an 'I love you' at least ten octaves higher than her normal voice. The woman shoves into my back, and I crunch into the iron fencing in front of me.

"Give it up for BLACK FALCON!" the rocker screams, and my insides jitter. I'm not sure why I'm nervous. It's not like he'll even remember me. He sees tons of women every night, and after a while faces probably all start to look the same to him.

My gaze instantly glues to the stage. The lead singer, Noel Falcon, enters from the right and looks just like I remember him—tall and lean with shaggy, dark-brown hair. He's not the goofy boy I knew anymore. The past four years have been good to him. Really good. He wears twenty-two well. The dark, scruffy hair on his jaw line brings out the blue in his eyes, and for a second, I kick myself for the night we broke up.

Noel stops center stage, wearing a sexy grin as he takes in the arena packed with his adoring fans. He's close. I can practically reach out and trace the intricate tattoos on his arm if I want to. The spotlight beams down on him, and he points a finger out to the throngs of people in the upper deck. The crowd goes nuts, but I stand there simply awestruck. Not because Noel Falcon, one of the hottest rockers on the planet is five feet in front of me, but because it's Noel Falcon, the first boy I ever loved. He used to be my best friend. The guy I thought at one time was my forever.

Noel pulls the microphone off the stand. "Wow!" He steps back and laughs as he stares around. He looks unbelievably hot in his jeans and tight, black t-shirt. "I can't tell you how great it feels to be back in my old stomping grounds. I grew up not far from here, so tonight—"

"I LOVE YOU NOEL!" shouts the lady behind me again, practically right in my ear.

Noel flicks his line of sight down and makes eye contact with me. Surprise registers on his face, and he pauses for a brief second, even though it feels like an eternity to me. "So tonight—" he says, still staring at me. "—is a very special night. It gives me a chance to revisit my past. See people I haven't seen since high school. The good and the bad." Noel's gaze leaves me, and he glances back out toward the crowd. "Are you guys ready to rock?"

Noel's band starts off with a fast song, and every person in the arena thrashes around. Pumping their fists and jumping around like crazy Mexican Jumping Beans.

"Oh my God, Lanie. He totally recognizes you!" Aubrey squeals in my ear while grabbing my arm.

"No he doesn't." I attempt to blow her words off. She has no clue how intense mine and Noel's relationship was back then. She's only heard stories.

"Hello? Are you kidding me? He even just said 'high school' when he looked at you. We have to put these passes to use and get back stage," Aubrey shouts as she bounces in time with the beat—her long, auburn hair trailing down her back. Tonight for her, is all about fun and the possibility of meeting one of the hottest bands around, but for me...I'm not really sure what I expect from tonight. Noel's always been the 'what if' for me. The one who got away.

Noel straps his guitar around his neck and then haphazardly slings it over his shoulder. He grabs the mic with both hands and brings it to his full lips. It reminds me of the way he used to kiss. He'd always put his entire soul into everything he did, which included the way he loved me.

"Look at me. I see you now. The way we used to be..." Noel sings in perfect rhythm.

The smoothness of his voice fills my ears, and it takes me back. I close my eyes and listen to his words and remember all the times we sat out on the old boat dock, overlooking the lake that separated our two childhood homes. That was our spot. The place we met in secret so many nights. The first place he sang to me. The first place we made love.

It was also the place where our love ended—where I told him to give up on his foolish dreams to become a rock star and do something sensible, like me, and go to college. I knew I broke his heart when I said I could never be with a dreamer because dreams don't pay the bills.

Look at what I knew.

He totally made it, while I'm still struggling to land my perfect job in this tough economy with my 'sensible' degree. Life without him, these last four years, has been lonely.

A tear rolls down my cheek. How silly was I to listen to people, that Noel was a loser going nowhere just because he loved music. We could've been happy. We could've beaten the odds. But, I guess that's something I'll never know. Just another old chapter in my life I need to walk away from because it's too late.

I open my eyes to take one last look at Noel. His eyes close as he belts out the chorus. Sweat beads illuminate his face under the spot light. He's truly beautiful. But he's a stranger now. Someone I used to know. It's time to quit torturing myself and move on. I'll just have to kiss the job at Center Stage goodbye.

"Aubrey, I need to get out of here. I can't do this," I shout to my friend.

Her pink lips twist. "Why? Because of him?" She points to Noel.

My eyes flit up to Noel's face, and at that very second, he looks down at me while he strums his guitar. His eyes hold mine for a second before I glance back at Aubrey and nod. "I have to get out of here. This is like torture."

Aubrey's whole body slumps like a deflated balloon. "You know we can't do that," she sighs. "You have to suck it up and talk to him. You won't get a job and I'll lose mine. Diana doesn't mess around." She takes my hand and pulls me through the crowd. I glance back and watch a pile of girls shove their way into our spot.

The outdoor arena is so loud I can hardly hear my own thoughts. We make it to the back of the crowd just as the song ends. People are screaming Noel's name while they're waiting for the next song to begin. When it's oddly silent, I think about taking one last look before I walk out on him again—one last look to remember him by.

"This next song goes out to the girl who shredded my heart without hesitation back in high school. It's called *Ball Busting Bitch*, and Lanie, this one's for you."

My entire body freezes and I feel my mouth go dry. What a dick! The blood in my veins boil and my fingers shake as I resist the urge to storm the stage and punch him square in the face.

On second thought that sounds like a fantastic idea.

I lunge forward and Aubrey snags my arm. "What the hell are you doing?"

"I'm going to kick his ass," I snarl.

Aubrey rolls her emerald eyes. "As much as I would love to see you do that, it's impossible and you know it. The guy probably has ten hunky bodyguards to protect him from the likes of you. Besides we have to be civil to that cretin, remember?"

My shoulders slump in defeat. Oh, right. I have a job riding on getting Noel to like me. The last thing I want to do right now is talk to him, let alone be nice to him, but what choice do I have?

"You're right. Let's just get through tonight, get the info we need, then get our asses back to New York where we belong."

Aubrey wraps her slender arm around my shoulders and gives me a little squeeze. "There's the Lanie I love. Come on. Let's weasel our way backstage and get to work."

My fingers rub over my aching forehead. This is a bad idea, but I reluctantly tell her okay. She grabs me in a tight hug—her vanilla perfume super strong in my nose—and leads me toward the restricted area sign with our backstage passes tight in hand.

Chapter 3

Being backstage at a rock show isn't as glamorous as one may think. It's filled with dirty, sweaty men—most of which are overweight and look like they haven't showered in six months. Plus, the way they leer at me is creepy, like I'm a dessert ready to be licked.

I shudder at the last thought and grip Aubrey's hand tighter.

"Damn, Lanie, loosen up. You're killin' my hand," she complains.

I drop her hand. "Sorry. Where the hell is the band? Their set has been over for at least fifteen minutes."

We come to a hallway filled with music equipment and people loitering about. Something tells me we've come to the right spot to find a rock band. The sheer volume of scantily clad women milling about shocks me. Some of them are even walking around topless like it's no big deal.

I smooth down my fitted leather halter and jean shorts, suddenly feeling like one of the only modestly dressed women around.

Do these girls have no self respect?

Aubrey runs a hand through her auburn curls. "How are we supposed to get any one on one time with him in this freak show? Harold is right, rock star accounts are definitely not the usual."

"I don't know, but we aren't leaving until we talk to him." I grab her wrist and tug her forward. "We'll check every one of these rooms if we have to."

Aubrey giggles uncontrollably as we rush from room to room throwing the red doors wide open in search of Noel Falcon. Somehow we've ended up turning this into a silly little game of shocking people as we slam open the doors. A majority of the rooms are either locked or empty, but I have the feeling if we keep this up much longer we are going to get thrown out of this place.

The last room we come to has music blasting on the other side of the red door. Aubrey twists the handle, throws open the door, and shouts, "Booyah!" at the top of her lungs, causing me to laugh so hard I double over.

"Oh, um, sorry," Aubrey says while yanking on my arm.

I stand up straight, trying to curve my giggles, and stare right into the eyes of Noel Falcon. The smile drops completely off my face.

Two topless women press against him, one on each side, and his arms wrap around them. A slow, lazy grin spreads across his face, and I suddenly feel the urge to hurl.

"Well, well, well. If it isn't my old pal, Lanie," Noel says. "Please, by all means, come in and join our little private party. I was going to take it easy tonight and settle for just these two, but you and your friend are more than welcome to join in. The more the merrier, right ladies?"

The blondes giggle and then run their hands up and down his chiseled chest while they lean in and kiss each other.

He continues smiling at me, loving that he's paying me back ten fold right now. I shake my head in disgust. "You're a real piece of shit, you know that? Come on, Aubrey."

Aubrey grabs my shoulders, holding me in place. "Lanie, we can't. What about our jobs? We have to talk to him."

I shake my head and glance at Noel. "Fuck the job. I'll pass."

I storm away from the door with Aubrey close on my heels. I don't know how I'm going to explain this to Diana Swagger, but this is just too much. It's way more than I bargained for. No sane person could speak to such a condescending, egotistical, prick of an ex-boyfriend, let alone work with him.

I'll just have to find a new dream.

Aubrey keeps up with me as I blast past all the people in the busy hallway. I'm so angry with myself. I can't believe I let myself think for a minute this would be easy or that I'm even capable of facing Noel.

The exit door flies open as I shove my way through. I gulp down the thick, Texas night air and push my hair back from my face. I'm not even sure how to find our rental car from this area of the parking lot, but I keep trudging forward. I need distance as much as I can from Noel Falcon.

"Damn, Lanie, would you wait up? These boots aren't exactly made for running a marathon," Aubrey complains behind me.

I sigh and stop in my tracks. "Aubrey, you just don't—"

"What?" her tone snaps. "Don't understand? If you tell me that one more time after I've listened to you pine after him for four freakin' years, then I'm going to murder you here and now. Capiche? I know what he meant to you and how much tonight hurt you, but now you know there isn't anything left for you there. You can move on. Forget about Noel Falcon and focus on your career. That douche is the only thing standing between you and your dream job, go back in there and face him. Get your answers."

She's right. I can't let my emotions come get in the way of the biggest career opportunity I'll ever have. "Alright. Jeesh. You don't have to go and get all mafia on me. I'll think about it."

Aubrey tilts her head and pops her bottom lip out. "Please, Lanie. Please? I need you as my coworker."

My fingers rub over my aching forehead. She's not going to let this go, is she? Even though I know this is a bad idea, I reluctantly tell her okay. She squeaks and grabs me up into a tight hug.

She pulls back. "You're doing the right thing."

I frown. Second thoughts plague me, and my gut twists into a knot. Maybe this isn't such a good idea after all.

When we return to the building, it seems even more crowded than before as we find ourselves weaving between people, like we're in a packed night club. The red doors in the hallway remain shut, and I cringe when I think about what's behind the last one.

Aubrey stops me. "Sure you don't want to wait for him to come out? I can only imagine what's going on in there now."

I shake my head. "No. If I wait, I'll lose my nerve. We are getting what we came for. Do me a favor, though?"

"Anything."

"When I toss the two hookerbots out, keep them out. I can't fight both of them and get info from Noel at the same time."

I turn and shove open the door and storm through. "Alright everyone get the—"

Noel glances up from his guitar and glares at me. "Can I help you?"

I shut the door, closing the two of us alone in the small room. "Where'd your sluts go?"

Noel's eyes narrow. "Why? You jealous or...maybe, they're more your type now."

"Fuck you." It slips out before I remember I need to stay calm here.

He laughs and then strums his guitar. "No thanks. For some reason, I'm not in the mood anymore."

I sigh and run my fingers through my hair. "Look, Noel. I didn't come here to fight with you."

Noel raises a pierced eyebrow. "Really? Tell me then, Lane, why *did* you come here?"

'Lane.' It's been so long since I've heard that. Noel is the only person alive who shortens my name.

I shake the memories away. This isn't a time to reminisce. It's time to get down to business. "Well..." I clear my throat. "I'm an intern at Center Stage Marketing, and my boss, Diana Swagger, flew me down here to discuss Black Falcon's charity with you."

"You?" He shakes his head. "Out of all the people in the entire fucking world, they send you down here to talk to me. Did they think because we've fucked before I wouldn't fire you?"

My hands ball into fists at my side. "How can you say that to me? I'm not one of your groupie whores, Noel. What we had was real!"

He lays his guitar down and stands in front of me—his six foot two frame towers over me. "Then why did you leave me, huh? Tell me that. If it was so real, why did you walk away from it?"

I can't look at him. The reasons for me leaving him that night, on the dock, are unbelievably selfish. Noel reaches out and takes a strand of my brown hair between his fingers and twirls it just like he always did when we were a couple.

I slap his hand away. His touch is just too soon.

The corners of his lips turn down. He reaches back up and tucks the loose strand of my hair behind my ear. His fingertips linger on my cheek. "Why do you always fight against the inevitable? You've always made things so difficult."

I take a step away from him, but he closes the gap between us even tighter—his chest against mine. "There is no inevitable with us, Noel."

"Sure there is. Fate brought you here, didn't it?" Noel cradles my face in both hands. I try to pull away, but he doesn't let me go. A smile flirts along his lips. "You look exactly the same. Still the most beautiful girl I've ever seen." He brings his lips toward mine. Warmth from his breath touches my face and all I can think about is kissing him. What it would feel like. Would it be just like old times? "How about a kiss? Don't you remember how hot things were between us?"

My heart thunders with anticipation, and I bite my bottom lip. He runs his nose along my jaw line and I close my eyes and inhale his spicy sent. He smells delicious. Noel's eyes search my face while his lips hover over mine. I can feel the heat of him against my face and my legs tremble.

He leans in closer but stops just short of my lips and whispers, "Now you know what it's like to want something you can't have."

His hands drop away from my face. There's no emotion on his face, but his eyes look pained and it crushes me to know I have this effect on him.

Noel steps back and runs his hand through his shaggy hair before stepping around me and walking out the door.

The breath, I didn't even realize I'm holding, expels from my chest when the door closes. I feel like I should say something, maybe even apologize for what I did to him four years ago, but I can't. The ground holds my feet steady as I hear the door open behind me. My heart falls around my ankles, and I think about how easy it's going to be for him to stomp on it while it's down. I know I don't deserve any kindness from him, but the blatant smack in the face of emotion still hurts like hell. This is my payback from Noel—to hurt.

A small pair of hands rest on my shoulders. "Did you get your answers?"

I nod, but can't bring myself to turn and face Aubrey. "Everything I needed to know."

Chapter 4

This is the first time since the start of my internship a month ago, that I hate being at work. It's going to be hard to admit I failed. Noel didn't tell me jack crap about his charity. The only information I have about it, is that it's some type of children's charity.

I pinch the bridge of my nose. He knows what the job meant to me. He took this away from me on purpose, and it pisses me off.

Aubrey leads us into the conference room for our scheduled meeting with Diana and the rest of the executive staff at Center Stage. My stomach rolls as I take a seat and scoot closer to the table. I fold my hands on top of the notepad I brought with me and take a deep breath.

Ms. Swagger takes her seat, and looks at me before slipping on her glasses. "Ms. Vance, would you care to fill us in on how your meeting with Mr. Falcon went?"

The finger nails of my left hand dig into the skin on the back of the opposite hand. Telling this woman I screwed up will be like nailing my own coffin shut, but what other choice do I have?

I readjust myself in the chair. "Actually, Ms. Swagger, I—"

She holds up a finger toward me, asking for me to pause, before she pushes a button on the intercom in front of her. "Jillian, dear, there isn't any water in the conference room. Could you see that some is brought in immediately?"

"Right away, Ms. Swagger," the secretary replies. I can tell by the response Diana always gets what she wants.

Without skipping a beat, Diana turns her attention back to me. "Ms. Vance, can I just say I've never received a phone call quite like the one I got from Mr. Falcon yesterday."

My heart leaps into my throat. Oh God. Here comes the boot. I need to do every thing I can to keep my internship. "I can explain about that."

Diana leans back in her chair. "Please do. It seems some of my account executives could learn a thing or two about reeling in a client."

My brow furrows, and I glance over at Aubrey who just shrugs in response. "I'm sorry, but I'm a little confused. What exactly did Noel— er, Mr. Falcon say?"

"We had a lengthy conversation about the long term goals of the marketing campaign for his children's literacy program, and Mr. Falcon is adamant that you take the lead on this project. He seems to think you are the only person on my team that understands him and his goals. Of course, I explained that you were only an intern and that I felt it best for someone with more experience head this up, but Mr. Falcon blatantly refused. He said he wants you, and you only, or he pulls the account from us."

My eyes widen. "Are you offering me a job?"

Diana smiles and removes her glasses. "Yes, with the stipulation that you are successful with the Black Falcon project. If it fails, then I'll have no choice but to let you go."

All the eyes of the other marketing team members focus on my reaction. Children's literacy hits home for Noel. He grew up with dyslexia and reading was always a struggle for him and he knows that I know that about him. It explains why he thinks I'm the best person for his job.

I rub the back of my neck as I feel the weight of the pressure push down. Even though I've known him forever, I don't understand why on earth Noel would make that kind of request? He hates me now. He made that perfectly clear back in Houston. Why would he want me around more—to torture me, probably.

Is a job really worth all of this?

I have to grab this opportunity with both hands and do my best to keep my relationship with Noel strictly professional.

I swallow hard. Those are some hefty stakes, but I'm willing to take it on. "Understood."

She nods. "Good. Welcome to the Center Stage family. Aubrey, see that Human Resources changes Ms. Vance's employment status to full-time."

I watch my best friend make a note in her elegant script. "Yes, Ms. Swagger."

"Oh, and Aubrey, find this young lady a desk so she can get to work." Diana winks at me before moving on to the next order of business.

After the meeting ends and everyone clears out of the room, Aubrey yanks me into a tight hug. "Oh my God, Lanie. What the hell just happened? Instead of getting the boot, you get handed a job on a platter. I thought you said Noel didn't tell you anything."

My head spins. All this doesn't seem real. "He didn't. When we were in Texas, it was like he couldn't get away from me fast enough."

She twists her ruby, red lips into a slight grin. "Sounds like he's doing whatever he can to keep you close."

I roll my eyes. "He only wants to punish me for breaking up with him. You saw how he loved shoving the two naked skanks in my face."

Aubrey sighs. "That was pretty gross, I'll give you that, but it wasn't like he meant to do that, Lanie. He didn't know that we'd come busting through the door unannounced."

"Yes, he did. He even invited us to join. Ugh," I growl in frustration. "Whose side are you on, anyway?"

"Yours, always yours, you know that. All I'm saying is he did go out of his way to make sure you got this job. Would he really do that just to get back at you? Give him a chance. Maybe it was an off night. He might actually want to be friends again."

I shrug. Damn her. Why does she have to be so rational?

Aubrey smiles, "When you meet up with him again, plaster on the biggest smile you can muster and win him over. He's the key to keeping your job. Remember the old saying, 'fake it 'til you make it'?"

I nod. That's exactly what I have to do "You're right. I'll do whatever it takes to keep this job."

"Of course I am. Now, let's go pick out your future shitty cubicle." Aubrey giggles and pulls me into the hallway.

An hour later, I sit at my new desk staring at Noel's contact information on the computer screen. What am I going to say to him? I mean, do I thank him for basically getting me this job or do I play it cool and pretend his phone call didn't pull any strings. Either way, I have to call him. Talking with Noel is the only way I can get things rolling.

The only thing I know about the charity he's trying to establish is, it's for children's literacy.

I rub my forehead vigorously. It's just a stupid phone call. How hard can it be?

The nerves in my hand twitch when I pick up the phone. Each number punch makes my stomach knot a little tighter and when it rings my skin grows cold and clammy.

Noel answers on the fourth ring. "Yeah?"

I tuck my hair behind my ear. "Noel? Hi. It's Lanie Vance and I'm—"

He chuckles. "Lane Vance, to what do I owe this pleasure?"

I squeeze the phone tighter in my hand. "Actually, I was calling on behalf of Center Stage Marketing. I've been assigned to your account and I wanted to touch base with you."

"Touch base?" He laughs. "Listen to you sounding all professional. If you really want to touch my base, that can be arranged. All you have to do is ask."

The nerve of this guy is unbelievable. "Ugh. You're a real asshole, you know that?"

"Yes, as a matter of fact, I do know that. Thanks to you. You made that quite clear last time I saw you."

Play nice, Lanie. Remember?

This is harder than I thought. The sweet, sensitive guy I knew once is long gone. This guy is self-centered and egotistical. It's taking every inch of my self control not to tell him to shove this job right up his leather covered ass.

I take a deep breath and remember what Aubrey said about smiling. "You're right, and I'm...I'm sorry about that. I was out of line, even just a moment ago. There's no reason two old friends can't get along and work together on a project."

Noel's silent for a moment and then he says, "Friend, huh? Ouch."

I shake my head. There's no way we are going down that old road. "You know what I mean."

"You're right, Lane. We should be friends, but there's only one problem with that scenario."

"And what would that be?" I bite my lip, hating the fact that I'm thinking of how sexy he probably looks right now. I picture him spread out on a bed, shirtless, still exhausted from the night before.

"I can't be friends with someone who hates me." The sexy vision of him bursts and I'm thrown back into reality.

"Noel...I never said I hated you."

"You didn't have to. I saw it all over your face," he says with a sharp tone.

"That wasn't hate, Noel."

"Then what was it?"

"Disgust," I say instantly. "Don't you have any self-respect? You just sleep with any slut that throws herself your way? That's not the Noel I know."

"It's not like that," he growls, frustrated into the phone. "Forget it. I don't have to explain anything to you."

"You know what? You're right. You don't owe me any explanations. Who you sleep with is none of my business. However, *my* business with you is now professional and I really need some details about this charity. My job is riding on how well it turns out, so you've got to give me something."

"So you got the job?" He sounds surprised and even a little excited.

I debate on which tactic to use, but I decide to play it straight with him. Noel's not stupid. "Yes, actually, thanks to you. That phone call you made to Diana Swagger made it possible."

"Good." I can hear a smile in his voice. "It's the least I could do after blowing you off the way I did."

"Well, thank you for that. This job means a lot to me."

"I know it does. That's why I felt like a total tool and had to make it right."

I chew on the inside of my jaw. It is kind of sweet that he cared enough about my feelings to make that phone call. Maybe he's not the complete dirtball I thought. This might work. A small glimmer of hope shines in my heart for a split second that we may be able to overcome our past and keep things civil.

"So...Noel, about this charity"—I clear my throat—"what is your vision for the project?"

Noel yawns into the phone, and my feathers ruffle. I'm boring all of the sudden? Two minutes ago we were fighting. I shake my head. I'll never get a good read on this guy with his crazy up and down signals.

"Lane, these business calls tend to put me asleep. I'd much rather see you in person to discuss all of this. Maybe you can wear something skimpy to keep me focused on you and what you're saying."

I roll my eyes. "Whatever, Noel." Before I let the severely rude things on my mind fly from my mouth I take a deep breath and remind myself, yet again, that I need to get him to like me. I soften my voice and say, "That's kind of impossible. It's not like you're here, right around the corner in New York."

"Actually, I *am* in New York."

My heart does a double thump against my ribs. "You—you are?"

"Yep. Did some press last night for our next album, and I decided to stay a couple nights and check out the local scene. So, what do you say to dinner with me tonight?"

This is a curve ball I'm not prepared to catch.

"I don't think a date is a very good idea. You're technically my client now and that wouldn't be very professional."

"Don't think of it as a date. Think of it more as a business meeting."

I look down at the notepad in front of me, and my hand freezes. Seven doodle hearts stare back at me. Is my subconscious trying to tell me something? I hope not.

"A business dinner would be fine." What's the harm in meeting him for job related purposes?

"Great. Give me your cell, and I'll text you the time and place."

We say our goodbyes after I give him my cell phone number. *Dinner with Noel Falcon?* It's been a long time since I've said that, and I'm wondering if it's a good idea to trudge down old paths. I only hope I can keep my head on straight and maintain a business relationship with him. God knows if he touches me the way he did in Houston, he'll be pretty fucking hard to resist.

FIND THE REST ON AMAZON NOW

Phenomenal X Playlist ▶ ⤬ ⏏

	▲ ✓	Name	Artist
1	✓	Love the Way You Lie	Eminem, Rihanna
2	✓	X Gon' Give it to Ya	DMX
3	✓	Save Yourself	My Darkest Days
4	✓	Die For You	Otherwise
5	✓	Hit Me Like A Man	The Pretty Reckless
6	✓	I Wanna Be Bad	Willa Ford
7	✓	Wrecking Ball	Miley Cyrus cover by Our Last Night
8	✓	Alone	Falling in Reverse
9	✓	Dark Horse	Katy Perry
10	✓	Mama Said Knock You Out	LL Cool J
11	✓	Do What You Want	Lady Gaga
12	✓	99 Problems	Hugo
13	✓	One For the Money	Escape the Fate
14	✓	Undressed	Kim Cesarion
15	✓	Talk Dirty	Jason DeRulo
16	✓	Kiss Me	Ed Sheeran
17	✓	Wrong Side of Heaven	Five Finger Death Punch
18	✓	All Around Me	Flyleaf

Acknowledgements

First off, I want to thank you, my dear readers, for embracing this book. Words cannot express how much you all mean to me. Love you all!

Emily Snow, and Kristen Proby (aka, The Wicked Mafia) this past couple of years with you all have been amazing. Thank you for your love and support. Love you guys hard!

Holly Malgieri you freaking rock my world. Thank you for EVERYTHING you do for me. I couldn't make it on a daily basis without you. Your encouragement and undying support means so much to me. Thank you. Thank you. Thank you.

Jennifer Wolfel thank you for always being in my corner! You are the one person I depend on to give it to me straight. Thank you for your honesty and keeping me on task. Love ya!

Jennifer Foor thank you for being you and always making me laugh. You are a rock star and you help keep me sane.

Ryn Hughes you kick so much ass, woman! Thank you for working with me through my crazy schedule. I always look forward to your red marks!

Jenny Sims thank you for your eagle eye on this book! You saved me a boatload of time.

Jillian Harbison thank you so much for your wrestling guidance and being my fact checker!

Keelie Chatfield thank you for reading this messy book as I worked on it.

My beautiful ladies in Valentine's Vixen's Group, you all are the best. You guys always brighten my day and push me to be a better writer. Thank you!

To romance blogging community. Thank you for always supporting me and my books. I can't tell you how much every share, tweet, post and comment means to me. I read them all and every time I feel giddy. THANK YOU for everything you do. Blogging is not an easy job and I can't tell you how much I appreciate what you do for indie authors like me. You totally make our world go round.

Last, but never least the two men in my life, my husband and son. Thank you for putting up with me. I love you both more than words can express.

About the Author

New York Times and USA Today Best Selling author Michelle A. Valentine is a Central Ohio nurse turned author of erotic and New Adult romance of novels. Her love of hard-rock music, tattoos and sexy musicians inspires her sexy novels.

Find her:

Facebook:
http://www.facebook.com/pages/Michelle-A-Valentine/477823962249268?ref=hl

Twitter:
@M_A_Valentine

Blog:
http://michelleavalentine.blogspot.com/

Website:
http://www.michelleavalentine.com

CPSIA information can be obtained at www.ICGtesting.com
Printed in the USA
LVOW01s1659070514

384806LV00018B/1219/P